CRITICAL ACCl

'A million readers can't be wror
day, sit l

'Leig
depe

'A b

'Bri

'DI G

'The
Russell

'An en

'Well
edge-
St

ALSO BY LEIGH RUSSELL

Geraldine Steel Mysteries
Cut Short
Road Closed
Dead End
Death Bed
Stop Dead
Fatal Act
Killer Plan
Murder Ring
Deadly Alibi
Class Murder
Death Rope
Rogue Killer
Deathly Affair
Deadly Revenge
Evil Impulse
Deep Cover
Guilt Edged
Fake Alibi

Ian Peterson Murder Investigations
Cold Sacrifice
Race to Death
Blood Axe

Lucy Hall Mysteries
Journey to Death
Girl in Danger
The Wrong Suspect

The Adulterer's Wife
Suspicion

LEIGH RUSSELL

FINAL TERM

A GERALDINE STEEL MYSTERY

NO EXIT PRESS

First published in 2023 by No Exit Press,
an imprint of Oldcastle Books Ltd,
Harpenden, UK

noexit.co.uk
@noexitpress

ISBN
978-0-85730-429-2 (Paperback)
978-0-85730-474-2 (eBook)

2 4 6 8 10 9 7 5 3 1

Typeset in 11.25 on 14.2pt Times New Roman
by Avocet Typeset, Bideford, Devon, EX39 2BP
Printed in Great Britain by Clays Ltd, Elcograf S.p.A.

MIX
Paper from
responsible sources
FSC® C018072

For more information about Crime Fiction go to crimetime.co.uk

To Michael, Jo, Phillipa, Phil, Rian, and Kezia
With my love

Glossary of Acronyms

DCI   – Detective Chief Inspector (senior officer on case)
DI   – Detective Inspector
DS   – Detective Sergeant
SOCO – scene of crime officer (collects forensic evidence at scene)
PM   – Post Mortem or Autopsy (examination of dead body to establish cause of death)
CCTV – Closed Circuit Television (security cameras)
VIIDO – Visual Images, Identification and Detections Office
MIT   – Murder Investigation Team

1

CASSIE APPLIED HER LIPSTICK quickly. It was different from the nude colour she generally wore to school. 'Luscious' was the description of that online, although it scarcely made any difference to her appearance. Until they reached the sixth form, pupils weren't even allowed to wear something as subtle as that. Not content with forcing pupils to wear uniform, the teachers had regulations governing make-up, jewellery, shoes, hair... everything they could possibly think of. But she was sixteen, and they couldn't stop her from doing whatever she wanted. It probably wasn't even legal for them to try. She popped another piece of bubble gum in her mouth and sighed. The initial burst of sweetness was almost sharp in its intensity, but after a few minutes the gum became tasteless.

She pouted at her reflection in the mirror. Her lips, now a gorgeous bright pink, were lush enough for her purpose. Satisfied, she set to work on her eyes. While the lipstick was the most important element of her make-up, there was no point in leaving the job half done. Deftly, she applied smoky grey eye shadow and more mascara. Seeing her eyelashes stuck together in tiny clumps, she swore aloud. The cheap stuff always ended up clogged, and she had to use her fingers to separate the lashes. Very soon she would be able to afford expensive make-up, instead of the shit she was reduced to using now.

Stuffing her cosmetics back in her school bag, she took one last look at her reflection. Commonplace enough on a night out, her make-up looked sensational with her school uniform, and her blonde hair could have been natural if you didn't look too closely. There was no way Sir was going to be able to resist at least a flicker of desire once they were alone together. And that was all she needed. She glanced at her phone, aware that timing was crucial if she was going to catch him on his own. Not long now. Undoing another button on her shirt, she yanked her tits up to deepen her cleavage.

Two sixth form girls came in and glared at her in the mirror.

'Slag,' one of them muttered, loudly enough for them all to hear.

Cassie stared pointedly at the speaker's frizzy ginger hair. 'Can't you do nothing with that hair?' she retorted.

The ginger's friend giggled.

'Stupid slag,' the girl repeated.

'I ain't done nothing. Anyone can see I'm hot,' Cassie replied smugly.

'That's because you get your tits out any time you see a bloke,' the ginger-haired girl said.

'We all know a slag when we see one,' the other girl murmured, barely loudly enough to be heard.

Cassie rounded on her, sensing her timidity. 'Who you calling a slag? You shut your fucking mouth.'

The ginger-haired girl sniggered. 'Slag. You open your legs for a stick of gum.'

'Fuck off, I never,' Cassie replied.

She spat her gum straight into the girl's frizzy ginger hair. The girl shrieked in indignation and swore at Cassie who darted off, laughing.

'Stupid bitch,' she called out as she left.

'Don't worry, she'll get what's coming to her,' Cassie heard one of the girls say before the door swung shut.

'Oh, fuck off,' Cassie muttered under her breath. 'I gotta go.'

She hurried along the corridor and chose a position from where she could watch Mr Moore's door unnoticed. It wasn't long before a class came charging out of his room, seconds after the bell. Jostling and jabbering, they barged past one another with barely a glance in her direction. Normally she would have been put out at being ignored by her peers, but right now she was preoccupied with more important matters. A rush of excitement flooded through her and she mumbled under her breath, rehearsing her painstakingly prepared script.

If only she'd been sixteen and streetwise when her stepfather had moved in with them. He had gone, thank fuck, and left them alone, but not before he'd taught Cassie more than she wanted to know. He had hurt her, really hurt her, but through that pain had come her power because he had shown her the way to use her body to get what she wanted. She hadn't been able to stop her stepfather, but now she knew better. And her sister was safe. Cassie would never have let her stepfather assault her sister like that. Just thinking about it made her angry. The other teachers had better not cross her or they'd end up going the same way as that pervert. She spat out her gum in anticipation and waited.

The class seemed to take forever to leave. Even when the door closed she couldn't be certain no one had stayed behind to ask a question. More likely, Sir might be keeping someone back for misbehaving. Pressing her lips together, she felt the greasy texture of her lipstick as she stole towards the door. Peering through the glass panel, she grinned, relieved to see he was alone in the room. She took a deep breath to steady herself, knowing that she might only have this one chance. Stealthily she opened the door and slipped into the room. Absorbed in rearranging a pile of papers on his desk, Mr Moore didn't hear her enter. By the time he was aware of her presence, she had reached his large wooden desk, its surface chipped and scratched from decades of use. Swiftly she dodged around it, until they were face to face without any barrier between them. They were almost touching.

'What are you doing here?' he asked, standing up.

'I had to see you,' she replied, her voice husky with the exhilaration of a sudden access of power. 'I know you been feeling the same way.'

His eyes widened in alarm. 'What are you talking about? I don't know what you want, but you need to leave. Now. You can't be talking to me like this. Not here.'

She revelled in his uncertainty. He had been careful to avoid potentially compromising situations, never meeting her alone in school. Now they were together, just the two of them, and she was standing in front of him, blocking his exit route.

'I know you want it too,' she murmured, relishing his discomfort. 'I seen you looking at me. You can't keep your eyes off me.'

'We're not having this conversation,' he said.

His voice was cold, but she could see the fear in his eyes as he realised he was hovering on the edge of an abyss. They both knew she could completely destroy his career, if she chose.

'I want you to leave right now,' he insisted, frowning.

Grinning, she licked her pink lips. 'I know what you want.'

His cheeks turned red. 'What the hell do you think you're playing at?' he snapped. 'This has gone far enough. We're in school. The bell's about to go. My next class will be here any minute.'

She shrugged, relishing his flustered response. 'So? What do we care? The others can think what they like. This is about you and me, innit? I know all about you, Sir.' She let the last word linger on her lips in a drawn out hiss.

With a frantic glare, Mr Moore fumbled in his pocket, muttering at her to stop her nonsense. He might be clever, but he was making a big mistake if he thought he could dismiss her so easily. Seeing the angry determination in his face, she hated him, not only as an individual, but for everything he represented. With a grunt of annoyance, she slapped the phone out of his hand and watched his mouth open in surprise as it went skittering across the floor.

'Stop this at once,' he exclaimed. 'You have no idea what you're doing.'

He was wrong. She knew perfectly well that she was toying with his future, and she understood exactly what was at stake for him. He thought she was just another girl with dyed blonde hair and clogged mascara, no different to many other girls who passed in front of him in the course of the day.

'Is it about your end of term grade?' he went on, although they both knew that wasn't what she was after.

She pushed her lips out in a practised pout. 'This isn't about school.'

She moved closer, until her breasts were touching his chest, close enough to see tiny blood-red threads in the corners of his eyes and a sheen of sweat on his forehead. Unable to move without physically grabbing hold of her, he was trapped. 'Step aside now,' he barked at her.

'You gonna make me?' she taunted him.

In desperation, he tried appealing to her. 'Cassie, you know as well as I do that this is inappropriate. You could get me in a lot of trouble if you don't leave right now.'

She didn't answer. He tried to reassure her that she could receive the attention she craved without approaching him like this in school.

'Listen,' he went on, no longer trying to conceal his panic, 'I can help you. I'll listen to whatever it is you want to say, but

13

not here. If you've got a problem, we can talk about it, but not now. The bell's about to go. This conversation can't continue, not like this.'

'We're not here for no poxy conversation.' She giggled at his indignant expression. 'Why don't you go on and kiss me? I don't mind, and you know you want to.'

'You need to stop this now, Cassie,' he urged her. 'I'm a happily married man. I'm twice your age. For Christ's sake, Cassie, you must know that what you're suggesting is out of the question, and it's far from funny. We're in school.' He broke off, lost for words, aware that his agitation had become obvious. 'You need to get away from me and leave the room right now,' he resumed in a calmer tone. 'This ends now. Go on, off you go, before anyone comes.'

She stood her ground, and they both knew he was powerless to stop her. It was a glorious feeling. Before she had even reached her teens, men had been teaching her about sex, and she understood its power only too well. But now she was the dominant one, and he was going to pay for the abuse she had suffered. It was only what he deserved.

As the bell rang, she leapt. Grabbing hold of his arms and pressing her body against his, she shoved him backwards. If his shoulders hadn't hit the wall, she might have knocked him over. He whipped his head sideways too late to avoid her kiss. His lips felt dry and rigid against hers but she persisted, determined to leave a bright pink stain as evidence of their physical contact. Through her glee, she was dimly conscious of footsteps and voices which stopped as suddenly as if a television had been switched off. Immediately she began to cry, pulling away from her physical contact with him.

'Get off me, you pervert!' she screeched.

Blinking furiously to force tears from her eyes, she stumbled backwards, sobbing.

'He's a bloody paedo,' a boy's voice shouted and other voices took up the chant in an eager chorus. 'Sir's a paedo! Sir's a paedo!'

Turning to her, he hissed, 'Why are you doing this to me? I never did anything to hurt you.'

Ignoring him, she continued wailing and shaking, abandoning herself to a wild hysteria. There was a sudden hush. Peering through her fingers, she saw Mrs Prendergast standing in the doorway among a throng of pupils who were staring at her with varying expressions of horror and joy at this diversion.

'He tried to rape me!' she shrieked, still keeping her eyes covered. 'I told him I didn't want to do it with him. I said no but he wouldn't stop.'

'Don't be absurd. That's the stupidest thing I've ever heard,' Sir snapped angrily. He looked over at Mrs Prendergast who was standing motionless in the doorway. 'If I wanted to do something so unprofessional, would I do it just when a class was about to come in?'

'He said he couldn't stop himself,' she sobbed, loudly enough for everyone to hear. 'He said I been asking for it. He told me he can't stop thinking about me.' Her voice broke into a wail.

Mrs Prendergast started shouting at everyone to line up outside in the corridor and be quiet.

'I'll make you pay for this,' Mr Moore muttered quietly to her, before he strode towards the door.

Leering pupils fell back to let him pass, muttering and sniggering. Sniffling, she fell to her knees and covered her face in her hands, furtively using a tissue to wipe off her eye shadow. It didn't matter if she made her eyes look puffy and bloodshot; everyone would assume it was from crying. No one could tell she was laughing.

2

'YOU'RE SURE YOU DON'T mind me going away for the weekend?' Ian asked again. 'I mean, it's not as if either of us is involved in a case right now.'

Suppressing a smile, Geraldine did her best to look disappointed. 'Well, it's going to be tough, of course, but I think I can probably survive without you for a few days.'

As a detective inspector working on murder investigations, Geraldine had always been singleminded in her devotion to her career, and somehow she had never found time to have much of a personal life when she was younger. Slowly the years had slipped away from her, like proverbial sand through her fingers. It wasn't until she reached forty that her fellow detective inspector, Ian Peterson, had moved in with her and, for the first time in her life, she found herself in a serious relationship. Now the initial joy of being able to express her love had worn off, she felt settled and paradoxically, at the same time unsettled. She wouldn't have changed her relationship with Ian for anything, but it was emotionally draining, like living in a permanent state of unreality, and she lived in fear of losing him.

She knew she could trust in Ian's unwavering affection. They had met while he was a young sergeant and, back then, she had been his mentor. Their friendship had taken years to develop into a romance, not least because he had been unhappily married for years. Now, it was hard for her to imagine life without him. Love might be dependable, but life itself was precarious. Her work on murder investigations had shown her that only too clearly. Nevertheless, she was looking forward to his going away for the weekend, giving her a few days to herself. She liked her own company, and much as she loved Ian, she sometimes felt crowded by his constant presence in her life.

'I'll be fine,' she assured him. 'For goodness sake, I managed perfectly well without you for twenty years. It's hardly going to be a problem for a few days.'

'Well, I hope you don't start to enjoy your solitude too much,' Ian replied, smiling and leaning down to kiss her. 'Tell me you'll miss me, just a little?'

She laughed. 'About as much as you're going to miss me at your stag party. You may think you don't want to go away, but once you're there you won't want to come home.'

Ian straightened up with a grimace. 'It's not really my kind of thing,' he admitted, a little shamefaced. 'But I feel I ought to go. Team solidarity and all that, you know.'

Geraldine nodded. Ian played five-a-side football, and one of his fellow players was getting married. The rest of the team had organised a trip for his last weekend of being single.

'I'm sure it'll be a blast,' she said.

'I'm not so sure. I mean, there was a time when I would have relished all that larking about. I think we're going paint balling.' He gave a mock shudder. 'And no doubt there'll be plenty of alcohol and lashings of unhealthy grub, kebabs and chips, and all the things I used to enjoy twenty years ago. But these days I'd rather put my feet up and watch the box with you than go out on the town with a gang of raucous blokes. We're all old enough to know better than to spend a weekend getting a massive hangover.' He heaved a sigh which Geraldine suspected was for her benefit.

She burst out laughing. 'All this time, I had no idea that I've been living with an old man.'

It was early May and the weather was changeable. April showers seemed to have come late that year. But that evening was dry and mild, and they walked into town and went for a drink before going out to eat. The pub was comfortable and welcoming, with fake wooden beams, leather benches, and straight-backed chairs arranged around the tables. They found a table in a corner of the bar and sat down with a couple of pints. A group of youngsters were gathered near the bar, drinking and chattering. Watching them, Geraldine speculated about whether they were under age.

'You're not on duty now,' Ian chided her. 'You can just ignore them. They're not doing anyone any harm.'

'It's impossible to tell how old they are,' Geraldine went on, ignoring the interruption. 'Once they're dressed up and plastered in make-up, many of the girls look a lot older than they should. You might think it's quite innocent, but they could be putting themselves at risk from sexual predators.'

'I suppose you never plastered your face in make-up and attempted to pass yourself off as older than you really were?' Ian asked her, grinning. 'I can just imagine you all dolled up, going to the pub and claiming to be eighteen when you were really still sixteen.'

'No,' Geraldine replied earnestly. 'I was always a responsible teenager. I never went off the rails. How about you?'

Ian laughed a little self-consciously. 'Well,' he said, 'I started going steady with Bev when we were sixteen, so that probably saved me from some of the worst excesses I might otherwise have indulged in.'

'Let's hope a midlife crisis doesn't hit you while you're off on this stag weekend, then!'

'Midlife? At my age? I hardly think so!'

'No, I guess it's too late for that now,' she teased him.

Leaving the pub, they walked slowly along Micklegate, chatting about their last case and what Ian was expecting to happen over the weekend. After a curry at an Indian restaurant they liked, they walked slowly home.

'That was a lovely evening,' Geraldine said when they were home.

'I don't know why we don't go out more often,' Ian replied.

'Because your curry's as good as anyone's and a lot better than most,' she replied.

'I'll take the compliment, even though it's a slight exaggeration.' He grinned.

She smiled. 'And we can't usually be bothered,' she added truthfully, and he grimaced.

It was true that once she was involved in a murder investigation, she tended to just grab a bit to eat in the police station canteen. There rarely seemed to be time to sit down to eat together in the evening, even though Ian insisted it was important she take better care of herself. She used to ignore him, even though she knew he was right, but lately she had been feeling more tired than usual, and decided to take his advice when she was on her next case.

'Now, how about a nightcap before bed?' he asked.

Listening to him humming happily as he went to the kitchen, Geraldine dismissed a familiar regret that they hadn't started living together earlier. But there was no point in dwelling on what might have been. When they first met, Ian had been with his wife, and Geraldine had been too focused on her career to be interested in a serious relationship with anyone. At least they had found happiness with each other now, and she was thankful for that. Not everyone was as fortunate as she had been. Life was good.

'Better late than never,' she murmured as he returned.

'What's that?'

'Nothing. I'm just feeling happy.'

'Well, I'm not sure whether to take that as a compliment or not, considering I'm about to go away for the weekend.'

'It was most definitely a compliment,' she replied seriously. 'I've never been happier than I am right now. Just make sure you come back in one piece because –' She broke off, unable to put her thoughts into words. 'Well, just make sure you come back safely.'

Ian raised his eyebrows. 'I'm going to a stag do in the Midlands, not to a war zone.'

He laughed at her anxiety, and she couldn't find the words to explain that being in love made her feel vulnerable.

3

'YOU CAN'T JUST HANG around the house all day,' Laura said as Paul stood up and began to clear the table. 'It's been three days.'

There was a tense edge to her voice that grated on him.

'What do you expect me to do?' he asked.

He dumped the bowls in the sink, leaving her to stack the dishwasher.

'You could go and speak to the head,' she replied. 'There must be a procedure to follow with this kind of thing.' Her words were suitably vague, but he could sense her distaste as she referred to the situation.

'There is a strict protocol for dealing with false allegations, and the school are following it, but it's going to take time.'

'So you're just going to sit around here, doing nothing?'

'I'm not sure what you want me to do.'

'You could go out and get a job.'

He frowned. 'I've already got a job.'

'Well, no, actually you haven't. Not any more. You had a job but you seem to have forgotten they've thrown you out.'

'No, they haven't,' he protested. 'No one's thrown me out.'

'Paul, you need to face up to what's happened. You can't keep up this pretence.'

Paul sighed impatiently. 'There's nothing to face up to. Listen, Laura, you clearly don't understand the situation. I haven't been sacked and I haven't lost my job. I've been suspended, which means it's just a temporary measure. The head made it perfectly clear he doesn't want to lose me, and in any case there are no grounds for sacking me. Nothing happened. Just some silly little slut made a ridiculous accusation about inappropriate conduct. It's risible, really. This will all blow over, and I'll be back at work in no time. You'll see.'

'If there's no reason to sack you, why did he send you home?'

'I've already told you, that's the system,' Paul explained with exaggerated patience. 'The head was very apologetic, but he had no choice. While the allegation is being investigated I have to stay away from school. That's all. There's no need to be melodramatic about it.'

'So in the meantime you're just expected to sit around doing nothing all day?'

'I'm not doing nothing.'

'That's what it looks like. And I'm not being melodramatic. I'm just concerned about our future now you've been thrown out of school.'

He understood the reason for her concern. They had recently been discussing the possibility of starting a family, but all at once their future seemed less secure. Still, there was no point in repeating himself if she refused to listen.

'So, what *do* you intend to do?' she asked.

'I'm waiting. And I've got lessons to plan,' he added, determined not to be needled by her frustration.

That was true. There was always plenty to do, but usually he was too snowed under with marking to take stock of where he was with his lesson plans. He could make use of this brief period of free time to get on top of his preparation so that when he returned to school he wouldn't be under constant pressure.

'We're due an inspection soon,' he added, with forced insouciance. 'I might as well be ready.' He made for the door then spun round to face his wife, dropping all pretence to sound jaunty. 'This isn't easy for me, you know. It would help if you were a little more supportive. Right now I feel as though the whole world has turned against me. And I've done nothing wrong. Nothing! You could at least make an effort to be sympathetic. This isn't my fault.'

Laura didn't answer. Staring into her blank eyes it struck him with a sudden cold certainty that she suspected he had done something to deserve this trouble. Without another word, he left the room and ran upstairs. Locking himself in the bathroom, he cast his mind back over the past few months, wondering whether he had actually done anything to incite Cassie to accuse him so publicly. Whatever she was thinking, she could have spoken to him discreetly, instead of denouncing him in front of an entire class, and consequently the whole school.

He wondered if anyone would believe he was innocent when even his own wife doubted him. It didn't say much for their relationship. Shocked that she mistrusted him, he sat on the edge of the bath and dropped his head in his hands, close to breaking down in tears. This whole episode had tested his usual resilience almost to breaking point. But throughout the shock, and the ensuing sleepless nights, it had never once occurred to him that he might not be able to count on his wife's unwavering support. They had always been so happy together, or so he had thought.

Downstairs he heard the front door slam. Laura had left for work without even bothering to say goodbye. With a sigh, he stood up and splashed cold water on his face. It wasn't fair of him to be angry with his wife. Of course, this was horrible for him, but it was hard for her too. It wouldn't help either of them if he crumbled under the pressure. Somehow he had to force himself to stay positive. Before long he would return to school. He might as well make good his claim, and take advantage of his unexpected time off to do some preparation. Seated at the dining room table with his iPad and a pad of A4 paper, he tried to focus on objectives and resources, learning outcomes and differentiation, but his thoughts kept wandering.

His worst fear was the possibility that he might never be reinstated. No one could prove he was guilty of any wrongdoing, but nor could he prove he was innocent. It was a stalemate. It seemed unlikely that he could convince the little bitch to retract her accusation, but on balance that was the only means he could think of to extricate himself from this mess. Unless he could persuade her to admit that she had lied in claiming he had attempted to force her to have sex with him, his career was over. Even if the head's investigation concluded that he was blameless, suspicion would linger. The accusation would remain indelibly on his record and he would never gain promotion or find another job. He would be trapped, and all because of that vicious little cow. It wasn't going to be easy, getting to speak to her, but he would wangle it somehow. The more he thought about it, the more he realised that was the only way he could ever hope to clear his name. He had to see her on her own and convince her to admit she had made a false allegation, or at least that she had been mistaken.

Used to the noise and activity and constant interruptions of the school day, he found it impossible to relax at home alone all day with his disturbing thoughts. By lunchtime he was feeling restless, so he went out to the pub. Entering the bar, he felt as though everyone was staring at him, whispering into their drinks. After gulping down a pint he gave up and left, stopping to buy a bottle of whisky in a corner shop on the way home. At least he could feel anonymous there. Nevertheless, the little man behind the counter gave him a suspicious glare as he handed over the whisky, and Paul scurried out of the shop like a guilty man. Pleased to get home, he poured himself a generous slug. The warm aroma hit him before the liquid burned in his throat, suffusing his mouth with a mellow glow. He slowed his breathing, aware of the tension leaving his muscles and his shoulders drooping as the alcohol reached his brain. Straightaway he started to feel better. The stress headache that had begun to plague him was replaced by a faint and welcome wooziness. Having refilled his glass, he hid the bottle in his school bag where Laura would never find it.

He needn't have bothered with the pretence because as soon as Laura returned home, she sniffed disparagingly and asked him if he had been drinking. All at once he was sick of having to justify himself.

'What if I have?' he blurted out testily. 'What's it to you?'

'Your breath stinks of whisky.'

'So now *you're* making accusations against me?'

'Don't be so ridiculous. I'm not accusing you of anything. I merely asked if you've been drinking.'

Gazing at her once familiar face, he felt as though he was looking into a stranger's eyes.

'I'm going out,' he muttered, unable to cope with her coldness.

Seizing his keys and wallet from the table, he rushed from the house. He hesitated before he slammed the front door, listening for his wife calling out his name, but the house was silent. The door closed behind him with an air of finality. Feeling sick, he realised that he had lost more than his job, thanks to one histrionic slut who had attacked him, when all she had to do was keep her stupid mouth shut.

4

CASSIE PAUSED IN UNBUTTONING her blouse and grinned nervously at him. There was barely enough light for her to see him, but she could tell that he wasn't looking at her.

She had thought everything would be back to normal between them, but there was something different about him this evening which made her uneasy. She couldn't work out what was wrong, but he seemed distant. Afraid she had annoyed him, she hesitated to challenge him for fear of alienating him further, but his coldness was difficult to bear.

'What's wrong?' she asked at last. 'I done everything you wanted. Whatever I done it's only so's we can be together all the time because we love each other, don't we? Tell me you love me. Tell me.'

'Oh, stop your whining.'

Taken aback by his aggressive tone, she fought to control her tears. 'I just want to be with you,' she stammered. 'That's all I want, and you said –'

'Just shut up, will you? And leave your clothes on, unless you want to freeze.'

Her fingers trembled as she fumbled to do up the buttons on her blouse and pull her jumper down. With a toss of her head she shook her shoulder length blonde hair, miserably wishing it was sleeker and shinier. Her friends at school assured her it looked fine, like a genuine natural blonde, but her mother was less complimentary. She was annoyed with Cassie for repeatedly bleaching it.

'Your hair's going to end up looking like wool,' she grumbled. 'And if you don't stop bleaching it, it's all going to fall out, you'll see. I don't know why you have to keep messing about with it. What's wrong with the hair you were born with?'

Cassie smoothed her dry hair with the palms of her hands before turning to him with a flirtatious smile. He had often told her she was irresistible. She saw no reason for that to have changed.

'I can't believe a girl as gorgeous as you would fall for someone like me,' he had said, several times.

But that was before she had made her accusation in front of the whole class. Now he seemed completely indifferent to her, and she was scared. As she looked out of the window, a light drizzle began to fall between the trees, scarcely visible in the gathering dusk. There was no one else about, just the two of them sitting side by side in the car, in a private world of their own. It was so romantic, she could scarcely control her disappointment at his coldness. Tentatively she reached across and placed her hand on his crotch, but he batted her groping fingers away with an impatient expletive. Instead of wanting sex with her, he told her to get out of the car.

'What about you?' she asked. 'Are you coming with me?'

He didn't answer.

She tried again. 'It's raining. We can do it here. Why do you want to go out in the rain?'

Quietly he explained that he was staying in the car. She was the one who was leaving.

'When will I see you again?' she asked, sudden fear clutching at her stomach.

'You won't.'

'I don't understand.'

'It's quite simple. This is over. I don't want to see you again.'

The finality in his tone made her feel sick. 'You can't –' she stammered. 'We have to see each other. You need me. You know you do. You said so. You said you wanted to keep me with you always.' Aware that she was sounding plaintive, she struggled not to cry.

'And now I'm saying it's over between us,' he said impatiently. 'Don't be a pain in the neck. Just get out of the car.'

She refused to believe him. 'What you talking about?' Tears would be smudging her mascara, but she didn't care. 'What's wrong with you? We're good together, you know we are. You said, you promised me –'

All at once she grew angry, her rage fuelled by the growing realisation that he really didn't want to see her any more. 'You can't dump me,' she snarled. 'Not after everything I done for you. It's not going to end like this. It can't. We mean too much to each other. I know you want me,' she went on, pleading frantically now. 'You said you can't stop thinking about me. You said –'

'Stop making a fuss and get out.' He turned to glare at her, his eyes seeming to bore into hers. 'Whatever you think you mean to me, you're fooling yourself. You mean nothing to me, nothing. Now get out of my car.'

'No, no, you can't do this,' she wailed. 'I know where you live,' she added, with a sudden flash of cunning.

'Do you think you can threaten me, you little whore? Get out before I throw you out.'

She leaned back in her seat and folded her arms to signal her refusal to budge. He was in a mood with her, that was all. He would think better of it soon enough. He couldn't resist her for long. She stared straight ahead, feeling the car vibrate when he slammed his door. The rain had grown heavier. If she went outside now, her hair would get wet and she wouldn't have time to straighten it before school in the morning. It wouldn't be the first time she had bunked off on a Friday, but she didn't want her hair messed up anyway. At the periphery of her vision she was vaguely aware of him running round to the passenger door. Too late, she realised his intention and reached forward to lock her door. He was already yanking it open. He leaned in to grab her, and hauled her bodily out of the car, his wet hair dripping on her face. She screamed, as much in rage as fear at the way he was manhandling her, but he slapped his hand over her mouth and hissed in her ear.

'Shut up, you little bitch.'

His glove pressed hard against her mouth, filling her nostrils with the stale smell of leather as he pushed her head right back, making her choke. She began struggling in earnest, terrified that he would break her neck, yet at the same time curiously excited by his closeness. He shoved her down on the ground and she let out a low grunt of relief, knowing that she was still irresistible and he had come to his senses. But instead of relaxing his grip to scrabble at her clothes, he pressed down harder, moving the position of his hand so that he was gripping her nose between his finger and thumb, all the while pushing down hard on her mouth. She tried to cry out, to warn him that she couldn't breathe, but she could only manage a faint moan. The back of her head was painfully squashed against the hard ground, and his hand kept pressing down on her mouth until she felt her teeth digging painfully into the soft flesh inside her lower lip.

Terror gripped her and she felt her guts turn to water. She wanted to cry out, to beg him to stop, to ask him who was going to take care of her little sister if she wasn't there to look out for her. Their mother was never home, but Cassie saw to it that her sister had something to eat after school, even if it was only chips. Cassie had to be there to make sure her sister wasn't so

LEIGH RUSSELL

grubby that she would be humiliated in front of her classmates and come home with tear-stained cheeks. Desperately she tried to push him away, but he didn't budge. He was crushing her chest with one knee now, without relieving the pressure on her mouth and nose. Panicking, she kicked out and flung her arms at him in a frenzy but she wasn't strong enough to push him away. A horrible lassitude seized her, and pain radiated from her chest like boiling lava spewing out of a volcano.

5

IAN HAVING LEFT ON Thursday evening, on Friday morning Geraldine woke up in rare and glorious solitude. When she stretched out under the duvet, instead of hitting the warmth of Ian's leg, her toes felt an unfamiliar coolness in the far corner of the bed. She drew her legs back, luxuriating in the warmth of her own body. Her sense of relaxation faded as she realised it was no longer dark outside, and after a few minutes she reached for her phone to check the time. It was nearly eight o'clock. She wasn't due at work yet, but she was wide awake. Abandoning any hope of sleeping late, she flung her covers off and jumped out of bed. She pulled the curtains open, and gazed out over myriad speckles of sunlight flickering on the river flowing past her veranda, before padding into the kitchen to brew some fresh coffee.

Still in her pyjamas, she went out on to her balcony. The sky was cloudless, promising a fine day, and she hoped the weather was equally sunny where Ian was staying until Monday evening. With a sigh of contentment, she settled down with a mug of coffee and a new book. She had scarcely opened her book when her phone rang. After hearing the message, she hurried indoors to dress and pull her fingers through her cropped black hair, before driving straight into work. She arrived just as Detective Chief Inspector Binita Hewitt was about to brief the team.

Geraldine glanced around the group. Naomi Arnold, recently promoted to detective sergeant, was staring fixedly at the DCI as though the intensity of her gaze might reveal her senior officer's thoughts. When Geraldine had first joined the team in York, she had been concerned that her young colleague was too skittish to be reliable, but Naomi had developed into a staunch member of the team. She and Geraldine had helped each other out several times in the past. Geraldine had rescued Naomi from a potentially dangerous predicament, as a result of which they had developed a strong bond. Since then, Geraldine had been acting as a kind of unofficial mentor to her younger colleague. Next to Naomi was an experienced detective sergeant, Ariadne Croft. She had recently married and was Geraldine's closest friend in York. Several constables were present, both men and women, but before Geraldine had a chance to study them each in turn, Binita cleared her throat loudly to signal she was about to speak.

The DCI's black eyes were gleaming and her expression earnest as she announced that a girl's body had been discovered lying beside a path in Fishponds Wood. No one spoke, although everyone present was familiar with the site, which was less than four miles from the police station. Geraldine's initial thoughts were that, although the wood was situated in York, areas of it were as secluded as some more remote places. It was feasible that a body could be deposited there by a careful killer unobserved, especially after dark. That suggested the murder could have been premeditated, which would make it harder for the police to track down the killer. But she dismissed such conjecture. Before starting to speculate about what had taken place, it was important to establish the facts and resist the temptation to blur any ideas with preconceptions.

'We haven't identified her yet, but the information we've received from those first on the scene is that she's young,' Binita went on.

'Are we looking at a child?' someone asked in a low voice.

'A teenager,' Binita replied. 'Her age hasn't yet been determined, but she's probably around fifteen. We should be able to identify her without too much trouble.' She paused. 'She's wearing what appears to be a generic school uniform.' Binita's black eyes looked around her colleagues, perhaps watching for any reaction to her words. No one's expression altered, and the DCI grunted. 'There seems to be little doubt that we're looking at a murder, so let's get moving quickly.'

In the absence of any further information, the team sprang into action. Evidence deteriorated quickly, especially out of doors, and witnesses' statements became less reliable with the passage of time, so it was important to work fast. A check on girls who had recently been reported missing was initiated, and Geraldine and Ariadne were despatched to Fishponds Wood to question the witnesses who had discovered the body.

'I do hate it when the victim's young,' Ariadne grumbled as they walked towards the car park. 'It just seems such a shame.'

'Worse than when an older person is murdered? Or a young mother?' Geraldine asked. 'Or any parent for that matter. And isn't an old person's life as valuable as a young one? What about a doctor? Or someone conducting groundbreaking research into a cure for cancer? Can we really place a higher value on one life over another?'

Ariadne sighed. 'No, of course you're right. It doesn't make any difference how old or young the victim is, or what they do. But it just gets to me more when it's a youngster. I can't justify feeling that way. It's not entirely rational.'

Geraldine nodded. 'I know what you mean. Somehow it seems more of a waste of a life when the victim hasn't even really had a chance to live.'

'Exactly,' Ariadne agreed, sounding almost relieved. 'That's what I meant. How much can any teenager really experience of life? A vague education of sorts? A few fumbling sexual encounters? When I was fifteen I hadn't lived at all.'

Ariadne drove them across the city. The traffic was heavy. She put her foot down whenever possible, but it took a long time to travel the short distance to the site. By the time they reached the woods, the area had been secured, a forensic tent had been erected, the mortuary van had arrived and scene of crime officers were already busy scrutinising the site and the surrounding area. The tent had been set up across a narrow pathway between the trees. The sun that had been shining brightly earlier on was obscured by ominous grey clouds and, under bright artificial lights, leafy branches cast eerie shadows across the grass and damp mud of the path.

6

GERALDINE AND ARIADNE PULLED on their protective suits in silence and approached the tent, taking care to keep to the common approach path.

'Have you found anything significant?' Geraldine asked the first scene of crime officer she passed.

'Well,' he said, his eyes creasing as though he was grinning, 'there's a body over there. I'd say that's pretty significant. I mean, it's why we were all dragged away from our breakfast to scratch around in the mud here searching for scraps of evidence.'

Geraldine grunted and rephrased her question, speaking rapidly so as not to hold the SOCO up for long. Any delay in examining a crime scene risked decomposition and contamination of the evidence.

'I meant, have you come across any indication as to how she died?'

'The medical officer's on his way,' the SOCO replied. 'He'll be able to tell you more. There's no sign of a weapon that we can see, but it does rather look as though she was bashed on the head with something. It's difficult to see how much blood has soaked into the ground and, of course, it rained last night, just to make our job more difficult, but there's a few streaks of blood still in her hair. Her face is bruised and battered. Someone definitely wasn't happy with her.'

'Was she killed here?'

'That's difficult to say, especially as it's been raining overnight. But there are some fairly fresh tyre tracks which haven't quite been washed away. So we think she was brought here by car; whether dead or alive is difficult to say. Once we've examined the soil we'll have a better idea of whether she bled here or was already dead when she was deposited here.'

'If she came here with someone, that would certainly help our investigation. But could she have been walking here and been attacked by a stranger?'

The SOCO's eyes looked serious. 'It's possible, but there's hardly any mud on her shoes, dry or otherwise, and no sign of recent footprints, and we have a couple of tyre tracks. But nothing's certain. She was found by a couple on an early morning run before work. Health freaks,' he added disparagingly. 'Catch me out of bed for a run before work. They're over there if you want to have a word, but they're both quite shocked and don't seem to have much to say for themselves. Nothing very coherent, anyway.'

He gestured towards a young man and woman standing beside a police van. They were both wrapped in silver foil sheets although the morning was mild. They gazed blankly at Geraldine as she approached, but didn't move. She flashed her badge and introduced herself.

'We always like to go for a run before work,' the woman blurted out, as though Geraldine had enquired what they were doing out on the path in the woods so early. 'That way we know we'll get the exercise.' She smiled anxiously. 'Unless it's raining.' She paused. 'She was just lying there, on the path. We called the police – you – straightaway. We could see she was dead. We didn't think it was worth asking for an ambulance –'

'We didn't know what to do,' the man added.

The couple had nothing more to tell Geraldine. They had

phoned the emergency services and waited for the police to arrive.

'We didn't know what else to do.' The woman repeated what her companion had said. Suddenly she became talkative. 'We weren't really sure if she was unconscious or – you know, dead. It could have been drink or drugs, or she could have collapsed and passed out because she was ill, diabetic or something. We didn't know. But she didn't move all the time we were waiting. And then they told us. We couldn't have done anything,' she added, with a shudder. 'We didn't know what to do. Should we have called an ambulance?'

Geraldine reassured them that they had done what they could. She hoped for their sake that the girl had already been dead by the time she was found, but there was nothing she could do about that. Either way, they had nothing with which to reproach themselves.

After thanking the couple she entered the tent and turned her attention to the body. One glance at the slender feet confirmed that the dead girl hadn't been out for a walk in the woods. She wasn't wearing hiking boots or trainers, and her high black heels looked scuffed but clean. She was lying on her back, her eyes wide open and her mouth gaping as though she was screaming. Badly dyed blonde hair was splayed out around her head and there was a dark streak on one side, where her hair was stained with blood. Dressed in a white shirt and dark green skirt which could have been a school uniform, she looked very young, but there were grey bags under her eyes and, together with thick smudged make-up, her face appeared somehow wizened and old. Her arms were extended sideways, the fingers curled as though she wanted to scratch her assailant with her long pink nails. Geraldine knew that muscles contracted in death, and the tension in the dead girl's hands could be a consequence of rigor, but her position made her look as if she was trying to fight someone off.

Around the tent several SOCOs were working in silence, taking care not to disturb the body. Geraldine was reluctant to interrupt them, but after a few minutes one of the white-coated figures came over to her.

'She looks very young,' Geraldine said, by way of greeting.

The SOCO answered in a hushed voice. 'That's what we all thought.'

'Can you tell us anything about her?'

He shook his head. 'Only what you can see, which isn't much to go on. The cause of death hasn't been established yet. Someone else was probably involved, if only because she must have got here somehow, and she doesn't appear to have walked far. She doesn't look too battered, except around the face. It looks as though she might have tripped or been thrown to the ground and hit her head, but that's just speculation, really. The medical officer should be here soon, and the PM will be able to tell you even more.'

'Was this a sexual assault?' Geraldine asked.

'It's hard to say, but she's fully clothed although she's not wearing a coat and there's no sign of one anywhere nearby.'

A light rain began to fall as Geraldine walked thoughtfully back to the car where Ariadne was waiting for her, looking glum.

'She was very young,' Ariadne said, shaking her long black curls. 'She could have been lying there all night. If those joggers hadn't spotted her, who knows how long she would have been here before she was found.'

Geraldine shivered and turned away. It made no difference to the dead girl, but it was pitiful to think of her lying there, abandoned.

7

THE ANATOMICAL PATHOLOGY TECHNICIAN, Avril, was a cheerful young blonde who had recently got engaged. Although Geraldine had only ever met her in the mortuary, they had formed an unspoken bond through their routine exposure to murder victims, while their shared stoical approach to death had engendered in them a mutual respect. The next morning, Avril greeted Geraldine like an old friend, and responded eagerly to a polite enquiry about her wedding plans.

'We really wanted a summer wedding,' Avril explained, 'but all the best venues are fully booked until the autumn. Bob suggested we go abroad, but we can't expect everyone to go flying off somewhere, and I don't want to get married without all our friends and family there celebrating with us, and my mother doesn't like flying. It would ruin it for her, I know it would. Honestly, it's been a complete nightmare to organise.'

Geraldine listened patiently to Avril's account of her wedding plans. Finally Avril turned her attention to the reason for Geraldine's visit to the mortuary.

'What's happened to Jonah?' Geraldine asked, when Avril told her that it wasn't the usual pathologist conducting the post mortem on the dead girl.

'Even Jonah's entitled to a holiday.'

'Not when there's a body to examine,' Geraldine protested, making no effort to hide her disappointment. 'Oh well, who have we got instead? Someone helpful, I hope.'

Avril's smile faded, and she lowered her voice as she answered solemnly. 'It's Catherine Collins.'

'I haven't come across her before. What's she like?' Geraldine enquired, slightly disconcerted by Avril's sour expression.

'You're about to find out.'

Geraldine gathered that Avril was unhappy about Jonah going away, and she sympathised. Jonah was good-natured, and he made light of his grisly job, which meant he was easy to work with. Anyone else would almost inevitably seem dreary in comparison. Entering the mortuary, Geraldine saw a gaunt woman with a stern expression. Fair hair scraped back severely off her face emphasised her prominent cheekbones, and her overalls contrived to look neat despite being smeared with blood. Her dour appearance was in keeping with the brutal nature of her work, but Geraldine missed the warmth and humour of Jonah's customary welcome.

'Catherine Collins,' the pathologist replied tersely when Geraldine introduced herself.

Preliminary greetings swiftly dispensed with, Catherine drew on fresh gloves, pulled up her mask and turned back to her work.

'The victim was young,' she said gruffly.

Geraldine sighed. 'That's what everyone's been saying.'

Catherine raised her eyebrows, as though surprised that anyone else would have commented on the age of the victim.

'She hadn't been sexually assaulted on this occasion,' the pathologist continued, sounding curiously offhand.

'On this occasion?' Geraldine echoed uneasily.

'Our victim here was no virgin. She had an abortion, possibly as long as a year ago. It's impossible to pin a time down with any degree of certainty. I'd say she was no more than seventeen when she was killed, maybe as young as a well-developed fourteen-year-old. Again, it's difficult to tell.

The soles of her shoes weren't muddy or scratched, so she was probably transported to the woods by car, but she could have cycled there.'

'There was no bicycle found anywhere nearby,' Geraldine said.

Catherine grunted and was silent. After waiting a while for her to resume speaking, Geraldine prompted her by enquiring about the cause of death.

Catherine nodded and spoke briskly. 'Someone attempted to strangle her.' She pointed to dark smudges on the victim's throat. 'You can see the contusions clearly. She also hit the back of her head.'

'Can you tell whether she tripped, or was thrown to the ground, or was pushed out of a car?' Geraldine asked.

Catherine's head jerked up. 'It's not my job to speculate about how it happened, but clearly someone did this to her.'

Geraldine nodded. She didn't need the results of a post mortem to tell her they were looking at a murder victim.

'So what was the actual cause of death?' she enquired. 'Strangulation or the blow to her head?'

'The head injury. She might have tripped and fallen backwards, or been pushed backwards from a car.' Catherine frowned. 'There's nothing to indicate that she tried to break her fall, or even spread the impact, by putting her hands out.' She paused. 'Someone attacked her, but there are no signs that she tried to resist.'

'Perhaps she was caught off guard, or knew her attacker,' Geraldine said. 'Or she might have been drugged and unable to defend herself.'

'She'd been drinking, but we'll know more when the tox report's back,' Catherine said.

'You just told me someone tried to strangle her,' Geraldine said. 'Could she have lost consciousness before she hit her head? Is it possible to tell whether the fatal head injury was caused by a fall or a blow?'

'That's difficult to tell with any certainty,' Catherine replied.

'Either way, someone else was there when she died.'

Catherine grunted.

'So to summarise,' Geraldine said briskly, 'it's looking like someone drove her there, strangled her and threw her from the car while she was unconscious but not yet dead, and in falling from the car she suffered a fatal blow to the head. She never recovered consciousness because there were no marks where her fingers tried to scrabble at the ground when she was thrown from the car.'

'Yes, that would fit, but she might have died from strangulation anyway, if her skull hadn't hit the ground. And she was run over,' Catherine added.

Geraldine stared at the pathologist. 'This is beginning to sound like Rasputin. What do you mean, she was run over?'

'After she died, she was run over by a vehicle. It didn't do much damage because there was a layer of mud and leaves on the path, so she just sank a little into the ground. Only one tyre of the car went over her, possibly as the car was reversing away. It didn't make any difference to her because she was dead by then anyway.'

'I wonder what she was doing in the woods at night,' Geraldine said.

'Up to no good, I dare say,' Catherine replied acidly.

'She was a teenager,' Geraldine said. 'Just a child, really.'

'Oh, I don't think you could call her a child any more. I told you, she was sexually active and she'd had at least one abortion.'

There was something unpleasantly cold about the way Catherine spoke about the dead girl. It wasn't merely that she seemed devoid of any emotion, which was necessary in her line of work. She sounded completely uninterested in the case, as though she was bored by the whole situation. There was even a hint of disgust in the way she referred to the victim. She didn't actually ask why the police were concerned about the death of a promiscuous teenager, but her attitude seemed to imply the question.

'Whatever her lifestyle, she didn't deserve to end up here, like this,' Geraldine said, more fiercely than she had intended. 'Her life had barely begun.'

Catherine didn't answer.

'What else can you tell us?'

Catherine gave a disapproving sniff. Geraldine couldn't see her mouth but could imagine her lips curling in disapproval behind her mask.

'We'll have to wait for the tox report, but her guts stank of beer.'

'Is there anything else you can tell me, while I'm here?'

Geraldine hesitated to add that Jonah would have been more forthcoming. He frequently went beyond the limits of what he was supposed to say, happy to offer his own speculation off the record.

'I won't quote you,' she added.

'If you can't quote it, then I won't say it,' Catherine responded tartly, before turning back to her grisly work.

Geraldine thanked the pathologist for her time and took her leave, grumbling to Avril on her way out that a morally judgemental attitude had no place in a mortuary.

'She seems very competent technically,' Avril said, as though she felt she ought to apologise for the pathologist's brusque manner.

'That's something, at least,' Geraldine said and they both smiled.

Driving back to the police station, Geraldine replayed her visit to the mortuary in her mind. Catherine's opinion of the victim seemed to be influenced by the knowledge that the girl had been sexually active. But that didn't alter the fact that she had been murdered. Geraldine hoped none of her other colleagues would be prejudiced by the victim's history, which had no real bearing on the case.

8

AT MIDDAY ON SUNDAY, a woman called Amanda came to the police station to report that her daughter was missing. Alert to the possibility that the missing girl could be the unidentified victim found in the woods, Geraldine found a small jittery dark-haired woman waiting in an interview room. She was clearly too stressed to sit still but fidgeted and squirmed on her chair as though desperate to leave. Noticing the woman's nicotine-stained fingers and the whiff of stale smoke that hung around her, Geraldine wondered whether she was primarily anxious about her missing daughter, or desperate for a cigarette.

'We'll keep this brief,' Geraldine said as she sat down, and Amanda nodded eagerly.

'You say your daughter's missing?'

The woman didn't seem to find anything strange in the fact that a detective inspector was questioning her. Probably she wasn't even aware of Geraldine's rank. In answer to an initial question, she gave her daughter's name as Cassie.

'That's short for Cassandra, but everyone calls her Cassie,' she added. 'She hates it when I call her Cassandra. She says it's pretentious. Well, no one likes their own name, do they?'

Amanda told Geraldine that her missing daughter was sixteen. 'Just sixteen, to be exact, although you wouldn't think it, not when you see her. She doesn't look much more than thirteen, although she manages to pass herself off as older than that.' She screwed up her eyes and squinted at Geraldine, as though sizing

45

her up. 'When she's all dressed up to go out, she looks a lot older, of course. They all do. She could easily pass for eighteen. And, of course, they all have their fake ID, don't they?'

Geraldine learned that Cassie was a natural brunette who dyed her hair blonde.

'She does it herself, and she doesn't do a very good job of it. I told her, if she carries on like that, all her hair's going to fall out before long. It's already dry as straw and looks more like wool than hair. I don't know why she does it. She's a beautiful girl. Why she needs to wear all that muck on her face and ruin her hair like that... I mean, some dark-haired girls do go blonde very nicely, when it's done professionally. But not Cassie. Not the way she does it. She won't go to a proper hairdresser. She says it costs too much, but I don't think it's the money. She's just bloodyminded. You know how it is with teenagers. They think they know best.'

She was evidently irritated by her daughter's insistence on dying her hair herself. Geraldine gathered they had disagreed and wondered what else they had argued about.

'How tall is she?' Geraldine asked, although she suspected she already knew the answer to any other questions concerning Cassie's physical appearance.

Amanda shook her head. 'Average sort of height for her age, I suppose. She's not particularly tall.'

'When did you last see her?' Geraldine enquired gently.

Irrationally, she wanted Amanda to say she had seen her daughter the previous evening. That would mean the body in the woods couldn't possibly be Cassie Jackson. Meanwhile, Amanda's description of her daughter could certainly match that of the body found in Fishponds Wood. Geraldine was keen to discover the identity of the dead girl, so that they could start investigating the people she had known, looking for her killer. Yet she hoped for Amanda's sake that Cassie wasn't dead. But whatever her identity while she was alive, nothing could alter the fact that a dead girl was lying in the mortuary, her eyes unseeing, her skin cold.

'I suppose you could say she's blonde,' the woman continued, staring at Geraldine with an expression that seemed to display irritation rather than concern. 'But she isn't a real blonde. I mean, she couldn't pass herself off as blonde, not really.'

She seemed unreasonably exercised by the colour of her daughter's hair. Aware that fear could manifest itself in unexpected ways, Geraldine continued with her questions.

'You said you last saw her on Thursday morning before you left for work?'

Amanda nodded, a trifle reluctantly.

'So that means she hasn't been home at all since Thursday morning?'

Amanda nodded again.

'Why did you wait three days before reporting her absence?'

Amanda looked uncomfortable, but she must have been expecting this question.

'She often stays with friends,' she said quickly. 'I wouldn't have come here bothering you like this, only she has a Sunday job and they phoned to say she hadn't turned up this morning. They said they'd warned her she'd be out on her ear if she didn't turn up again without letting them know. So I just wondered if something might have happened to her. I'm sure it's nothing.'

Her voice broke and she pressed her hand to her lips, suppressing a sob, mumbling that she was sure her daughter was fine.

'Did you contact her friend?'

'What friend?'

'The one she was staying with? She could still be there.'

Amanda shrugged and muttered that her daughter had lots of friends.

'Didn't she let you know where she was spending the night?'

'She's a popular girl,' Amanda replied, refusing to meet Geraldine's eye. 'She stays with lots of – girls. Cassie's not a bad girl, but she's – she's a little wild. That is, she's going through a difficult phase. Puberty and all that. You know, discovering boys. And I'm a single parent. It's not easy. Do you have any daughters?'

Remembering the pathologist's words about the dead girl's abortion, Geraldine wondered how well Amanda knew her daughter. Instead of answering her question, she acknowledged that teenagers could be wilful. If she was honest, she was reluctant to tell the anxious mother about the girl lying in the mortuary. Of course, she couldn't put it off for long. All that remained was to ask to see a picture of the missing girl. Amanda pulled out her phone and immediately scotched any question that Cassie was dead. The girl pouting flirtatiously at the camera looked very different to the grey-faced corpse lying in the mortuary, but there could no longer be any doubt.

'I'm so sorry,' Geraldine said. 'I'm afraid I have some bad news for you.'

The other woman shook her head, perhaps anticipating what Geraldine was going to say. Amanda grew hysterical on hearing that her daughter's body had been discovered abandoned in Fishponds Woods. Bursting into noisy tears, she wailed that Cassie was all she had. There was no one else in her life, just her and her daughter. Her initial outburst rapidly switched to disbelief. Cassie couldn't be dead, she insisted. She was barely sixteen. It wasn't possible.

'She's run away before,' she said, her eyes gleaming with frantic conviction. 'She's a teenager. That's what teenagers do, isn't it? But she always comes home. She always comes home in the end. She never goes to Fishponds Wood,' she added, wiping her eyes and glaring furiously at Geraldine. 'Whoever you found there, it's not Cassie. It can't be. She's never gone there. Never. Not Cassie. She always comes home. She always comes home.'

But Geraldine had seen images of Cassie on her mother's phone, and they both knew Cassie was dead. All that remained was for Amanda to identify her daughter's body. A constable brought Amanda tea and sat with her while Geraldine called the mortuary and arranged for the identification to take place.

'It's just a formality,' she told Avril, before ringing off. 'It's definitely Cassie Jackson.'

'I don't know what to do,' Amanda wailed when Geraldine told her a constable could take her to the mortuary that afternoon. 'I don't know what to do. How can I bury my daughter?' Suddenly decisive, she sat up straight. 'The funeral – I'll arrange it as soon as possible. I want to lay her to rest.' She began to cry again. 'I want to lay her to rest.'

'I'm afraid that won't be possible just yet,' Geraldine said gently.

As tactfully as she could, she explained that Cassie had not died from natural causes. 'We are looking into whether or not her death was an accident,' she added. 'I'm so sorry.'

9

DETECTIVE CHIEF INSPECTOR BINITA Hewitt gazed calmly around the assembled team. Her air of quiet determination made a pleasant change from their previous senior officer, who had rushed at murder enquiries like a ferocious bull charging across a field. Following the detective chief inspector's glance, Geraldine saw that several of her colleagues were bleary eyed, as though they were only just waking up. Many of them were clutching mugs of tea or, more likely, strong coffee, and one or two were blinking sleepily. It was earlier than most of them would usually have been at work on a Monday morning, but all personal concerns were swept aside now they had a murder to investigate.

Binita's black eyes looked bright, and she spoke briskly, showing no sign of fatigue. Somehow her slender frame gave a tough impression, and she held herself very upright. Geraldine wondered how wide awake she herself appeared as she lowered her head to stifle a yawn. Blowing on her scalding hot coffee, she took a sip and stared at Binita, doing her best to look alert and attentive.

'Now we have a confirmed identity for the victim, it's time to start looking into the circumstances of her life, and not just focusing on the manner of her death,' Binita was saying. 'We can't afford to waste a moment in finding out who did this. We want him behind bars as soon as possible.'

She didn't need to add that, while the attack on Cassie could have been a one off, there was a chance this killer might seek out another young victim.

'If you ask me, prison's too good for him,' Ariadne muttered fiercely.

'Why are we convinced the killer is male?' Geraldine asked.

'Assume nothing,' Binita replied, 'except that Cassie Jackson was murdered and we're going to do everything we can to find her killer right away. So come on, let's get to it.'

Tasks were swiftly allocated. First on the list for Geraldine was to take a small team to visit the school Cassie had attended. The head teacher's secretary was a thin middle-aged woman. Dressed in a matching turquoise jumper and cardigan, she peered at Geraldine through the lenses of her tortoiseshell-framed glasses. Smelling faintly of talcum powder, she was wearing a gold wedding ring and an engagement ring with a tiny diamond. As soon as Geraldine introduced herself, she was escorted to the head teacher's office. Mr Wilson rose to his feet and greeted her solemnly. He was a tall man, his hair shot through with grey. Shrewd eyes gazed directly at her from beneath overhanging brows, as they sat down on either side of his desk.

'This is a terrible shock to us all,' he said solemnly. 'The pupils are understandably in pieces. We're doing our best to carry on as normal but it's difficult, especially for her class, and teaching has been completely disrupted. She was a popular girl.'

He hesitated ever so slightly before the word 'popular', making it sound almost like an insult, and Geraldine wondered about the reason for the dead girl's popularity. The pathologist was sure Cassie had been sexually active for a while. In death she had lost the allure of youth, but the images on her mother's phone had shown her to be attractive, despite her gaudy make-up. Her brash appearance might well have appealed to teenage boys. And there was no reason to suppose that older men

51

might not have been tempted by her provocative appearance as well.

'How would you describe Cassie? A sensible girl? A good student?' Geraldine questioned him about the dead girl's lifestyle.

'I hardly know what to say.' The head teacher heaved another sigh. 'To be frank with you, she has come to my attention more because of her absences than anything she did. And there have been repeated infringements of the rules, mainly those relating to uniform. Those were relatively trivial matters. What is more concerning was that she hasn't been regular in her attendance, and from what I understand from Cassie's form tutor, her mother doesn't seem to care. At any rate, she's been complicit in confirming Cassie's excuses for her absences. It's not unusual,' he added as though he felt the need to defend the school for not taking issue with Cassie's mother for her irresponsible attitude towards her daughter's education. 'She suffered a series of stomach aches, toothaches, headaches, none of which was corroborated by any medical certification. It's a disappointing situation, but it happens, especially with teenagers. They can be very strong willed and it's not unusual for parents to struggle to control them. I've seen little of Cassie, personally. Until her allegation, that is,' he added grimly.

'What allegation is that?'

He looked taken aback, then nodded. 'Of course, you'll need to hear it from me. Very well. There has been an allegation.'

Unsure where this was leading, Geraldine sat perfectly still, waiting.

'Cassie Jackson made an accusation against a member of staff.' Mr Wilson cleared his throat. 'A serious allegation of a sexual nature.'

Geraldine concealed her surprise. 'When was this allegation reported?'

'We suspended the teacher with immediate effect, and are conducting an internal enquiry.' He raised his hands in a gesture of resignation. 'The allegation was only made last Monday, and it was possibly –' he hesitated and lowered his eyes before continuing. 'We need to gather statements from all the witnesses before taking the matter further.'

'There were witnesses?' Geraldine said.

'Not to any misdemeanour, you understand,' Mr Wilson reassured her quickly. 'Only to the allegation. If we had confirmation it was actually true we would have handed the matter over to the police – to you – straightaway. But a man's career is at stake, Inspector, and we wanted to be sure about what we were dealing with before taking this further. Once the complaint is in the public domain, there is no going back, you understand? Of course, we can't stop pupils from sharing their reactions on social media, so any attempt on our part to be discreet proved entirely futile.' He sighed. 'We wanted to protect the teacher's reputation while we were looking into the accusation.'

'Are you saying you don't believe the allegation was true?'

The head hesitated. 'The circumstances made it appear unlikely that there is any substance to the claim.'

'Circumstances?'

'The assault is alleged to have taken place just as a class was due to arrive in the room. That naturally raised some doubt. The accused is an experienced teacher, and a happily married man. It seems unlikely he would have risked everything – his career, his marriage, his whole future – in so reckless a manner. There are clocks in every classroom and, of course, there are bells. He couldn't have mistaken the time. So he would have been expecting his next class to arrive, as would the girl who made the allegation. Given the time of the alleged assault we decided, on balance, to conduct a rigorous internal investigation before taking this further. On being questioned, one of the girl's close associates told my colleague that Cassie had confided to her that the allegation was untrue. But, of course, we are still obliged to take this situation very seriously and we are looking into it thoroughly.' He paused. 'In the meantime, we have been held up by Cassie being away from school since Thursday, and we have been unable to contact her mother. We are conducting our investigation as swiftly as possible and, should any doubt remain, we will hand the matter over to you.' He sighed again. 'As things stand, I'm afraid there's not much more I can tell you. If Cassie refuses to retract her allegation, as I suspect she will –'

Geraldine interrupted him. 'Cassie won't retract her allegation.'

'I see. Well, it seems Cassie has decided to take the matter into her own hands and report it to you. Why else would you be here?' He smiled sadly. 'So, let the official process begin. The staff member concerned has no doubt been in contact with his union –'

'Cassie hasn't reported anything to the police,' Geraldine said.

Mr Wilson looked surprised. 'Then how did you know about the allegation?'

Geraldine told him she had been ignorant of the incident until he had told her about it.

'Then I'm afraid I don't understand – what are you doing here?'

'I'm very sorry to tell you that Cassie Jackson has been murdered.'

10

FOR A MOMENT MR Wilson stared at Geraldine without saying a word.

'Murdered?' he repeated at last in a curiously strangled voice, as though he was struggling to draw breath. 'You're telling me Cassie was murdered? Oh good lord. Cassie Jackson? Are you sure? I mean, I had no idea. This is terrible. When did this happen? And how did it happen?' Without waiting for Geraldine to respond, he blurted out more questions. 'Do you know who it was? Are you quite sure it was deliberate? I mean, it couldn't have been an accident? What happened, exactly? Have you arrested whoever was responsible?'

Geraldine repeated her condolences and explained that a murder investigation was under way.

'We have a team of trained officers waiting outside, ready to question all Cassie's classmates, as well as the pupils who entered the room while the alleged assault was taking place. We will require a member of your staff to accompany the pupils while we talk to them.'

'Yes, yes, of course, of course,' Mr Wilson said, recovering his outward equanimity and turning his thoughts to what needed to be done. 'We must tell the whole school as soon as possible, before any rumours start. I'm afraid the pupils are going to assume that Paul Moore was responsible. They're already convinced he's a paedophile. He'll never be able to return here, even if he proves his innocence. Oh dear, oh dear, what a terrible thing to happen.'

Geraldine wasn't sure if the head teacher was referring to the ruin of a man's career, the alleged sexual misconduct, or Cassie's murder.

'I'll call a staff meeting at first break so pupils can be given the sad news in their own classrooms by their form teachers. After that, we will need to contact the parents.'

'We would like to speak to the pupils concerned individually, and as soon as possible.'

The head suggested the pupil interviews take place in the afternoon, to allow the children time to process the shocking news. Geraldine would have preferred to begin at once, before the pupils had time to discuss what they had seen,

but she acceded to Mr Wilson's request. It was probably far too late to prevent the witnesses from comparing notes. They were unlikely to have been discussing anything else since the allegation had been made.

'And it goes without saying that my staff and I will do everything we can to help,' the head added, nodding at Geraldine. 'Is there anything else you need to know?'

Geraldine said she was keen to find out as much as she could about Cassie's time at the school.

'What was she like? Who were her friends? To your knowledge, did she have any enemies? And can you tell me anything about her family and her home life?'

Cassie's family members were of more interest to the police than her schoolfriends, but at this early stage in the investigation no one could be discounted. Repeating that he knew very little about Cassie, the head teacher summoned the head of year, Jane Delaney, the teacher who had been responsible for Cassie's wellbeing. Mr Wilson hurried away to make his arrangements, and a few moments later Geraldine was joined by a youngish woman with a sharply pointed nose. In repose she wore a sullen expression but she had a ready smile and her voice was low and gentle. Once introductions were over, Geraldine explained the reason for her visit. Although shocked, Jane didn't appear surprised on hearing that Cassie had been killed.

'I'm afraid Cassie was a little wild,' she said with a grimace that could have signified disapproval or regret, or possibly both.

'Wild?' Geraldine queried. 'Are we talking about drugs?'

'No. That's not what I meant. She wasn't taking drugs, at least not in school. We don't have that problem here. We have a zero tolerance policy on drugs. But, of course, we have no control over what our pupils get up to off the premises. But no, I don't think Cassie was involved in drugs as such, not as far as I know, anyway. She might well have smoked cannabis, and cigarettes, and she probably drank, but not in school.' She sighed. 'It's so frustrating, but a lot of our pupils seem to spend their weekends getting wasted, as they call it. And it's an appropriate name for how they waste their time, getting drunk or stoned. We just can't get through to some of them that there's more to life than knocking their brains out with various substances, legal or otherwise. They have their whole futures ahead of them, but they just don't see the value of education. I'm not talking about our pupils as a whole, you understand,' she added, suddenly anxious. 'I wouldn't want you to think badly of us here. The majority of our pupils are extremely sensible hard-working young people and we're justifiably proud of their achievements. But I can't deny there's a minority of pupils who go off the rails. It's more to do with their home background than anything that goes on in school. I'm afraid our influence is very limited.'

'I'm guessing Cassie wasn't one of the sensible ones?' Geraldine said, and Jane sighed.

'Cassie was wild,' she repeated. 'She was – she was trouble in a certain way. It wasn't just that she caused trouble. She *was* trouble, but – have you read *Of Mice and Men*, Inspector?'

Puzzled by the question, Geraldine shook her head. 'Not for a very long time,' she replied.

'Perhaps you recall the girl in it? The only female character in the book. She doesn't have a name. She's just known as a wife to indicate how, as a woman, she has no value and no identity in a male environment other than for sex. She's seductive, so she's viewed as "jailbait" by the other characters, who are wary of her. They're all afraid of the havoc she might wreak in their lives, if they succumb to her attractions.'

'And you think Cassie was sexually provocative in the same way?'

Jane shrugged. 'You make it sound as though I think she was some kind of sexual predator, responsible for what happened. Look, she was a sixteen-year-old girl who was interested in boys. That's only natural in a teenager. But – I'm telling you this in confidence – there was something slightly off kilter about her attitude towards sex. A lot of teenagers are obsessed with sex but with her it was an unhealthy fixation, and it started very early. Even at thirteen she was manipulating boys into doing what she wanted by offering them sexual favours. I'm afraid her sexual experience may have begun when she was very young. It seems likely she was sexually abused as a child. There was an investigation a few years ago, when she first joined us, but it all came to nothing. In the absence of any proof, there's not much that can be done and Cassie was adamant she hadn't suffered any abuse. But many of us suspected she was covering something up.'

The teacher sighed before resuming her account. 'Anyway, by sixteen she had a history of casual promiscuity. I'm not saying this to be judgemental, you understand. I'm just trying to give you an idea of the kind of girl she is – was. Plenty of sexually precocious teenagers mature into adults who have stable relationships, and Cassie might well have done that if she'd lived. I'm just telling you she was promiscuous. You understand I'm not saying that to criticise her, I'm just trying to describe what she was like.' She gave a helpless shrug. 'Her mother gave her no support at all. And then there was the incident with Paul Moore. What's going to happen to him now? I mean, if he's guilty, of course, we'd all want to see him thrown out of the profession to face criminal charges. But Cassie was sixteen and she was – well, like I said, she wasn't exactly innocent. Where sex was involved, she knew what she was doing.' There was a touch of bitterness in her voice, and Geraldine wondered if she had been friendly with the teacher Cassie had accused of assaulting her.

'Paul Moore?' Geraldine repeated. 'What can you tell me about Paul Moore?'

Jane looked worried. 'Cassie made an allegation against him, it's true. But have you met Paul Moore?'

Carefully, Geraldine explained that she had only heard about the allegation against Jane's colleague that morning, from the head teacher. There was no need to point out the coincidence of his accuser being killed just three days after he had been suspended.

'If it's his word against hers, I'd take whatever she says with a massive pinch of salt. I don't think she –' She broke off suddenly, perhaps remembering that Cassie was dead. 'I don't want to say anything –' She fell silent, biting her lower lip. 'What I mean is, I know the poor girl's dead, but – well, Paul's a good man. He's conscientious, and decent, and there's no way he would have assaulted that pupil. As for killing her, that's just impossible.'

After thanking the teacher for her help, Geraldine said that when questioning of the pupils began, she would like to speak to Cassie's closest friend first.

11

ASTUTE EYES STARED AT Geraldine from a sullen childlike face. Cassie's friend and alleged confidante was pale, her shrewd expression at odds with her slender figure and wispy white blonde hair. At first glance she looked as though a gust of wind might blow her away. Closer study revealed a determination in the rigid set of her mouth and the way her chin jutted out, as though warning an observer that she was not as soft and delicate as she appeared. Before Geraldine had finished her reassuring introductory remarks, Ella interrupted her with a moue of impatience.

'So was it that paedo done her in?' she demanded in a shrill nasal voice.

'I'm sorry?' Geraldine replied. 'Tell me exactly who you're talking about.'

Geraldine knew perfectly well the girl was referring to Paul Moore. All the same, she threw a questioning glance at the teacher in attendance. The woman was sitting perfectly still, staring at her hands which were clasped in her lap. She didn't look much older than the pupil she was chaperoning. From the set of her jaw, and her raised shoulders, Geraldine had the impression she was tense. Whether she was feeling apprehensive about her charge, or about the visiting detective, was unclear.

'I'm talking about Mr Moore. The paedo, innit. Was it him done her in?'

'The allegation against him is currently under investigation.'

'Yeah, well, why would he do her in if he wasn't guilty?'

Glaring at Geraldine with an air of having proved a point, Ella seemed to be waiting for a response. Accustomed to taking charge of interviews, Geraldine returned the girl's defiant stare uneasily. Members of the public were often unnecessarily defensive, and sometimes that translated into aggression. More typically they were unresponsive, afraid of saying something that might appear incriminating even though they were innocent of any crime. But however knowing she might be, Ella was still little more than a child, and probably terrified, in addition to being traumatised by the sudden death of her best friend.

'I'm so sorry about what happened,' Geraldine said, carefully avoiding mentioning Cassie directly. 'This must be very difficult for you, but there are just a few questions I'd like to put to you, if that's all right.'

'If it's about Cassie, I already told Miss Penwright what I think.'

'I'd like you to tell me, if you don't mind. It might help us find out who killed her. I know she was your friend.'

'That tart?' Ella let out a shrill yelp of nervous laughter. 'She was a right cow. She got what was coming to her, innit? Ran around like she was some A-lister sleb, when the only reason guys noticed her at all was because she flashed her tits. She wasn't so much.' She gave a derisive snort. 'She had Max running round after her, so why did she have to be so needy? Still, the perv got her in the end and if you ask me, it was her own stupid fault. A girl needs a fella, right? But once she got him, she shouldn't be putting it about, innit?' She shook her head. 'She should've been satisfied. Max is buff.'

Geraldine decided she could stop being so delicate in her questioning.

'Were you one of the pupils who entered the classroom while the alleged assault on Cassie was taking place?'

'You know. There's a list, innit? You got my name.'

'Very well. Can you tell me exactly what you saw?'

For an instant, uncertainty flickered in Ella's eyes, and she licked her lips apprehensively.

'What you want to know, then?'

'Tell me what you saw.'

The accompanying teacher shifted in her seat but didn't look up.

'I saw them, innit?'

'Who did you see? Can you tell me exactly?'

Ella hesitated and glanced at the teacher, who reassured her that she wasn't obliged to answer any questions if she felt uncomfortable.

'That's right,' Geraldine confirmed. 'You don't have to say anything. But if you do tell me what you saw, it might help us to find out who is responsible for the death of your friend. You do want to help us catch him, don't you?'

Ella grunted. 'I saw her – Cassie – and him, the paedo.'

'You mean Paul Moore?'

'Yeah, the paedo.'

'Yes, very well. And what were they doing?'

'He was a paedo. What do you think they were doing?' Ella scoffed.

'Just tell me what you saw.'

'She was yelling for all she was worth. "Get off me! Get off me!" And he jumped away from her like she was red hot, you know. Hot like hot. And he had this guilty look on his face, like he knew he was doing something he shouldn't be doing.'

'Can you remember anything else? Where were his hands when you entered the room? Was his clothing disturbed at all?'

'Disturbed? How should I know? You think I'd be looking?'

Ella sniggered and put her hand over her mouth. Her nails were bitten to the quick and flecked with vestiges of green nail varnish.

'What about Cassie? Did you notice anything unusual about her?'

'She was yelling blue murder and her shirt was flapping open, with her tits hanging out. Everyone knew what he was after, bloody paedo. You won't catch me in the same room as him again. He's a rubbish teacher anyway, always nagging and pestering us for our books.' She giggled. 'You won't find nothing in my book. Bloody paedo. He can go fuck himself.' She turned to the teacher. 'Can I go now, Miss?'

The teacher nodded her permission and the girl fled. The door swung closed behind her.

'Was that helpful? I mean, did you find out what you wanted to know?' the teacher asked.

'I found out that Cassie doesn't seem to have had any friends,' Geraldine replied miserably.

'These things go in phases,' the teacher replied with a feeble smile that was no doubt intended to be reassuring. 'Popularity comes and goes at that age.'

Geraldine gave a polite response to the teacher's fatuous comment.

'If I had a best friend like Ella, I'd probably top myself,' she added later when she was back at the police station, telling Ariadne about the interview.

None of the other pupils seemed to have had much to say about Cassie, other than that she was willing to use her body to cajole boys into buying her gifts.

'This boy's statement doesn't even make sense,' Ariadne said, reading aloud. 'I give her a phone and then we did it. Was rubbish but she never give me back the phone. Bitch. Still, it was only an old one. Had no credit on it.'

Cassie's boyfriend, Max, had not yet been questioned. He was absent from school, and Geraldine was tasked with driving to his home that evening to see if he had anything to add to the picture they were building of Cassie. So far it had been one-sided, with all of her classmates deriding her as a nymphomaniac. Clearly no one had liked her. Universally despised by the girls, she had been friendless, using her body as her only means of gaining attention from boys.

'What a sad life,' Geraldine said, when the interviews had all been logged.

'What are the chances she could ever have become a functioning adult?' Ariadne replied.

Geraldine shrugged. 'She might have grown out of her desperate need for attention and achieved some success in life. Maybe she would have found help, if she'd lived.'

'If she'd lived,' Ariadne echoed.

'But she didn't, and we have to find out why,' Geraldine concluded decisively.

12

IT WAS DIFFICULT TO believe that sitting across the room from Geraldine was the good-looking boy she had seen in photos online. Max's cheeks were blotchy and his eyes were bloodshot and puffy from crying. His black hair looked greasy, and his T-shirt was rumpled and stained. He seemed more upset about losing Cassie than her mother, who had reportedly appeared resigned to the death of her daughter when she had identified her body at the mortuary.

'She's done with it all now,' the police officer who had accompanied Cassie's mother had reported her as saying. 'It wasn't much of a life, was it? She's better off out of it.'

Max's mother was sitting beside him on a chintz sofa, while his father hovered beside them, looking uncomfortable. Mrs Dean was small and mousy, with brown hair, beady eyes, and a narrow face with a tiny nose and chin. Despite her diminutive stature and soft expression, she had an air of underlying strength. Geraldine had the impression she would fight to defend her son from any hint of criticism. Her husband was tall and good-looking, his black hair speckled with white. Geraldine studied their son closely as she spoke, aware that Max was a suspect in a murder investigation. He was well built and looked strong. If Cassie had been messing around with other boys – and men – as Ella claimed, then it was conceivable Max had attacked her in a fit of jealousy, perhaps killing her by mistake.

Geraldine was careful to put her questions tactfully. 'I'm very sorry for your loss, Max. You do understand that we need to find out who did this to Cassie, and we would appreciate your co-operation in answering a few questions.'

'He'll do whatever he can to assist you,' Max's father replied, with an anxious glance at his son.

Max had hidden his face in his hands when Geraldine began to speak, and he appeared to be sobbing silently.

'Come on now, Max,' his mother urged him. She spoke slowly, as though she was addressing a small child. 'The policewoman is trying to find out what happened to your friend. Let's hear what she has to say, shall we?'

Geraldine took a deep breath. 'I'm sorry to tell you that Cassie's death wasn't an accident,' she began.

Max dropped his hands and looked up, his eyes wet with tears. 'Who was it?' he demanded hoarsely. 'Who did it? I'll smash his fucking face in. He won't never walk again.' He punched the arm of the sofa with his fist.

'Calm down, son,' Mr Dean said, with a worried glance at Geraldine. 'The policewoman doesn't want to listen to this. Remember, she's come here to help.'

'Help? How can anyone help? She's dead, innit? Dead,' the boy muttered, his rage subsiding as rapidly as it had erupted.

'He's very upset,' Max's mother murmured, stroking her son's arm. 'It's not like Max to fly off the handle like that, but he's just learned that he's lost his girlfriend. He was very fond of her.'

Geraldine did her best to appear sympathetic, but she couldn't help wondering what might have happened if Cassie had fallen foul of her boyfriend's temper. He was clearly struggling to control his feelings. He was only a teenager, of course, and was understandably distressed, but he had hit the arm of the sofa with some force.

'When did you last see Cassie?' she asked.

Max frowned, blinking furiously. 'After school on Thursday. We went to McDonald's, me and her.'

'What time was that?'

'Like I said, after school,' he repeated morosely.

'Surely you can check that?' Max's father asked. 'CCTV and all that. You'll find he's telling you the truth.'

'Our boy doesn't lie,' his wife chipped in.

'Very well,' Geraldine said, still looking at Max, 'so you and Cassie went to McDonald's after school. What did you do after that?'

'I drove her home. I wanted to go for a smoke –' He broke off, and glanced up at Geraldine uncertainly. 'For a drink,' he amended his original statement, unconvincingly. 'But she said she wanted to go home. She *said* she wanted to wash her hair.'

His undue emphasis on the word 'said' led Geraldine to ask whether he had believed her.

'It's what she said,' he replied doggedly, staring at his feet.

'And what did you do then?'

He shrugged. 'I drove her home. That's what I said, innit.'

'Did you go straight to her house after you left McDonald's?' Geraldine asked.

He nodded, staring at the floor.

Geraldine decided not to push the boy, although she had a suspicion there might have been an argument between him and Cassie, and that row could have become violent. But this was speculation. She needed facts. She wanted to enquire how Max had felt on Monday, when Cassie had accused her teacher of molesting her at school, but she decided it was best to invite him to the police station for a taped interview. She kept the sobering thought to herself, but it was clear that Max would have had both motive and opportunity to kill his girlfriend. And with his large, powerful hands, he certainly had the means.

After thanking the youth for his co-operation, she left the house, summoned back-up and rang the bell again once her colleagues arrived.

'What is it now?' Max's mother asked irritably. 'The poor boy's in shock. He needs time to process his grief. He's just lost his girlfriend for Christ's sake. Have you people no decency? He cared about that girl.'

'Yes, give it a rest, can't you?' her husband added, joining Mrs Dean in the doorway. 'Max is distraught. He needs some space to come to terms with what's happened. All your questions aren't helping him.'

Geraldine looked from one parent to the other, wondering if they knew more than they would be willing to divulge. Perhaps they too had their suspicions about their son. Certainly they were keen to shield him from any further questions.

'I'm sorry,' she said gently, 'but I'd like Max to accompany me to the police station for a few more questions. He was possibly the last person to see Cassie, before she met her killer. We need him to make an official statement. One of you might want to accompany him and, of course, you have the right to bring your own lawyer.'

'A lawyer? What does he need a lawyer for? He's already given you his statement,' Max's father objected, his face reddening with exasperation. 'Look, he took the girl to McDonald's and then he drove her home. And that was it. He had nothing whatsoever to do with what happened to her after he left her.'

'We'll be checking his movements that evening,' Geraldine replied evenly. 'And I'm sure CCTV evidence will confirm his story.'

'Story? What do you mean by that?' Max's father began, but his wife put her hand on his arm to restrain him.

It seemed that a short temper ran in the family. Although they were all feeling stressed and possibly not behaving normally, it was still interesting to see how Max and his father reacted to pressure.

'Can't this wait?' Max's mother asked.

'It would be better for Max if he came with us now. Surely he's keen to assist us in finding out who committed this crime? Now please, can you ask Max to join me or do I need to send one of my officers in to fetch him?'

Without the boy present, Geraldine dropped her soft tone and gestured towards the handcuffs at her waist. Both parents looked at one another aghast.

'You people make me sick,' Mrs Dean hissed between clenched teeth.

'We just want to ask him a few questions,' Geraldine said, resuming her earlier gentle tone. 'It won't take long. You'll all be back home in no time.' She smiled reassuringly.

Although she was keen to apprehend Cassie's killer, now that she was planning to interview Max as a potential suspect, she remembered how young he was, and how distressed.

'I'll get him,' Max's mother replied angrily.

With a sigh, Geraldine followed Mrs Dean back into the house.

13

STARTLED, LAURA DROPPED HER biro.

'What? Oh, sorry,' she stammered.

Lunging, she reached for the pen too late; it rolled forward and dropped to the floor. She clambered off the high-backed stool to retrieve it. When she looked up, Gina was glaring at her across the white desk.

'You're supposed to be answering the phone,' Gina said. 'All you have to do is greet clients with a smile, and answer the phone. How hard can that be? Jesus, what the hell is wrong with you? It's like you've been in a trance all week.' Her eyes narrowed. 'Are you coming to work high?'

'I'm sorry,' Laura repeated, hauling herself back on the stool. 'I'm fine, really I am. And I'm quite sober.'

'If I didn't know better, I'd think you were hungover.'

Struggling to maintain her composure, Laura fidgeted with the pen and mumbled about having a problem at home.

'A problem?' Gina retorted, bristling with indignation. 'You're telling me *you've* got a problem?' She snorted and glanced around, lowering her voice. 'Listen, Laura, I don't give a damn about what's going on in your private life, you don't bring your personal problems into work, not if you want to keep your job. Capiche?'

Laura was tempted to tell Gina to stuff her job, and stalk right out of the salon, but there was a possibility Paul might lose his income. They couldn't afford to lose hers as well. So she mumbled that she was sorry, and promised she wouldn't mess up again.

'What's wrong?' Gina leaned over the desk and spoke in a confidential whisper.

They didn't look over at her, but Laura knew her colleagues were listening.

'Nothing, it's nothing really,' she stammered. 'Nothing's wrong.'

The last thing she wanted was for her colleagues at the salon to learn about the humiliating circumstances that had led to Paul's suspension. She supposed they would all find out eventually, but they weren't going to hear it from her. Looking irritated, Gina relieved Laura of her usual duties and banished her to the tiny kitchenette at the back of the salon to spend the day sweeping the floor and serving coffee. The new junior, who had been doing the menial tasks, was promoted to shampooing. Laura welcomed the penance, relieved not to have to put on a show, smiling and chatting to clients.

Gina summoned Anna. 'You're on the desk today. All you have to do is sit here and greet clients and answer the phone. It's not rocket science,' she added pointedly, as Laura scrambled off the stool. 'Anyone can manage it if they stay awake for long enough. And if anyone asks for Laura, share her clients out among the girls if you can,' she concluded, glancing angrily at Laura.

'Yeah, yeah, I know what to do,' Anna replied. 'I have done it before.'

'You youngsters think you know it all,' Gina murmured under her breath.

For all her brash ways with her staff, Gina wasn't a bad boss. She was a kind woman who was determined to run her salon efficiently. Laura understood why Gina was exasperated with her. Failing to answer the phone could lose them business. A client entered and Gina hurried forward to greet her, all smiles and friendly chat, while Laura retreated to the kitchenette to prepare the coffee machine. Serving coffee and sweeping the floor were mindless tasks she would normally resent, but today she was relieved to be left alone to pursue her own thoughts. Paul had been at home for a week, and his assurances that everything was fine were beginning to wear thin, not least because he was so obviously stressed. Usually equable, overnight he had become snappy and jumpy, and she knew he wasn't sleeping. Several times she had woken in the night to find his side of the bed empty, but he had refused to discuss the situation with her, saying that this was his problem, and she shouldn't worry. He must have known that was pointless because, of course, it was her problem too. She was his wife, and they were supposed to love one another and support each other for better or worse, whatever happened.

The worst of it was that she suspected he wasn't being honest with her. Something was going on that he hadn't shared with her. Maybe he hadn't even admitted it to himself. She was tempted to challenge him but, at the same time, she was scared of hearing the truth, because what if he really had behaved inappropriately towards a pupil? Such things happened. She had always believed they were happily married. Certainly they both seemed content with their life together. But perhaps Paul craved a passion that was lacking in their marriage. When she and Paul had first met, he couldn't get enough of her. In bed he had been all over her, but gradually the energetic sex had grown less frequent. She had thought it was inevitable he would become less eager in bed after six years together, but what if there was another reason, and his weariness wasn't really caused by his demanding time at work, as he claimed, but by something else altogether?

She tried to recall whether he had been more attentive to her during the school holidays, but her memory was hazy. Certainly he was happier to cook and help around the house when he wasn't working, but she wasn't sure he had been more demanding in bed. She could hardly bear to contemplate the possibility that he had been having an affair with another woman, a woman barely out of her childhood. But nor could she pretend the idea had never been raised.

'Laura, did you hear me?' Gina's strident tones recalled her to her surroundings.

'Sorry, what was that?'

'White coffee, no sugar!'

'Coming right up.' Laura forced a smile.

Whatever her private concerns, everything had to continue without a glitch on the surface, so the clients were happy and Gina stopped prying. More than anything, Laura had to maintain a pretence that everything was fine, just as Paul was doing with her. She hadn't told anyone that Paul was home from work. The thought of telling John made her cringe. She could just imagine him pestering her for details, under the guise of affectionate concern. No, she was going to keep this mortifying secret to herself, at least until Paul was back at work and the evil accusation had been scotched, once and for all. Because, she told herself fiercely, the allegation was a lie. It had to be.

Once Paul's name had been cleared, Laura would have no truck with anyone who tried to suggest there was 'no smoke without fire'. She would explain that the allegation had been thoroughly investigated and it had been proved beyond any doubt that the girl was a liar and a fantasist, and her story was groundless. With any luck, it would turn out that Paul wasn't the only man she had accused of interfering with her. Everyone would accept that the girl was unhinged, and Paul would be exonerated as a blameless victim of a delusional teenager. Either she was mentally disturbed, or she was on drugs. Probably both.

Once the truth about Cassie was known, no one would hold Paul responsible for her lies. Laura realised her fists were clenched and she made a conscious effort to relax. The truth had to come out, and it had to absolve Paul of any hint of guilt. It just had to. The alternative was too painful to consider. Savagely, she dismissed the possibility that Paul could be responsible for what had happened. It just wasn't possible. It couldn't be.

She had put the broom away and switched off the coffee machine, and was rinsing out the jug when her phone rang.

'I just called to see how you are,' a familiar voice said. 'And to ask if you'd like a lift home. It's no trouble,' he went on, without giving her time to reply. 'It's on my way. We could go out if you like,' he went on cheerily. 'I haven't seen you for weeks. Let me take you out.'

Laura seized the chance to escape the suffocating atmosphere of home and blurted out that she would love to meet up for a drink. She told herself she deserved to relax and enjoy herself. Even if it was only for an hour, it would be a break.

'I'm just leaving,' she added. 'Give me a few minutes. I can meet you somewhere if you like.'

She didn't dare take him home, but Paul wouldn't mind if she was a bit late. She could easily tell him she had been held up at work. Smiling, she agreed to meet in the pub. Paul need never know.

14

MAX AND HIS MOTHER had to wait over an hour for their lawyer to arrive. After joining them for a brief consultation, she explained to Geraldine that she wasn't exactly a 'family lawyer' for the Deans, but a criminal solicitor in the firm that had conducted the conveyancing for the family's house purchase. She was young, and looked as though she might have been preparing to go out for the evening when she was summoned. Her clothes were appropriately formal, but she was heavily made up, and Geraldine caught a whiff of a perfume that was probably more expensive than she would usually wear for work.

'I've no idea why they called my firm when they could just as easily have made do with the duty brief. This isn't going to take long, is it?' She glanced at her watch. 'I'm assuming it's merely a formality? Only time's marching on.'

'We could have left it until the morning, but given the seriousness of the possible charge, we wanted to question him without any delay.'

Geraldine looked pointedly at the lawyer who had kept them waiting for over an hour.

The solicitor sighed, perhaps seeing her plans for the evening vanishing. 'Let's get on with it then, shall we? I'll need to see my client before you start.'

By the time the interview finally began, Mrs Dean was looking decidedly restless, fidgeting with the strap on her bag, while her eyes flicked around the room as though she was searching for an escape route. Max, on the other hand, didn't appear at all intimidated. If anything, he seemed to be bored by the situation.

'Now can I have a fag?' he asked as they all sat down.

'I'm afraid we don't allow smoking here,' Geraldine replied.

'That's just great, innit?' Max grumbled. 'How am I supposed to think straight?'

'You go all day at school without a cigarette,' Geraldine pointed out.

'Hardly all day,' he muttered, with a grimace.

The opening stage of the interview was a waste of time, as Geraldine had expected. Asked about his movements on Thursday evening, Max repeated what he had already told Geraldine. After dropping Cassie off, he had gone home. His mother confirmed that he had not gone out again that evening, but she said she and her husband had gone to bed at eleven.

'So you can't be sure of Max's whereabouts after eleven?' Geraldine asked.

'He was at home in bed,' Mrs Dean replied promptly.

'My client has already told you he didn't leave the house that evening,' the lawyer piped up.

Max smirked at Geraldine, as though to say that his lawyer must be privy to the truth by virtue of her profession.

Geraldine moved on to question Max about Cassie's relationship with her teacher, Mr Moore.

'What relationship?' Max asked sulkily. 'She weren't in no relationship with that old guy. She was my girl, innit?'

His lips twisted momentarily when he spoke about Cassie. Geraldine was afraid he was going to lose his temper, or break down in tears, but he managed to control his emotions.

'Were you there when Cassie accused Mr Moore of molesting her?'

'Me and the rest of the class,' he conceded. There was no point in denying it. 'So what?'

'So how did that make you feel?'

Geraldine was hoping he would respond without thinking, but Max considered carefully before speaking. He was not as callow as he appeared.

'Cassie's – Cassie was always on about other guys,' he said at last. 'Gurning about the way they pestered her. I don't know what she expected me to do. Cassie's – Cassie was a babe and guys came on to her. I couldn't kick off with all of them, innit?'

'Did you often fight with other boys because they showed an interest in Cassie?' Geraldine asked.

'He doesn't get in fights,' Mrs Dean interposed quickly.

'Max said nothing about fighting,' the lawyer added, shaking her head at Mrs Dean.

'He said he couldn't kick off with all the men who looked at Cassie. Max,' Geraldine smiled encouragingly at him, 'what do you mean when you use the term kicking off?'

'Having a row with a classmate is hardly relevant to this case,' the lawyer interposed, 'unless you intend to attempt to defame my client's reputation without any substantive evidence. Have the school noted anything on Max's records about any violent outbursts?'

The lawyer sounded fairly confident that she was on safe ground. Nevertheless, Geraldine decided to have that checked with the school. She was also interested in recording the names of any other boys Max had accused of pestering Cassie, and made a note to task a sergeant with following up that potential line of enquiry. For now, her own focus remained on Max. The lawyer could be bluffing, hoping to deter Geraldine from making a thorough investigation into Max's history. But, of course, the lawyer was right. Even supposing Max had been in a few brawls at school, that was no indication that he was capable of murder.

'Max,' she said, 'did you see anything that convinced you Cassie was being pursued by Mr Moore?'

The boy shrugged. 'You calling Cassie a liar?' he asked. 'She weren't interested in some old geezer.'

'No, but was he interested in her?'

'That's what she said, innit?'

He sat back and folded his arms as though to indicate he had nothing more to say. Geraldine decided there was no point in continuing to question him.

That evening, Ian returned home from his weekend away. Geraldine was happy to see him, and she tried to listen attentively to his account of his weekend. Despite his protestations to the contrary, it sounded as though he had enjoyed himself. His blue eyes sparkled with mischief as he described what had happened. After a while he fell silent and, reaching out, took both of her hands in his.

'Geraldine, you haven't been listening to a word I said.'

'What? Oh, sorry, yes, of course.' She smiled, appreciating the warmth of his hands. 'You were telling me how someone ended up in the river with all his clothes on and two of you had to jump in and pull him out.'

Ian laughed. 'He was in the canal, not the river.'

'And I suppose you were one of the ones who pulled him out?'

'We could hardly leave him there to freeze to death on his stag weekend, could we? Seriously, he was lucky at least two of us weren't too pissed to help him out.'

'I'm sure it was great fun. And I'm glad you weren't pissed enough to let your friend drown.'

Ian looked at her. 'You're thinking about the case you're working on, aren't you?'

'No, not at all. I was listening to you.'

Ian laughed and pulled her towards him. 'You're a useless liar. So come on, tell me all about it.'

'I want to hear more about your weekend first,' she fibbed.

'No, you don't,' he replied, smiling at her. 'I told you, you're a useless liar. Now tell me everything there is to tell about the case you're working on and we'll see if we can't get to the bottom of it. My anecdotes can wait. To be honest, nothing much happened.'

'Apart from the bridegroom nearly drowning.'

'Yes, apart from that.' He smiled. 'I missed you. Now, tell me all about it.'

Geraldine sighed. She had a horrible feeling it wasn't going to be an easy case to solve, but at least she now had a sympathetic listener to share her thoughts with, someone who could be relied on to be absolutely discreet. She told Ian about Max, and the teacher Cassie had accused of molesting her.

'Do you think it's possible her boyfriend lost his temper with her, and attacked her in a jealous rage?' she asked. 'On the grounds that anything's possible, I don't see why not,' she continued without pausing, answering her own question. 'And then there's Paul Moore, the teacher who was suspended pending an investigation into an allegation of sexual misconduct. Cassie's sixteen, but he was her teacher. Even if her accusation is discredited, his career has been destroyed.'

'Is that a motive for silencing her?' Ian asked. 'Surely his career could only be rescued if she retracted her allegation. Now she's dead she can't change her statement.'

'That's true, but he had a very powerful reason to want revenge. She's ruined his career and quite possibly his marriage too. So the first problem is that we seem to have two suspects.'

'That's better than none,' Ian replied cheerfully.

'You always manage to put a positive spin on things.'

'I'll take that as a compliment.'

'But it doesn't really help.'

'I'd say it gives you plenty to work on.'

Geraldine smiled. It was good to have Ian back. 'I missed you,' she told him.

'That's the most sensible thing you've said since I came home.'

15

BY THE TIME LAURA arrived, John was already ensconced at a corner table. He must have been looking out for her because as soon as she entered the bar he jumped to his feet, eager to greet her. She walked quickly over and sat down opposite him, registering straightaway how smart he looked in a white shirt and dark sports jacket. She was still in her work clothes and wished she'd had time to change. After a day spent sweeping the floor and cleaning up, she felt grubby, while he had obviously made an effort with his appearance. But then, John was always well turned out.

'What's it to be?' he asked with a smile, handing her a bar menu. 'We could go somewhere else if you like?'

'This is fine,' she assured him.

The pub was comfortable, with plush chairs, polished wooden tables, and soft lighting, and it was a welcome change to be with a man who was actually pleased to see her. Recently Paul had been so weighed down with his own problems that he hardly paid her any attention. Often he didn't seem to notice she was there at all. Trying to ignore the comparison, she smiled at John and let him buy her a shandy. Watching him as he returned from the bar with a tray of drinks, a packet of crisps, and peanuts, she was concerned to see that he had lost weight. He was a good-looking man, but he seemed older than she remembered. His hair was turning grey.

He gazed at her as she sipped her drink and his concern was almost palpable.

'Please don't look at me like that,' she said, afraid that he was going to ask her about Paul. 'I'm fine.'

He dropped his eyes.

'How are you?' she asked.

He shrugged and gave the ghost of a smile.

'I got salt and vinegar crisps,' he told her, wrinkling his nose.

He didn't like them, but he knew they were her favourite flavour. Knocking back a whisky chaser, he cleared his throat.

'You're looking a bit under the weather,' he said. 'Are you sure everything's all right?'

She nodded and reached for the crisps to avoid having to reply.

'I saw in the paper there's been a spot of bother at Paul's school,' he went on, cautiously probing for information. 'He's not involved, is he? Do you want to talk about it? You know you can speak freely to me.'

He glanced around as though to show her they were alone, and no one was listening to them. The bar was half empty at that time on a Monday evening. She wondered if that was why he had called her that afternoon, although there was no reason why they shouldn't meet at any time. It wasn't as if they were doing anything wrong. She lowered her eyes and continued crunching mechanically.

'I'm here if you ever want someone to talk to. You know you can trust me not to blab.'

'That's very nice of you, but it's nothing, really,' she assured him, putting the crisp packet down. 'There's been a stupid mix-up, nothing to do with Paul,' she added brightly.

'Excellent,' he replied, smiling broadly. 'That's really good to hear. I'd hate to see either of you getting into trouble. Life's hard enough without any additional unnecessary hassle.'

Laura smiled at hearing the horrible allegation against Paul dismissed as 'hassle'. John always had a way of making problems seem insignificant, even when they really weren't. It was a sensible approach to life's difficulties, and she resolved to feel more positive about the future. They chatted about other things: a scandal that had broken about a member of the royal family, the ridiculous shenanigans going on in government, and a celebrity's very public spat with her husband, which they both agreed was a transparent publicity stunt. They had always enjoyed talking about the gossipy items in the news and the conversation and the alcohol made her feel more relaxed than she had been for a long time, certainly since the allegation had been made against Paul. She finished her shandy and reluctantly reached for her bag.

'I'd best be going,' she said.

He pulled a little moue of dismay. 'But you've only just got here. I was hoping to take you out for dinner. We can go anywhere you fancy. Your choice. It's my treat.'

Laura felt a spasm of guilt, hearing the desperation in his voice, although it wasn't really her fault she hadn't seen him for a few weeks. She had been preoccupied by what was happening to Paul and, if she was honest, she was depressed by her own secret suspicions. She hadn't exactly been avoiding John, but nor had she made any attempt to see him, and she had deliberately ignored his recent calls. He had left several messages asking her to give him a ring, but she hadn't got round to it. She apologised now, claiming that she had been busy.

'Too busy to give me a quick call, just to tell me you were all right?' He leaned forward gazing closely at her. 'You are all right, aren't you?'

She squirmed. He came to her rescue, as he always did. 'Never mind, we're here now. I don't want to make you feel uncomfortable. I know you've got your own life to lead now, and it's good that you're busy.' He sat back, and she felt a rush of relief.

'This has been really lovely, but I'd better get going. We mustn't leave it so long in future.'

His smile vanished. 'Are you sure I can't take you out for dinner?'

'Thank you, I would have loved to, but it's such short notice, and Paul will have made supper. He'll be waiting for me. I'd better not be home too late.'

'At least have another drink,' he said. 'One for the road.'

'You and your one for the road,' she smiled, but she let him buy her another half and, of course, he came back with a pint.

'I said a half,' she protested weakly, but like he said, she hadn't seen him for a few weeks.

She gulped down her pint while he talked.

'I have to go, I don't need a lift, but thank you' she said quickly, rising to her feet before he could remonstrate. Woozy after drinking so quickly, she spoke very carefully. 'It's been lovely to see you. Thank you for the drink and the crisps.' She hesitated, aware that she was sounding rather formal.

He smiled thinly at her. Turning from him, she made her way stiffly to the door, feeling self-conscious; she knew he would be watching her. She left without looking back.

16

PAUL GLANCED SURREPTITIOUSLY AT his wife. Her fair hair had fallen over her forehead, and she sat perfectly still, her eyes fixed on the television.

'How's things at work?' he ventured. 'They kept you late today. I tried to call you. I called the salon too, but there was no answer, just a recorded message to say they were closed.'

She just grunted and he decided not to pursue the matter. At least she was still going to work. He supposed she was tired. Perhaps she had been kept late cleaning the place. That had happened a few times in the past. She didn't even look round when his phone rang.

'I'll take it in the kitchen,' he said, clambering to his feet. 'I don't want to disturb you.'

Laura didn't look up. It was as though she no longer noticed his presence.

He would have to be patient with her. He was confident the situation would blow over. Once he was back at work, they would get themselves back on an even keel. At least he had been suspended on full pay. Without his salary, he would have no means of paying the mortgage. Laura had a job but that only brought in enough to feed them both. They couldn't survive for more than a few months on what she earned. Besides, Laura had set her heart on starting a family soon. How was he going to manage to support a child if he had no job? They would be destitute. He knew he was flirting with despair, but it was hard not to feel discouraged in his present situation. And he suspected that Laura was bitterly disappointed at the interruption to their plans.

With a sudden burst of elation, he registered who was calling.

'Headmaster,' he replied, trying to sound nonchalant. 'It's good of you to call.'

It was important to remain professional in his dealings with the head, and keep his excitement under wraps, although he could hardly stand still. He had to behave as though he had never doubted for one moment that he would be swiftly reinstated. But his relief was short lived. Far from telling Paul he was expected back in the classroom the following day, the head teacher shared the grim news that Cassie Jackson was dead.

'Dead?' Paul echoed stupidly. 'I don't understand. How can she be dead? She was –' He broke off, uncertain what to say to convince the head teacher how shocked he was.

But there was more. Stunned, he listened to the voice at the other end of the line as it explained that the police suspected Cassie had been murdered. It took a moment for the implication of the head teacher's words to sink in. When they did, Paul felt a horrible tightening in his chest, constricting his breathing.

'When?' he stammered. 'How? When? When did it happen?'

'She was killed on Thursday evening.' The head teacher hesitated before adding, 'I thought I ought to warn you.' He hesitated again. 'There's a certain – faction – that seem to think you might be implicated. You might need to prepare yourself.'

The room seemed to spin. Paul reached for the edge of the sink and held on to it, afraid his legs might give way. 'What do you mean?' he demanded. 'Prepare myself for what? I don't understand.'

'The pupils are naturally confused by what's happened. Parents have been calling to ask what's being done about it.'

'About what?' Paul asked. 'What specifically are they asking about?'

A sigh reached him from the other end of the line. 'What happened to Cassie Jackson, it's all very unfortunate timing. There's been some talk, in the staff room.'

'What kind of talk? What do you mean?'

But the head clearly felt he had said enough. 'I just thought you ought to know,' he repeated and he hung up.

Reeling, Paul returned to the living room and waited until Laura's programme finished before broaching the topic. He spoke as casually as he could, while his heart hammered in his chest and his throat was so dry he struggled to move his tongue.

'What sort of bother?' Laura asked without looking up at him. 'What are you talking about? Aren't you in enough trouble already? How much worse can things get?'

Paul cleared his throat. 'Listen,' he said, speaking as clearly as he could. 'There might be an inquiry into what happened, questions asked and so on. No,' he raised his voice as she started to respond. Somehow he just had to blurt out what was necessary. 'Just shut up and listen, will you? For once in your life, just listen to me. I need you to say we were both at home on Thursday evening. All evening. You have to say we were both here, together, all Thursday evening, from when you got home from work until you left the house on Friday morning.' He could hear himself babbling. He had to make sure she understood what was at stake. 'Have you got that? I'm talking about Thursday evening. Last Thursday. This is important.'

Laura shook her head. 'I always go to the supermarket after work on Thursday,' she said slowly.

'Yes, well, that doesn't matter, does it? No one's going to check. It's no big deal, but I need you to do this for me. Do you promise?'

Seeing her bewilderment he struggled to conceal his panic. If Laura refused to comply, he would have no alibi for Thursday evening when Cassie was killed. And he could see how that might look. He had left school on Monday vowing vengeance on the girl who had recklessly destroyed his life, and three days later she was killed.

'Why? What's happened?' Laura asked. 'Who called just now? It's about that girl, isn't it? What's happened? Paul, you have to tell me what's going on.'

Paul hesitated to tell her the girl had been murdered.

'It's nothing, nothing,' he gabbled, 'just – if anyone asks, you were here, we were together all Thursday evening. Promise me you'll say you were here at home with me all evening.'

'You want me to lie?'

Paul hesitated. 'Yes. Yes. It's – it's necessary. You just have to trust me that it has to be done. It's the only way to keep us safe. I can't explain.'

'I think I understand only too well.'

There was a hardness in her voice that made him tremble.

'So you'll do this? For me? For us?'

In his agitation he realised he had approached her and was standing right in front of her chair. He was tempted to fall to his knees, pleading for her help. He turned away to hide his consternation, but he couldn't hide the alarm in his voice.

'Laura, you know I never touched that little slut.' He turned back to look at her but her head was lowered. 'For fuck's sake. Laura, look at me. I'm asking you to do something for me, for us. It's a little awkward, I know. I don't want to make you feel uncomfortable, but I have to ask you to tell this small fib, a white lie. If there was any other way out of this, I wouldn't ask. You have to believe me. I've done nothing wrong. I don't deserve any of this. We don't deserve what's happening to us.'

'What happens if I refuse?'

'The consequences if you refuse would be catastrophic, for both of us.'

To both their surprise, he burst into tears and sobbed uncontrollably for a moment.

'I'm sorry, I'm sorry,' he mumbled incoherently when he had recovered a modicum of self-control. 'It's just all the pressure lately, the stress of it all.'

Instead of rushing to comfort him in his distress, she sat perfectly still, watching him as if from a great distance.

'You know I love you,' he stuttered, reaching out for her hands. 'I never meant any of this to happen. You have to believe me, none of this is my fault. I've done nothing wrong. Nothing.'

'I'll go and put the kettle on and make us some tea, and then you can tell me exactly what's going on,' she said.

Her eyes were cold, and he knew she didn't trust him. Four years of marriage and it had come to this, he thought bitterly. It was all Cassie's fault. Whatever happened next, he was glad the little bitch was dead. She deserved it.

17

ON TUESDAY MORNING GERALDINE was up early because she wanted to visit Paul and his wife before Laura left for work. She thought Ian probably needed to catch up on his sleep after his weekend away, so she padded from the bedroom in her slippers, and closed the front door softly. She drove along Nunnery Lane, turning off at Blossom Street and then right on to the Holgate Road through a steady drizzle that made everything look grey. It was hard to believe it was spring, and that summer was on its way. Paul Moore and his wife lived in Grantham Drive off the Holgate Road, not far from the woods where Cassie's body had been found. Geraldine found the house easily and rang the bell, and the door was opened by a young man. It was still early, and he was in a blue dressing gown which he had probably thrown on before coming downstairs.

The man looked at her warily, seemingly poised to slam the door in her face. 'Yes?' Not merely cautious, she thought he looked frightened.

'Is your name Paul Moore?' she asked.

'Who wants to know?' he snapped.

Since he hadn't corrected her assumption, she concluded that she must be speaking to Paul Moore. As he scrutinised her identity card, Geraldine studied him. She would have guessed at his being no older than twenty-two although she knew he was in his early thirties. With his fair hair and youthful features, she could appreciate that a teenage girl might find him attractive. The question that hung over him was whether those feelings had ever been reciprocated.

'What do you want with me?' As he registered who she was he sighed, his broad shoulders drooped and he seemed to deflate. 'It's about that poor girl, isn't it? Cassie Jackson. I was afraid you were a journalist. Well, I suppose you'd better come in. Let's get this over with. I've been expecting you.'

He listened sullenly as she explained that, given the serious nature of the allegation that had been made against him, they wanted him to accompany her to the police station to answer some questions. She didn't mention the murder. Heaving a sigh, he gestured at his dressing gown and asked her to wait a moment. She nodded. He didn't need to know yet that he was a suspect in their investigation, nor that there were uniformed constables watching the house, front and back, in case he tried to do a runner. She heard him go upstairs, and he reappeared five minutes later dressed in faded jeans and a grey sweatshirt.

Seated in an interview room at the police station, facing Geraldine and Ariadne, he ran his hand through his hair, inadvertently leaving it sticking up comically, in a gesture that reminded Geraldine of Ian. But where Ian would be smiling quizzically at her, Paul's expression was dark and brooding.

'I never touched the girl, you know,' he said faintly. 'You might not believe me, but it's her word against mine, and she was a well-known troublemaker and a fantasist.'

Hearing him refer to Cassie in the past tense indicated that he knew the pupil was dead.

'Ask any of my colleagues,' he went on earnestly. 'They'll tell you. We were all careful to avoid being alone with her.'

'Yet that's precisely what happened.'

'No, it wasn't like that. What you just implied is a complete misrepresentation of the truth.' He scowled. 'I don't expect you to believe me,' he repeated wretchedly.

'Tell us what happened, Paul.'

'I was in my room, waiting for my next class. Cassie came in just as the bell rang. She must have been waiting outside. I was on my own, between lessons. There was nothing unusual about that.' He paused and when he resumed speaking, there was an edge of panic in his voice, although his face remained curiously impassive. 'She walked in and came right over to me. I was there, alone in my room, like a sitting duck.' He sighed. 'She came in really quietly. I mean, I just looked up and she was there, standing between me and the door, blocking my escape. And she waited, you know. I didn't know exactly what she wanted but I was feeling pretty uncomfortable. I told her to go and stand outside until the others arrived, but she told me she knew what I wanted and then she asked me to kiss her. She said that was what I wanted.'

He shuddered. 'She was chewing gum and she reeked of it. I didn't say I'd as soon kiss a stinking ashtray as go anywhere near her, but that's what I was thinking. I asked her if this was about her mid-term grade, but she just stood there telling me she knew what I wanted, when all I wanted was for her to leave. By now, I was feeling more than uneasy. She clearly had an agenda, and I was scared. It didn't feel like a prank. So I told her again to go and wait with the rest of the class. Then the bell went and as soon as she heard it, she – well, she launched herself at me, grabbing hold of my arms and shoving me backwards. I almost lost my balance. I'm not sure if she wanted to knock me to the floor, but my head and shoulders hit the wall with the force of her pushing me. Then I heard a din of voices and she leapt away from me, shrieking that I was a pervert.'

He closed his eyes, lost in the horror of the recollection. 'The other pupils starting yelling that I was a paedophile, and then there was a sudden hush. I looked up and saw my colleague, Annie Prendergast, standing in the doorway. And that was it. Cassie was crying, the kids were repeating the foul accusation, and I was summoned to see the head who suspended me on the spot. He was very apologetic. He knew it was all nonsense, but he had to follow procedure.'

'Had you ever done or said anything to encourage Cassie?'

'Not at all. I avoided contact with her. We all did. She was dangerous – damaged. The allegation against me was just a poisonous attempt to attract attention. She was an only child of a single mother and we – that is the staff – were all pretty much convinced she'd been abused as a child. We'd watched her attempting to use her precocious sexuality to control the boys in her class as far back as year nine, when she joined the school at thirteen. I dare say the problem went back further than that. I don't know her whole history, but I was certainly aware of her reputation when she was put in my class. A girl like that – well, she was trouble. Everyone knew it. We'd been warned to keep an eye on her. If it hadn't been me, she would have picked on someone else. It was just a bid for attention, at my expense,' he muttered bitterly. 'I don't blame her for that,' he added quickly. 'She was disturbed and she needed help. If anything, the school let her down. We all did. This was a disaster waiting to happen. You have to believe me, I'm an innocent bystander, caught up in this girl's desperation to whip up some melodrama in her life.'

Before Geraldine could comment on his use of the past tense, he resumed speaking.

'I'm sorry about what happened. The head phoned me and told me about it,' he added when Geraldine raised her eyebrows.

That was a blow. It confirmed he would have had time to concoct an alibi for the time of the murder. But it was possible he hadn't yet learned when it happened.

'Can you account for your movements last Thursday?'

'Thursday? Is that when it happened?'

'Just answer the question, please.'

Paul shook his head.

Geraldine hid her irritation. 'I'll ask you again. Where were you last Thursday evening?'

'I can't remember exactly, but I would have been at home. I didn't go out last week. I haven't left the house for a week, not since I was suspended from work. I didn't – I couldn't –' He shrugged and fell silent.

'Can anyone else confirm that?'

'Ask my wife. She was home. She works during the day, but she's always home soon after five. I've been there on my own during the day, but you wanted to know about Thursday evening? We were at home together.'

Geraldine went to speak to his wife, who had been driven to the police station in a separate car. Laura was a neat-looking woman in her late twenties. With tight blonde curls and widely spaced blue eyes, she wore a permanent air of surprise. She sat down opposite Geraldine and smiled anxiously at her.

'Laura, I'd like to ask you a few questions.'

'Of course.'

'Where were you last Thursday evening?'

Laura looked down, and her clasped hands tightened until her knuckles turned white.

'I was at home,' she replied, 'with my husband. Paul was –' She raised her head and gazed at Geraldine. 'He was – he is – desperately upset by the allegation that's been made against him. He's been understandably worried.'

'Of course. And did you go out at all last Thursday evening?'

'Thursday evening?' Laura repeated. Her eyes widened even more, as though it was a ludicrous question.

Geraldine waited.

'I – We were at home all evening,' Laura replied.

'Are you sure neither of you left the house at any time during the evening or the night?'

Laura looked agitated, but her voice was even as she repeated that neither she nor her husband had gone out after she returned home from work before six on Thursday. Telling her that an officer would be with her shortly to take a sample of her DNA, so she could be eliminated from the investigation, Geraldine thanked her and withdrew. She was fairly sure that Paul Moore had been telling her the truth, but she wasn't convinced by his wife. As a teacher, she wondered if he might be more skilled at bluffing and massaging the truth than his wife. Somehow, she felt that she had been hoodwinked, but she couldn't have said how. Why a suspect in a murder enquiry might lie, on the other hand, was blindingly obvious.

18

THE DETECTIVE SEEMED TO be questioning him for hours, and Paul felt exhausted by the time he and Laura were allowed to walk out of the police station, so he was startled when Laura announced she was going to work. Glancing at his watch, he was surprised to see that it was only twenty to ten. They had been at the police station for less than an hour. The most worrying moment had been when the detective had gone to quiz Laura about her movements on the evening of the murder. Laura understood how crucial it was for the police to believe that he had been at home all evening. He couldn't be sure how much credence they would give to his wife's statement, but at least she assured him she had stood by him, and between them they had done their best to present an alibi.

He felt his guts churn as the injustice of the situation shook him like a physical blow. He shouldn't be having to prove his innocence like this, when he had done nothing to set this terrible sequence of events in motion. Far from being guilty, he was the victim in this case, while everything that had happened to Cassie was her own fault. Now he was having to persuade his wife to lie for him. She didn't deserve to have to deal with this any more than he did.

'Come on,' Laura said as they reached the Fulford Road. 'The bus will be here soon.'

'I think I'll walk,' he replied. He had no reason to hurry.

'I'll see you later then,' she said. 'You will be all right, won't you?'

He grunted in response. It was difficult to know how to reply to her when he didn't know if he would ever be all right again. But she had lied for him, so it was his turn.

'I'll be fine,' he said, forcing a smile. 'This will all blow over soon and we'll be able to put it behind us and get back to our lives.'

He realised his fists were clenched at his sides. With an effort, he relaxed his fingers and tried to release the tension in his jaw and shoulders. He failed. With his whole world spinning out of control, he couldn't even restrain his own physical responses.

'Don't worry about me,' he said, making an effort to speak calmly. 'This can't go on much longer. It's all a bloody nonsense. We'll get through it. For now, we just have to be strong and wait it out.'

He heard his voice rise slightly in agitation and pressed his lips together, as though afraid different words would escape against his will. Laura kissed him lightly on the cheek and hurried off to the bus stop. A whiff of her scent lingered for a moment and he savoured its subtle hint of lilac. But then he recalled the cloying perfume of his accuser, and he shuddered, wondering how long he and Laura could continue to keep up the pretence that everything was all right. She had gone off to work, all fragrant and neat, as she did every day. He wondered if she put his troubles out of her mind as soon as she left him, and went about her daily routine as though nothing had happened to disturb the agreeable equilibrium of their lives.

Alone, he tried to put his predicament out of his mind, but that proved impossible. It was a pity the girl was dead. She had been his one chance of completely rebutting the allegation. As it was, there might always remain a cloud of doubt over his name. But if she had survived, she would probably have stuck to her vicious story anyway. On balance, he was glad she was dead, even if her murder placed him in an even trickier position than before. If he had been a religious man, he might have believed he was being punished for his sins, maybe even for a sin he hadn't committed himself. How did it go? There was something in the Bible about children being punished for the sins of the fathers. But he didn't believe in any of that. He was suffering from a random and terrible misfortune that he had to endure and ride out.

All he could do now was stick to his story and cling to the belief that in time his life would return to some kind of normality. That was the only thing worth believing in. As long as he held his nerve, and didn't let this break him, he'd come through it without ending up behind bars. He sighed. Not going to prison seemed to be the best he could hope for now. He doubted he would ever find another teaching job after all the publicity the case was attracting in the media. He pulled himself up short, determined not to give in to such negative thoughts.

He hadn't left the house much for days. Now he was up and out, he had no reason to go straight home and loaf around all day, casting a desultory eye over the daytime television where all the programmes struck him as vulgar or dreary, or both, with grinning presenters wishing him 'Good morning' when there was nothing good about it. Their professional cheerfulness made him feel even more depressed. He told himself this period of enforced idleness would be over soon enough. In the meantime, he needed something to occupy his mind. Somehow he couldn't settle to lesson planning. There seemed to be no point, when he didn't know if he would ever be able to return to the classroom. Instead of following Laura to the bus stop, he walked the mile and a half back to Holgate Road, and made his way to the supermarket. After spending the rest of the day at work, Laura would appreciate a decent meal when she got home. It was the least he could do after all he had put her through.

Reaching his local store, he made his way around the aisles. It wasn't busy at that time in the morning, just a few middle-aged women scanning the shelves, a youngster who probably ought to have been at school, an elderly man who struggled past with his trolley, and a couple of young women with toddlers in tow. Paul chose his items with care, dropping them into his basket. To begin with he wasn't quite sure what to get, so he looked up the recipe online on his phone, to check he hadn't missed anything. Satisfied that he had everything he needed, he joined a short queue at the checkout. The woman in front of him glared at him over her shoulder and seemed about to speak. Instead of addressing him, she turned and muttered to the woman at the till, who scowled at him. Suddenly he felt uncomfortable. Although he had no idea who the customer in front of him was, he thought she looked familiar. She turned and scuttled away and he moved along beside the conveyor belt, trying to ignore the woman at the checkout. There was something threatening about the way she was staring at him, and he packed up his purchases and paid as quickly as he could.

By the time he left the supermarket, he was close to panicking. But the sun was shining outside in the street. Pedestrians passed by without so much as glancing at him, and he basked in the warmth of his anonymity. He told himself the incident in the supermarket had been a manifestation of his own feelings of paranoia. In reality no one had been giving him filthy looks. They were just in a hurry to complete their shopping, or bored with their repetitive work. He felt the tension flow out of his shoulders as he walked, enjoying the sunshine.

Turning into the side street where he lived, he heard footsteps behind him. Dismissing his misgivings, nevertheless he walked faster. The footsteps speeded up. He stopped and waited for the other person to walk past him. The footsteps stopped too. Resisting the urge to turn round, he resumed walking, and the footsteps started up again. Someone was following him. All his strength seemed to seep out of him, until he could barely move his legs. He forced himself to keep walking. After what felt like an inordinately long time, he saw his own house, not far away. With a burst of adrenaline he sprinted home, rummaging in his pocket for his keys as he ran. He didn't slow down until he swerved through his gate, fumbled to unlock the front door and bounded through it, slamming it behind him. Panting, he sank down on the stairs and began to shake. It took him a few minutes to recover his composure. Hauling himself to his feet, he took the shopping into the kitchen and turned his attention to the dinner he was planning to prepare. It gave him something to think about, other than his growing paranoia. He couldn't even bring himself to consider what had just happened.

19

THAT AFTERNOON, THE DETECTIVE chief inspector summoned the team to a briefing. Cassie's bedroom at home, and her locker at school, had both been searched, but this wasn't a television crime drama, and no illuminating diary had come to light. Her social media accounts were similarly unhelpful in moving the investigation forward, consisting entirely of images of Cassie in different poses and varying stages of undress. Her contacts were schoolfriends, and random men who had all been located. None of them lived in the UK.

A young constable had been tasked with looking into Max Dean's history, and her enquiries had revealed some interesting information. Before the briefing, Geraldine had the report, which detailed the boy's history of petty violence.

'He's been in numerous scraps with other boys,' the young constable said to the assembled officers. 'None was reported to the police but they're all on his school record. What happened to Cassie Jackson doesn't seem to fit his history. His offences have all been relatively minor cases of brawling with other boys, and there's no mention of any weapons in any of the reports.'

'They might have been relatively minor skirmishes, but he had to leave his previous school after a particularly violent outburst,' Binita said. 'Clearly he has a temper.'

'Yes, there's no question he has a temper,' Geraldine agreed. 'But there's nothing in his past that suggests he's capable of murder.'

'Cassie was his girlfriend. If she was cheating on him, and he lost his temper with her, who knows what he might have been capable of?' Ariadne said. 'As for minor incidents, shouldn't we regard all violence as potentially significant? Is there such a thing as "insignificant" or "petty" when it comes to violence?'

'He's eighteen and old enough to know what he's doing,' Matthew said.

'He's eighteen now,' Geraldine pointed out. 'But he was thirteen when he was expelled from school for fighting, and another boy was expelled for the same incident. Max denied all along having started the fight. He may have had a violent temper when he was thirteen, but we can't necessarily assume that means he's capable of murder now.'

'Either way, we need to have another word with that young man,' Binita said grimly.

As soon as the briefing was concluded, Ariadne drove Geraldine to the Deans' house, as Binita wanted him questioned again. After a delay, Max's father opened the door.

'I seem to spend my life waiting on doorsteps,' Geraldine muttered.

'What do you want now?' Mr Dean snapped, making no attempt to conceal his annoyance.

'We'd like another word with Max.'

'Well, you're out of luck because he's not here.'

Mr Dean moved to shut the door, but Geraldine stepped forward to prevent it closing.

'Can you tell me where he is?' she asked, speaking as lightly as she could.

Mr Dean shrugged. 'He's eighteen. I don't keep tabs on him twenty-four seven. He's out with his friends. That's all I know.'

His wife joined him in the hall. Seeing Geraldine on the doorstep, she looked worried. 'Oh no,' she wailed, 'what do they want now?'

'We'd like to have another word with Max,' Geraldine explained patiently. 'Do you know where I can find him?'

'I'm sorry, I've no idea.'

'Max has lots of friends,' his father added. 'He could be at any one of their houses. He's a popular boy.'

'Yes, I'm sure. Well, when he comes home please ask him to call me.'

Geraldine held out her card. Neither of Max's parents made any move to take it from her.

'Is he suspected of having committed a crime?' Mr Dean asked gruffly.

'He wouldn't do anything to break the law,' his wife interjected earnestly. 'He's a good lad. He doesn't break the law. None of us does.'

'He's not a suspect,' Geraldine fibbed. 'But we think he may be able to help us find someone.'

She spoke in an even tone. It was true that the police didn't know the identity of Cassie's murderer. Unless there had been any witnesses, only one person knew for certain who had killed her. But it wasn't strictly true that Max wasn't a suspect. It just wasn't official yet.

'Then he doesn't have to answer to you and he won't be contacting you. If you want to speak to him, you're going to have to find him yourself,' Mr Dean snapped and he slammed the door.

'There's nothing unusual in parents not knowing where an eighteen-year-old boy has gone for the evening,' Ian said, when Geraldine told him what had happened.

'That's as maybe,' she replied crossly, 'but I'm going to be on their doorstep at seven o'clock tomorrow morning, before any of them have left the house, and I'm going to speak to Max Dean, if I have to drag him out of bed myself.'

'I wouldn't do that,' Ian said thoughtfully. 'If you want

my advice, I think that sounds like a very bad idea.'

'No teenage boy is going to intimidate me, not even one suspected of murder,' she fumed.

'I meant that his bedroom probably stinks,' Ian said. 'If I were you I wouldn't want to go anywhere near his bed. The smell might knock you out and then how are you going to apprehend your suspect?'

He wrinkled his nose and Geraldine laughed.

'Very well,' she said, 'you can come with me, if you like. And we'll take a couple of uniforms with us as well, just in case he tries to make a run for it.'

'In that case, as long as you're being sensible about this, I think I'll stay at home,' Ian replied. 'Much as I love the thrill of the chase, I'm not sure I like the sound of being up and out before seven.'

'His parents weren't at all co-operative,' Geraldine continued, 'but he's not getting away this time. Even if he didn't touch Cassie, with his record it won't do him any harm to have a bit of a scare. If you ask me, he needs a serious talking to. Kids these days think they can get away with anything.'

Ian hesitated, but he clearly thought better of trying to respond to her tirade. Instead he offered to make supper.

'Who used to calm you down when you were living on your own?' he asked her, when they had eaten and were relaxing with a glass of red wine.

Geraldine shrugged. 'I didn't spend much time at home,' she replied.

'I didn't have you down as a social butterfly.'

'No, more of a workaholic.'

'So no change there.'

She laughed. 'You are joking, aren't you? Honestly, Ian, I never know when you're pulling my leg.'

Ian looked surprised. 'I wasn't joking,' he said solemnly.

'Don't you regard yourself as a workaholic?'

Geraldine thought about it. 'I was a lot worse before you came along,' she said at last.

Ian whistled. 'Well, then, I'm glad I came along to save you from yourself.'

Geraldine didn't join in his laughter.

'I haven't offended you, have I?' he asked. 'You know what they say: it only hurts if it's true.'

'Well, it doesn't hurt, and it's not true,' Geraldine replied, but she suspected Ian didn't believe that any more than she did.

She had always regarded the majority of her colleagues as inappropriately lighthearted when working on murder investigations. Recently she had begun to wonder whether she wasn't the one who was out of step, with her earnest approach to cases. It wasn't that she lacked a sense of humour, rather that she found it difficult to laugh about her work. A colleague had once accused her of treating her job like a religion. At the time, she hadn't really understood what he meant. She had appreciated it wasn't a compliment, although she had pretended to treat it as one. Now she began to see what he had been getting at.

'Do you think I'm too serious?' she asked Ian.

He looked at her and smiled. 'Ask someone who isn't in love with you if you want a sensible response to a question like that,' he said.

'So you do think I'm too serious,' she replied and sighed. 'I need to try and take things more lightly.'

'No,' Ian said, no longer smiling. 'Don't do that. We need people like you if we're going to catch these tricky bastards. I've seen some colleagues give up when it all seems too hard, but you never do. If you were to lose your obsessively driven approach to our work, we'd all be worse off. Except for a few psychopaths who would be free to carry on going around killing people, that is.' He bent down and kissed her. 'Promise me you won't change.'

20

'WHAT WAS THAT?' LAURA asked.

Paul just grunted. They had finished their dinner in front of the television. Since Paul's enforced idleness they had virtually stopped talking to each other. With only the television to fill the awkward silences that had begun to characterise their relationship, Paul could scarcely bother to respond to her question.

'Be quiet,' Laura said.

She raised one hand and sat staring at Paul with startled blue eyes. He felt an urge to rush over to her chair and put his arms around her, but he suppressed it, unsure how she might respond. Since he had asked her to lie for him, she had seemed wary of him. They had not discussed his request again, but Laura was no fool. She would draw her own conclusions about his reasons for wanting her to claim they had been at home together all evening on Thursday. She hadn't even asked him what had happened on Thursday, and he didn't know if she was aware that Cassie had been killed that evening, but it was hard to see how she could have failed to reach that conclusion.

'I thought I heard something,' she whispered. 'Mute the telly.'

He obliged and they sat listening to the silence for a moment.

'It was nothing,' she said at last. 'I thought I heard something outside, that's all.'

'Probably a fox,' he replied. 'Or someone putting out their rubbish.'

Before he could turn the sound up on the television, there was a noise at the front of the house. They both heard it this time.

'What was that?' Laura asked.

She sounded curious rather than frightened, but Paul felt a dark suspicion uncurl itself somewhere deep in his guts, remembering how he had been followed home from the supermarket. Perhaps someone had wanted to know where he lived.

'There's a faction that blames you,' the head teacher had told him. 'There's been some talk… I thought you ought to know…'

He regretted not having pressed for more information, but the head had been keen to end the call, and Paul had not had time to question him.

'I need to make a quick call,' he said, and hurried from the room before Laura could remonstrate.

But the head didn't answer. He was probably in school. There might be a governors' meeting. They could be discussing Paul's future at that very moment. Agitated, he tried the school switchboard but was diverted to an automated message that told him the school was closed and offered him an extension to report a child who would be absent the following day. Cursing under his breath, he hung up. There was no way he could contact the head that evening, but he resolved to speak to him in the morning. He had to know what was being said about him, and by whom. It was unnerving to think that people were talking about him behind his back, allowing him no chance to defend himself. This was more than mere gossip. If someone believed Paul was responsible for murdering a young girl, there was no knowing what might happen. Cassie's family might blame him for her death, and decide to take matters into their own hands. If not her family then her boyfriend, Max, might be out for revenge. The police hadn't arrested Paul, but other people might be too impatient to wait for evidence before meting out what they believed was just punishment for a murderer who appeared to have got away with the crime.

He returned to the front room. The television was still muted and Laura was sitting on the edge of her chair, wringing her hands. Paul had never seen her looking so frightened, and so fragile, but somehow his urge to comfort her was stifled by apprehension. She ought to have realised by now that he had his own fears to contend with. He didn't have the emotional space to support her as well. Nevertheless his voice sounded more gruff than he had intended when he asked her what was wrong.

'I heard something,' she murmured. 'I definitely heard something.'

'It was just someone putting out their rubbish,' he said.

'No, no, it wasn't,' she stammered. 'I heard – I heard –'

'What did you hear?'

She shook her head, helpless in the grip of her apprehension. 'It was a kind of scratching,' she said, 'and then someone shouted.'

'Shouted?'

'Yes, yes, someone shouted.'

'What does that mean? What did they shout?' he asked, growing impatient with this guessing game. 'Tell me what you heard.'

'Someone shouted "Pervert",' she whispered.

Rage flared in Paul's mind, as though someone had let off a firework in his head.

'That's it,' he exclaimed loudly. 'I've had more than enough of this nonsense.'

He turned and walked to the door.

'Where are you going?' Laura cried.

She leapt to her feet and seized his arm to detain him.

'I'm going out there to confront whoever it is hanging around the house. I'll send them packing. Don't look so worried,' he added, seeing her terrified expression. 'It's just kids from school.'

'I'm calling the police,' she said.

He shrugged. That wasn't a bad idea, but first he wanted to see for himself what was going on, and who was behind it. He had a feeling it might be Max Dean. He was a nasty little shit, who had been soft on Cassie Jackson.

Laura followed him to the hall. 'Stop,' she snapped, fear making her angry. 'Don't you dare go out there alone.'

She slipped on her shoes and grabbed an umbrella.

'Don't be ridiculous,' Paul blurted out, seeing her brandish her impromptu weapon, but at the same time he felt a rush of relief that she was demonstrating her solidarity with him.

He had been feeling so alone.

Cautiously he opened the front door. There was no sound. He peered out, but there was no one in sight. Slowly he stepped through the door, with Laura at his heels. The front garden was empty. Relief flooded through him and he chuckled softly as his tension ebbed away.

'It must have been a fox or a cat,' he said. 'And there we were, getting all worked up for nothing. Come on, let's go back in.'

He turned and his whole body went rigid as he read what had been written on the front wall of his house, in large spray painted letters. The message seemed to burn itself into his brain: PEDO.

21

A FINE DRIZZLE WAS falling just before seven o'clock the following morning when, true to her word, Geraldine stood on the Deans' doorstep and rang the bell. A drowsy-looking Mrs Dean pulled the door open a crack and peered out, clutching a faded maroon dressing gown around her. Evidently startled to see Geraldine, together with a burly police officer in uniform, she scowled and took a step back.

'What the hell is going on?' she burst out irritably. 'You can't just go around ringing people's bells at this hour.'

'Mrs Dean, we'd like to ask Max a few more questions,' Geraldine replied firmly. Mrs Dean's frown darkened as Geraldine continued in an even tone. 'We'll wait here, and two of my colleagues are standing outside your back door, so if you've got any sense you'll tell him to come quietly. We don't want to keep him away from school any longer than necessary, so it's in everyone's interest to get this over with quickly.'

Muttering that it would be in everyone's interest for the police to bugger off and stop harassing her family, Mrs Dean turned back into the house and shut the door. Geraldine heard the sound of feet pounding up the stairs, followed by raised voices. A few moments later, someone came pounding down the stairs and Mr Dean came to the door, also in his dressing gown. He hesitated on seeing the broad-shouldered Police Constable Bert Brown standing beside Geraldine.

'What's this about, Inspector?' Mr Dean asked, politely

enough, although his eyes were burning with fury. 'Is there something I can do for you this early in the morning?'

'We're waiting for Max,' Geraldine replied.

'Is there anything I can help you with?' he repeated stubbornly.

Geraldine frowned at the delay. 'You can help us by telling Max to get a move on. If he keeps us waiting much longer, he's going to be late for school.'

Max seemed to be in no hurry to come downstairs. Only when Geraldine proposed sending her colleague upstairs to fetch him did Mr Dean scurry back upstairs to summon his son who appeared at the top of the stairs in his underwear, remonstrating angrily at being disturbed.

'Max! Max! Get down there and speak to the policewoman right now,' Mr Dean said.

'You might want to get dressed before you come with us,' Geraldine called up to him.

Mrs Dean came hurrying back to the front door, her face creased in a fake smile. 'You can talk to him in the living room. Why don't I put the kettle on and make us all a cup of tea?'

'That's very kind of you, but I'm afraid we do need to question Max at the police station. It's for his own protection, so we can conduct the interview in the presence of his lawyer.'

'Shall I go up and fetch him, ma'am?' the constable asked.

'No, that won't be necessary. Just wait there and I'll tell him to get dressed,' Mrs Dean replied, clearly agitated by the way things were going.

At last, after a lot of palaver, Max was seated in the back of a patrol car, with uniformed constables for company, and they were on their way. It had taken Geraldine just over an hour to bring him in.

'If you're late for school, that's entirely your own fault,' Geraldine said sharply, once the interview had formally begun.

113

'For the record, we were ready to drive you here over an hour ago but it took us a long time to persuade you to come with us.'

'Whatever,' the boy replied sullenly without looking up.

'Why were you reluctant to be questioned?' Geraldine asked.

'It was dead early,' he repeated. 'Way too early to be outta bed. I need my sleep, innit? You got no business getting me outta bed like that. It ain't cool.'

'I understand you're not bothered about being late for school. You don't care much for school, do you?' Geraldine went on, hoping to catch him off guard by moving quickly on to her next question. 'But you did care about Cassie Jackson, didn't you?'

He looked down at the floor and didn't answer.

'Tell me about her,' Geraldine urged. 'What was she like?'

Max shrugged. 'She was all right.'

'She was your girlfriend, wasn't she?'

'Yeah, whatever.'

'But she was also seeing other boys, wasn't she?'

He didn't answer.

'How did that make you feel?'

'Whatever,' he repeated.

Geraldine continued trying to coax him into speaking, but the boy just sat hunched over and taciturn, less forthcoming than many criminals who had been instructed by their lawyers to keep their mouths shut. When Max persisted in denying that he knew about anyone else Cassie was seeing, Geraldine ended the interview, accepting that it was a waste of time.

Her next visit was to Cassie's house, to see if her mother knew the names of any other boys who might have been interested in their daughter. This time, when she rang the bell, a girl of about twelve opened the door. She glared sullenly at Geraldine.

'What?' she demanded. 'I'm off with a virus, innit? You can ask my mum.'

Geraldine stared at the girl. Her face looked uncannily familiar and was framed by badly dyed frizzy blonde hair. Even the girl's nails were long and painted the same shade of pink as Cassie had used. Geraldine wondered if she was making use of her older sister's possessions now Cassie was no longer there to stop her, or whether the two sisters used to paint their nails together.

'You must be Cassie's sister,' she said gently. 'Belle, isn't it? I'm not here to chase you for truancy.'

'What?' the girl replied. 'I ain't bunking off. I told you, I got a virus.'

'Can I speak to your mother?' Geraldine asked. 'It's about Cassie.'

'Course it is. Everything's always about Cassie, innit? Cassie, Cassie, Cassie, that's all anyone talks about,' the girl burst out angrily. 'Ever since she was –' She broke off suddenly, and her eyes filled with tears.

'I'm so sorry,' Geraldine said. 'I didn't mean to upset you. Can I speak to your mother?'

'She ain't home.'

Geraldine hid her dismay that the girl had been left on her own. Even if she wasn't actually ill, she was clearly distressed about losing her sister. But perhaps her mother had only nipped out to the shops.

'When are you expecting her? I can come back later.'

The girl shrugged. 'I dunno, do I? She said not to wait up as she might be late.' She shrugged. 'I got to go. I got to get back to my game.'

'Wait,' Geraldine said. 'Do you know Max?'

'No.'

'He was Cassie's boyfriend.'

'I don't know no one called Max. She never told me nothing about no Max.'

'Did she have any other boyfriends?'

The girl shook her head and her crinkled hair jiggled about. 'She never said.'

Abruptly she shut the door.

'Well, that was all one big waste of time,' Geraldine grumbled when she returned to the police station and joined Ariadne in the canteen for lunch.

'What did you expect?' Ariadne replied. 'That someone would suddenly decide to tell us who killed Cassie?'

Geraldine frowned. 'There's something Max isn't telling us,' she said, 'but I don't know what it is. I thought it would be easy to persuade him to talk, once we brought him in, but he's determined to hold out on us. He's hiding something all right, and we need to find out what it is. As for Cassie's mother – well, I wonder how much parental supervision there was before Cassie was killed. Not a lot, judging by her younger sister.'

22

In a way Laura was glad to be relieved of her usual workload because it meant she could avoid having to watch what she said. Gina insisted the stylists nattered endlessly while they worked. It didn't matter what they talked about, as long as they kept going. She said it relaxed the clients, and made the experience of having their hair cut more enjoyable.

'They could go anywhere,' she liked to say, patting her neatly arranged curls and glancing at her reflection in the mirror across the salon. 'The competition is humungous, so we have to make sure we give them an enjoyable experience when they come here. That's what keeps them coming back, because we offer them more than just a simple haircut. They come here to feel pampered and valued. Our regular clients regard us as their friends. We *are* their friends.'

'I'm not friends with some old crone who comes here once a week to have her bald patch covered up,' Anna murmured, loudly enough for the other stylists to hear.

'That old crone pays your wages,' Gina snapped. 'So you make sure you treat her like a queen when she comes in. Make out that she really matters to you, because you know what? She does, if you want to keep your job.'

There was a lot more along those lines. Once a week, the staff had to sit and listen to Gina spouting forth in what she called the 'staff training'. In addition to their hairdressing skills, which had to be top notch, everyone had to smile and look cheerful, the coffee machine had to kept topped up in readiness, and the floor swept regularly. Everything had to be in place to present an image of effortless luxury. In a way, Gina was right. Somehow the job of washing and trimming hair seemed to encourage friendly chatter, and for over a week Laura had been constantly on edge, afraid her colleagues would find out that her husband had been accused of molesting one of his pupils. One careless comment was all it would take to betray her secret. She wasn't sure she could bear the pitying glances, and the whispering behind her back that would inevitably follow the discovery. They would no doubt gossip with their wider circles of friends, as well as with the clients at the salon, and it wouldn't be long before everyone Laura knew, and a lot more people besides, heard all about her troubles. So on balance she was glad not to be cutting and styling hair, even though it was costing her money.

She shuddered at the memory of the message that had been painted on the front of the house. It was enough to put her off returning home at all. Remembering how happy she and Paul had been there, it was a wonder she didn't explode with rage against whoever had daubed their home in that horrible way. If only she knew who it was, she would tell them exactly what she thought of them before reporting them to the police. They deserved to be locked up for what they had done. Paul was convinced it was just kids, messing around, but she wasn't so sure. Paul had run back inside to fetch a pot of paint from the loft, left over from a bout of home decorating he had carried out one summer. While his efforts to paint over the graffiti had been messy, at least he had covered up the message.

'I'll wash it all off,' he had assured her, stepping back to survey his handiwork. 'I'll go to the homeware store and get some paint stripper. But for now, at least no one's going to see the graffiti. I mean, it's not the kind of thing you want your neighbours to see, is it?' He had let out a queer hollow-sounding laugh.

'What if they come back and do it all over again?' she had asked, unable to conceal her apprehension. 'You can't keep covering it up every time they paint something on our house. We have to stop them doing it! Can't the police do anything? There must be a law against it. They're trespassing on our property. It's criminal damage.'

'They won't be back.' He had smiled reassuringly at her, glancing around as though he was afraid someone might hear her.

'How can you be so sure?'

'It was kids from school messing around. By tomorrow they'll have forgotten all about this, and they'll be on to the next thing. They never stick at anything for long. They're just kids mucking about.'

At the time, Laura had grudgingly accepted what Paul had said. She had been pleased the offending graffiti had been covered up. But now she wasn't so sure. Paul had been very quick to paint over the graffiti. Their neighbours couldn't see it now, but nor could the police. In painting over the words, he had effectively stopped her from reporting the incident to the police, and that meant there was no possibility the vandal might ever be apprehended. He – or perhaps she – might have left fingerprints or DNA, or something that could have enabled the police to trace whoever had done it. But now, any evidence the writer might have left at the scene had been destroyed. She wondered if Paul could have had a secret motive for obliterating the message so swiftly before they had a chance to report it to the police. There might have been something Paul wanted to keep hidden. She sighed, pouring the coffee, and carrying it carefully to the client. Everything was so confusing and so worrying.

'You look cheerful,' one of the stylists chided her.

It was hard to believe that only a week ago she would have responded with laughter, joking with her colleague. Feeling Gina's eyes on her, watchful and concerned, Laura forced a cheery grin.

'I didn't want to spill the coffee,' she replied.

She turned and retreated to the kitchenette where she rinsed the coffee pot and tried not to think about Paul. She felt safer hiding away in the kitchenette with the cups and the broom. At the same time, being restricted to sweeping the floor and making coffee meant she missed seeing her usual clients who were being eagerly snapped up by the other stylists. It also meant that she was missing her tips. Admittedly Paul had been suspended on full pay, but she didn't know how long that was likely to continue. He insisted there was no need for her to worry because the problem would be satisfactorily resolved very soon. But he had no way of knowing whether that was true. Before long, they might need every penny she could earn, and without tips that didn't amount to much. Overnight, her whole life had been turned upside down, and she was more frightened than she would admit, even to herself. Because what if the accusation were true? It seemed almost impossible to believe that of Paul. Almost.

Perhaps she would never know the truth, and would have to live with this horrible uncertainty, a dark cloud that would hover over them for the rest of their lives. Because how could she ever be sure her husband wasn't a paedophile? It was possible to prove something *was* true, given enough evidence, but Paul could never actually prove that he was completely innocent, in thought as well as in deed.

23

SITTING AT HOME BY himself, he considered his next move. Everyone else was an oblivious pawn in the game that he had initiated, a game in which there would only ever be a single player. As soon as someone else joined in, his game would be over. It was down to him to make sure that didn't happen. In a way the police had already entered the contest, but they were playing blindfold, and he was never going to reveal the truth to them. He had no desire to spend the rest of his life behind bars. Besides, there was no point in throwing his victory away when he had already won. The amusing thing about it was that none of the other players even knew what game they were playing. Only he was privy to the rules, and they were bent in his favour because he alone knew what was going on. The sound of his laughter echoed around the empty room.

Lately he had been spending a lot of time on his own. It had given him an opportunity to think. Killing the little slut had been a sudden impulse which he almost regretted now it was done. He hadn't planned to despatch her so early in the game, if at all, not least because killing her had been risky. At the very least it had complicated matters because by now the police must have realised that her death was no accident. But it would probably have been necessary to silence her in the end because there had always been a chance she might reveal what had really happened between them. He had the impression she had already begun to waver, so it was her own fault she was dead. If he could have trusted her to remain unswervingly loyal to him for the rest of her life, she would still be alive. But he knew only too well that lifelong loyalty could never be guaranteed. When the opportunity to rid himself of her had arisen, he had taken advantage of it, that was all. No one ought to blame him for that, only, of course, they would.

In retrospect, he was satisfied that he had been smart to silence her, and so far he had no cause to change his view. She should have kept her mouth shut, instead of running away with the foolish idea that she had some kind of hold over him. As if he was ever really going to be interested in a little tramp like her. At first he had considered himself lucky to get away. On reflection, he realised that luck had nothing to do with it because there was no way the police could prove he had killed her. No one knew he had driven her out to the woods in the old car he kept hidden away in a lock-up. With typical prudence, he had bought the car for cash, and had never registered it with the DVLA. Even if the police managed to make out its registration number, they wouldn't be able to trace it back to him. He was almost sure it had been stolen by the guy who had sold it on to him. It was certainly cheap enough, and the owner had no papers to go with it. Having a secret means of transport had come in handy on several occasions. But even that hadn't come about by luck. He had been clever, and his foresight had paid dividends. In contrast to the carefully thought-out acquisition of his secret vehicle, killing Cassie had been work of a moment: thrashing limbs, a few muffled cries, and it was over. Reviewing the incident, he smiled. It couldn't really have been much easier. Next time would be just as straightforward. All he had to do was be careful, and that came naturally to him.

It was annoying, but there had to be a next time; Cassie's friend knew too much. Ella had seen him and Cassie together.

If she ever realised the truth, she was never going to be discreet. He couldn't risk that. Even now, the police must be investigating what had happened to Cassie that evening in the woods. As long as Ella was alive, he would never be safe. Girls like her were bound to blab, sooner or later, and with the police badgering everyone who had known Cassie, it was only going to be a matter of time before Ella talked. He had no choice but to protect himself. If Ella was as trusting as Cassie, silencing her would be easy, but he would have to be careful, and he had to act soon. She might be stupid, but he was running out of time.

Fortunately young girls were gullible. All it took was a little flattery. He had experimented on Cassie and had it down to a fine art. It didn't do to exaggerate too much. The best approach was to select a genuinely attractive feature and focus on that. With Cassie it had been easy because she was ridiculously vain of her voluptuous figure. She could have been quite pretty if she hadn't made herself look trashy and cheap with fake eyelashes, and fake blonde hair. He had selected Cassie for a reason; Ella had been forced on him. She might not be so easy to fool, but he would just have to work a little harder to win her round, that was all.

A mousy little creature, Ella's face was all pointy nose and chin, and her beady little eyes seemed to bore through his skull, making him feel quite uncomfortable. Ella had only seen him once with his arm around Cassie, but she had understood straightaway what was going on. Her piggy little eyes had positively blazed with salacious suspicion. On the other hand, she probably didn't attract much attention from boys. That could make his task much easier. He just had to work out how to approach her and then proceed carefully. How difficult could it be to butter up a young girl like Ella? At her age they all wanted to believe they were attractive. He just had to convince her that he had fallen for her and get her alone, away from prying eyes. But he needed to do it very soon, before she had time to draw her own conclusions about Cassie's death. He took a deep breath. It was important to remain calm and think clearly. He couldn't afford any mistakes, knowing the tiniest slip-up could lead to discovery. But after years of practice, he was confident in his own powers of persuasion.

24

IN ADDITION TO STUDYING CCTV from the area around Fishponds Wood, a team of visual images, identifications and detections officers had been given the task of studying footage from any security cameras in the vicinity of Paul Moore's house. They were beginning their retrospective surveillance with any available film taken on the evening of the murder. No one really expected to see footage of Paul Moore creeping furtively out of his house on Thursday evening, but the scrutiny continued. There was always a chance that a previously unseen fragment of evidence might be discovered. And they all knew that one tiny scrap of evidence might feasibly start a chain reaction that could eventually lead them to the killer. Such things happened quite frequently in the course of murder investigations. So the search continued and any available CCTV footage was examined, frame by frame, centimetre by centimetre.

The team were tenacious and their patience was rewarded when early one morning a VIIDO officer spotted a figure arriving in the car park of the local supermarket. Enhancing the image revealed the registration number of the car, and close inspection of the figure itself confirmed the suspicion. Laura Moore had gone to the supermarket on the evening of the murder. Not only had she lied to the police about being at home all evening, but Paul had been alone for over an hour. That would have given him enough time to drive to Fishponds Wood, strangle Cassie, and be home again before his wife returned. Laura might even have known about his movements. Certainly she had lied to give him an alibi.

As soon as she heard about Laura's outing to the shops, Geraldine drove to Paul's house with a couple of constables: stocky PC Bert Brown who had accompanied her to the Deans' house, and PC Will Nash, who was fresh out of training. There was a messy splodge of white paint on the front of the property beside the front door that Geraldine didn't recall seeing on her last visit to the house. Paul opened the door as soon as she rang the bell. He looked surprised to see her.

'I was just going out,' he said. 'I need to get to —' He broke off in apparent confusion before concluding lamely, 'I need to do some shopping.'

'We need to ask you a few more questions,' Geraldine said.

'Okay then. Ask away,' he replied, making a feeble attempt to appear nonchalant.

'We'd like you to come to the police station with us.'

Paul dropped his fake composure and looked at her in unmistakable panic. 'What's this about?' he asked. 'Do I need a lawyer?'

'That's your choice.'

'Oh heck, it's not about Cassie Jackson again, is it? I've already told you everything I know. She might conceivably have had a silly schoolgirl crush on me, without my knowing anything about it, but that's all. It's not uncommon for girls her age to have these hysterical fantasies for absolutely no reason. I certainly did nothing to encourage her. On the contrary, I scarcely spoke to her, except to threaten her with sanctions for not handing in any work. She wasn't exactly diligent. That was the extent of my communication with her and, believe me, it was minimal on both sides. Neither of us wanted to have anything to do with each other. She was put out when I gave her a poor grade, and that might have provoked her to accuse me, but that's the only reason I can think of why she might –'

'Save it for the interview,' Geraldine said curtly, nodding at the patrol car.

'You want me to go in that? Oh, very well. Might as well give the neighbours a show,' he grumbled.

Paul's lawyer was tall and very thin, with unnaturally yellow hair that flopped untidily over his forehead. His bulbous eyes looked unfocused but his voice was sharp and clipped.

'How would my client benefit from the death of the girl who accused him of sexual misconduct? Surely his best hope of clearing his name would have been for her to withdraw her false allegation.'

'It's quite possible the murder wasn't premeditated,' Geraldine responded quietly. 'Your client might have killed his victim in a fit of temper. She had accused him of sexual assault.'

'Oh please,' Paul blurted out. 'We've been over this again and again. She was a fantasist, a hysterical teenager who was desperate for attention.'

Geraldine noted he sounded irritated but not angry. Perhaps he wasn't easily goaded, but that didn't mean he never lost his temper. And an allegation of inappropriate sexual conduct with a pupil was about as serious a provocation as a teacher could face.

'This is mere speculation,' the lawyer drawled. 'In a situation where a man's liberty is in question, supposition has no place, however reasonable you may consider it – or however determined you may be to find a culprit.' His eyes flicked at Geraldine as he implied that she was keen to make an arrest, regardless of whether or not the suspect was actually guilty.

Refusing to respond to the lawyer's veiled accusation, Geraldine changed tack and put a direct question to Paul.

'Why did you and your wife lie about her whereabouts on the evening Cassie Jackson was murdered?'

Paul mumbled something incoherent and cast an apprehensive glance at his lawyer who stared impassively at him.

'I'm sorry, I didn't hear that,' Geraldine said. 'Can you speak up for the tape, please?'

'What? What makes you say that?' He shifted awkwardly in his chair and glanced at his lawyer again. 'We didn't lie.'

'I'm afraid that's not true,' Geraldine said. She sighed. 'Your wife left the house and went to Sainsbury's on Thursday evening.'

Paul rallied quickly. 'It's not a crime to go to the supermarket, is it?' he asked with a nervous laugh.

'The point is,' Geraldine explained, choosing her words with care, 'your wife told us she was with you all evening, and neither you nor she left the house. But that's not true, is it?'

'You're right.' Paul shrugged. 'I guess we both forgot. With everything that's been going on, that's hardly surprising. Yes, I remember now, she went shopping. I can't be expected to remember everything, can I? It was stupid to be so careless, I know, but I panicked. I wasn't thinking clearly. I was frightened,' Paul went on, fidgeting uncomfortably. 'That is, we were both frightened and confused. We both panicked. The girl – Cassie – had just made a vicious and totally unfounded allegation against me, and the next thing I hear is she's dead. I was afraid you'd suspect I had something to do with it. But I've told you, I had nothing to do with her. I never touched her in any way, at any time. Forensic evidence is going to prove I'm innocent of any wrongdoing. She threw herself at me.'

'I'm afraid forensic evidence won't establish who instigated any touching,' Geraldine said.

'I've done nothing wrong,' Paul insisted.

'Other than lying to the police in the course of a murder investigation,' Geraldine pointed out.

'My client has explained that he was given the impression you suspected him of murder. It was natural for him to seek to defend himself when he knew his innocence might be difficult to establish.'

'But according to what you said just now, there was no reason for the allegation against you to be taken seriously by anyone.'

'That's right,' Paul said.

'My client has already stated he's innocent,' the lawyer said in his slow voice.

'Why were you so worried we would suspect you?' Geraldine asked.

'My client has already answered that question.'

'Can you explain why Cassie Jackson accused you of molesting her?'

Paul shook his head helplessly.

'Obviously my client can't speak for her,' the lawyer replied, frowning at the question.

'I've no idea what was going through her mind,' Paul cried out. 'Christ, I didn't even know her. She was just one of the pupils in my class. There was no reason for her to say what she said. Teenage girls often indulge in fantasies. I happened to be the subject for her fantasy on that day, that's all. It could just as easily have been someone else. I don't think there was a sensible reason for her choice. She just picked me at random.'

Geraldine had a feeling Paul was hiding something, but she couldn't work out what. In the meantime, they had no physical evidence to place him at the site where Cassie's body had been found. There was no trace of his DNA there, and nothing to connect him with the victim apart from her allegation against him. Telling him not to leave York, she let him go.

'Leave York?' he repeated. 'I've barely left my house since I was suspended from work. Except to come here,' he added sourly. 'Some outing this turned out to be!'

25

BACK AT HOME, PAUL stewed over what had just happened. He had thought the police had finished with him after they had questioned him and Laura, and taken a sample of his DNA. But as it turned out it had only taken them a couple of days to come back and drag him off to the police station to question him again. He wasn't quite sure what it all meant, but it couldn't be good. He had managed to stay outwardly calm while they interrogated him, but inside he had been too flustered to think clearly. All he could really remember clearly, now that he was home again, was his feeling of panic as he was driven away in a police car, and his cold terror when facing a pair of detectives across a table. Inspector Steel had a gentle smile and a sympathetic air, but he could tell she was internalising every word he uttered, dissecting and analysing his meaning. For all her soft way of speaking, he doubted she missed much. As for his lawyer, he might as well not have been there at all for all the help he was.

He tried to remember exactly what the detective inspector had said to him, but he had been too agitated to listen carefully. He recalled her calling him a liar, and challenging him as to why Cassie would have accused him of behaving inappropriately if there was no substance to the allegation, which was a stupid question. Anyone who worked with teenage girls knew how volatile and hysterical they could be. The boys weren't much better. He thought he had answered the detective's questions reasonably well, despite feeling intimidated by the situation. Even now, he could scarcely believe that he had been carted off to the police station for more questioning. Ever since Cassie had thrown herself at him in school, his life had become unreal, as though he had become detached from his body and this was happening to someone else. It was like watching a series on television about someone being psychologically tortured.

What was really concerning was that the police had discovered Laura had gone to Sainsbury's on Thursday evening. Now that the interview was over, he wasn't sure if the detective had told him how they knew Laura had gone out. The more he thought about it, the more he realised there was only one conclusion to be drawn: they could only have found out from Laura herself. They must have questioned her again while she was at work where she had blurted out the truth and landed him in real trouble. He fretted while he waited for her to come home and, by the time he heard her come in, he felt ready to burst with irritation.

'What did you say to the police?' he demanded, rushing out to the hall to confront her before she had even taken her coat off. 'What the hell do you think you were doing?'

Laura looked up, startled. 'What are you talking about?'

She turned calmly away to remove her shoes, as though she hadn't shattered his whole world.

'Why were you talking to the police?' he asked her again, stepping towards her and making no attempt to moderate his voice. 'Answer me! What did you say to them?' He was shouting now, but he didn't care.

She turned to face him, putting on a show of bewilderment. 'What do you mean? What are you shouting for? You were there as well, weren't you? You know what I said to them.'

He shook his head impatiently. 'After that,' he said, barely able to speak for the emotion choking his voice. 'I'm talking about after they took us to the police station. What did you tell them? Don't lie to me.'

Laura backed away from him, an expression of alarm crossing her face. 'I'm not lying. I've never lied to you.'

The fact that she had lied *for* him hung in the air between them, unspoken. 'I haven't told the police anything. I haven't spoken to them since we were there together. Why would I?' She smiled anxiously. 'I'll go and put the kettle on and we can have a nice cup of tea before I start the supper. You go and sit down and I'll bring it in. You're just feeling overwhelmed with it all. It's a lot to deal with. You'll feel better tomorrow.'

Haltingly, Paul told her that the police had called and taken him to the police station where he had been questioned for over an hour. Laura's face grew even paler than usual as she listened to him.

'They knew,' he said darkly. 'They knew.'

Now she looked really frightened.

'What – what do they know?' she whispered. 'Did you – what did you do?' She backed away from him, edging towards the front door.

He shrugged. 'What could I do? I told them we lied about it because I was frightened they wouldn't believe me. But they knew what had happened.' He glared at her. 'There's only one person who could have told them.'

'Who?' she whispered.

'You, of course. Don't act dumb with me.'

'I don't know what you're talking about. What could I have told them?'

'That you went to Sainsbury's on Thursday evening. That my alibi was a pack of lies. No one else could have known that.'

She heaved a deep sigh as though she was somehow relieved, and began to shake. 'Oh,' she said. She reached out and leaned one hand against the wall for support. For a moment he was afraid she might collapse. 'You mean they knew we weren't together on Thursday evening. They knew I'd gone out. That's what they know.'

'What else did you think I was talking about?'

She shook her head and avoided looking directly at him. Realisation dawned on him slowly.

'You thought –' he said. 'You thought they knew something else. What the hell do you think I've done?'

If even his wife refused to believe he was innocent, what hope did he have of convincing the police he had done nothing wrong? With a despairing cry, he pushed past her and ran out of the house. Not until he reached the end of the road did he realise that he had come out without his keys or his phone. He was all alone in the world, stranded and helpless. As he swore under his breath, a light rain began to fall, dusting his shoulders with a sprinkling of sparkling drops that soaked slowly into the fabric of his sweatshirt. A chill sensation crept down the back of his neck. For the first time in his life, he had nowhere to go, and absolutely no idea what to do.

26

GERALDINE AND IAN WERE discussing the case over a glass of beer and one of Ian's curries.

'It almost feels like sacrilege to be talking about work when we're eating this,' Geraldine said. 'It's sensational.'

Ian laughed, but she could tell he was pleased. 'It is one of my better efforts,' he agreed modestly.

It was Geraldine's turn to laugh. 'You know perfectly well your curries are always perfect. Why else do you think I stay here?'

'Because it's your home?' Ian replied, suddenly serious.

Geraldine had been living in the flat for several years before Ian moved in. Although it was beautiful, with a spacious living room overlooking the river, they both knew that Ian had moved in with her on a temporary basis, expecting that they would move to a place of their own.

'It's not that I don't like living here,' he had explained soon after he had moved in. 'It's just that this feels like your flat. I want us to live somewhere that feels like *our* home. Between us we can afford somewhere with a garden, and a bit more space. We don't have to live right in the centre of town. It's beautiful here, but it wouldn't be my choice. I'm used to living in a house, with stairs and – well, a house.'

The discussion had continued, on and off, ever since he had moved in. Now Geraldine held out her plate. 'Is there any more?'

Ian smiled, accepting the diversion before they could become drawn into a serious discussion about where they lived.

'So he just crumbled when you challenged him about his alibi?' Ian asked when they had finished eating. 'He didn't say he'd forgotten she went out?'

'He tried. But he had to say they'd both forgotten. Of course, it doesn't mean he's guilty.'

An alibi from a suspect's wife was never considered robust, but clearly Paul and Laura hadn't thought their story through. People rarely took into account the fact that it was almost impossible to move around the city without being caught on camera. Nevertheless, it had taken hours of scrutinising CCTV footage before Laura had been spotted, and she could easily have escaped attention. It was quite unlucky for Paul that she had been recognised emerging from the store. If Laura hadn't inadvertently drawn attention to herself by dropping a bag of shopping, the VIIDO officer admitted she might not have noticed her.

'She lied to protect him,' Geraldine murmured, wondering idly if Ian would do the same for her.

'Don't ask,' Ian said.

'Ask what?'

'If I would lie to save you from being arrested for murder.'

'The fact that you've entertained the possibility that the situation might ever arise doesn't say much for your faith in my moral rectitude.'

'Oh, you are the most morally upright person I've ever met,' he replied. 'Even if you do exaggerate how good my curries are. That's a form of lying, isn't it?' He grinned. 'Not so squeaky clean after all, are you?'

'Don't be daft. That's nothing compared to what Paul Moore is suspected of doing.'

'So you admit you exaggerate when you praise my curries?'

'Oh do shut up,' she laughed. 'I love your curries almost as much as I love you. And that's saying something.'

She stood up and walked round the table to bend down and kiss the top of his head and he pulled her on to his lap.

'This is the kind of argument that will win me round every time,' he said, kissing her on the lips. 'But no,' he added gravely as she stood up, 'I'm not sure I would lie to cover for you. That is, maybe I would. I don't know. It's difficult to say when you're not put in that position, isn't it? And it would depend on what you'd done.'

'If I believed you'd lie to cover for me if I'd committed a serious crime, I wouldn't be able to love you as much as I do. You wouldn't be the kind of person I'd want to spend the rest of my life with.' She frowned. 'I wonder why Laura lied for him like that?'

'I guess because he asked her to.'

'Yes, yes, I know, but what I meant was, did she lie because she believes he's innocent of killing Cassie Jackson, or because she loves him so much she doesn't care if he's innocent or not? Or did she lie because she was afraid of what he might do to her if she didn't back him up?' She paused. 'He might have wondered how we knew Laura went out on the evening Cassie Jackson was murdered. Paul doesn't know she was caught on a security camera. He might think she informed on him.' She looked thoughtful. 'If he is guilty of Cassie's murder, then it's fair to suspect he has a temper, and he's capable of killing.' She paused again. 'We never told them Laura was seen on CCTV, did we? I wonder what's happening in the Moore household right now. Perhaps we ought to go and have a word with them? What do you think?'

Ian frowned, but he followed Geraldine's drift. With a sigh, he stood up and followed her.

Laura looked surprised to see them when she opened the door. Geraldine smiled, relieved to see she was safe.

'He's not here,' Laura said straightaway, before they had a chance to ask to see Paul. She looked as though she had been crying. 'He went out. He was – he was very upset.'

'Are you all right?' Geraldine asked. 'You look upset.'

'How do you expect me to look, when everyone seems to think my husband's committed some terrible crime?' she replied miserably.

'Tell me what you think.'

Laura scowled. 'I think you should be looking for whoever killed that stupid, crazy girl, and I think you should leave my poor husband alone. He's done absolutely nothing wrong and now his whole life's been destroyed.'

Geraldine handed her a card. 'When he comes home, if you're at all concerned, call us.'

'Of course, I'm concerned. Paul's finding all this very difficult, and it's so unfair. He's done nothing to deserve this, nothing.'

'I mean, if you're concerned for your own safety,' Geraldine said gently.

Laura's jaw dropped as she realised what lay behind Geraldine's words.

'You think he did it,' she said, her eyes wide with shock. 'You think Paul's capable of doing what people are saying he did. You think all those horrible accusations are true. You think he's a monster. You're wrong, you couldn't be more wrong.' She burst into tears and slammed the door.

'You know where to find us if you need to talk,' Geraldine called out before she turned away.

'Well, she clearly believes he's innocent,' Ian said.

'That's what she's telling herself,' Geraldine murmured. 'It doesn't mean she believes it.'

27

EVERY WEBSITE AND MAGAZINE mentioned the benefits of regular exercise, so Mary and Susan made a point of going for a walk together every Friday morning. The sun was shining as Mary tapped on Susan's door, and they made their way to the nearby woods, talking as they walked. Mary had watched her granddaughter's tenth birthday party on Zoom, all the way from Australia, and they brought each other up to speed on their various aches and pains. It was a beautiful morning, fresh and bright, with a hint of summer in the air. Birds were twittering in the trees all around them while overhead the sky was a clear blue, so pale it was almost white. Chatting companionably, they entered the woods, and followed a muddy path between the trees. One area had been blocked off by the police a week earlier, when a body had been found lying on the path. There had been next to nothing about the incident in the papers, and after their initial shock on hearing about it, the two friends had settled back into their usual routine.

'I'm pleased I put on my walking boots,' Susan said.

'Yes, it's a bit muddy, isn't it?'

'It rained a bit during the night.'

'But what a glorious day,' Mary replied. 'It's like summer.'

Instead of answering, Susan halted abruptly and grabbed hold of Mary's arm, staring at the path ahead where a girl lay on the ground, flat on her back. She was naked, her arms and legs flung out on either side of her skinny torso, as though she had been dropped from a great height to land in a disorderly heap. Eyes the colour of the dirt on which she lay stared up at the sky, unseeing. Traces of mud had splashed on to her legs and flanks, and there was probably more in her hair, although it was impossible to tell because her hair, like her eyes, was the colour of mud.

'She's got no clothes on,' Susan blurted out, as though the dead girl's nudity were the most shocking aspect of her situation.

'Call the police,' Mary said, with more than a hint of panic in her voice. 'Tell them there's another one. Call the police. We have to call the police.'

'Don't you think we ought to cover her up?' her friend said. 'We can't leave her exposed like that.'

'No, no!' Mary cried out, shock making her testy. 'Don't touch her. We mustn't go anywhere near her. We have to call the police, now! Do it now! Can't you see she's dead? There's nothing we can do that can make any difference to her. Don't go near her or you might trample on evidence.'

A fly buzzed around the dead girl's face. Susan shrieked in alarm and flapped her hand, shooing it away. By now Mary was on her phone, gabbling about the body she and her friend had stumbled across.

'And she's dead,' she repeated, her voice rising to a shriek. 'She's dead. She's just a child and she's dead. Oh, it's horrible, just horrible.'

They seemed to be waiting for hours for the police to arrive. After that everything moved swiftly, as though someone had hit the fast forward button on a film that was being played in slow motion. It seemed no time at all before the two friends were ushered away, and the area was cordoned off to prevent anyone from contaminating the scene.

'We didn't touch anything,' Mary assured the policewoman who was taking their statements. 'There's nothing to tell you, really. We were taking a walk. We see each other every week and – well, that's not really important, is it? – anyway, we were walking here and we just saw the poor thing, lying there. Susan wanted to cover her up because she was just lying there, exposed, but I told her not to go anywhere near the dead body and not to touch anything, and we called you straightaway. I've no idea who she is. I mean, we don't know her. That is, I don't and I'm pretty sure Susan doesn't either because she would have said something. And – well, there's nothing else I can tell you, really. It's not the kind of thing you want to come across when you're out for a walk. Was she –' She broke off, unable to formulate the question she wanted to ask.

'I'm afraid she's dead,' the policewoman replied gently.

'Yes, we could see that for ourselves,' Mary snapped. 'Oh, I'm sorry, I didn't mean to be rude. I'm just a bit upset by all this, you know. She looks so young to be lying there dead.' Unexpectedly, Mary burst into tears, mumbling about the shock. The dead girl couldn't have been much older than Mary's granddaughter. 'It's not what you want to see, is it? Such a young girl, so – so very dead. And why hasn't she got any clothes on? It's so – so awful.'

She fell silent. The girl's nakedness seemed to express an obscene disrespect for life that was somehow more shocking than the futility of her death. Faced with so stark a reminder of mortality, it was hard not to succumb to despair about the darkness that would engulf them all in the end. An irrational anger seized her. She and Susan both lived alone, and they weren't young. All they had wanted was to enjoy a pleasant sociable walk in the trees, and maybe have a bit of a laugh. Life afforded her so little pleasure since her husband had died, and she had been so happy telling her friend about her Zoom call with her granddaughter. And now this.

Nearby a bird began to trill, oblivious to the tragedy playing out below its leafy perch and, beyond the trees, life continued uninterrupted for everyone else. Only Mary and her friend had been caught up in this waking nightmare. A police van arrived, and several white-suited officers climbed out. Disturbed by the commotion, the bird flew off, tweeting its outrage at this invasion of its territory. Susan was walking towards her, and Mary saw her own delayed shock reflected in her friend's unnatural pallor and shivered, although it wasn't cold.

'I'm not sure I want to walk here in future,' Susan muttered. 'Another girl was found here just a week ago. It's – it's –' She broke off, lost in the horror of what they had just seen.

Mary nodded dumbly, hoping their weekly walks wouldn't be another victim of this tragedy. More police cars arrived, and she watched as the white-suited officers scurried around the body.

The two friends barely exchanged a word on the way home. The bond that had developed between them seemed to have dissolved, as though a cold blade had sliced through the warmth of their friendship. Mary wondered if she would ever be able to look at Susan again without being reminded of another face, the eyes staring blankly at a white sky, the limbs splayed out awkwardly from a scrawny body. Muttering a hurried goodbye, she refused her friend's halfhearted invitation to join her for their usual cup of tea, and walked home alone.

28

THE TEAM WERE ALL troubled to learn that a second murder had taken place. What was even more worrying was that the site where the second victim had been discovered was very close to where Cassie Jackson's body had been found. To begin with, that appeared to be the only similarity between the two incidents, and the members of the team discussed the likelihood of it being a coincidence that the two bodies had been deposited so close to each other. There was a possibility the second murder had been some kind of copy-cat killing. It could even have been a macabre coincidence, two girls being killed in such close proximity to one another, just a week apart, and left in more or less the same location.

'The second victim was naked, but we don't yet know why,' Binita said heavily.

There was a faint murmuring among the officers present. The fact that the girl had been naked when she was found indicated a sexual motive.

'We don't know if she was killed there, or even if she was naked when she was killed,' Geraldine pointed out. 'The killer could have undressed her once she was dead, perhaps in an attempt to remove any trace of his contact with her.'

To begin with, other than the fact that the second victim had been found naked, the main difference between the two murders lay in the toxicology reports. Where Cassie had been discovered with a moderate amount of alcohol in her blood, along with indications that she had been drinking beer, the second victim had not only drunk a large quantity of whisky, but traces of the drug ketamine had been detected in her blood.

'So this could have been date rape?' a constable asked.

'Why do we always assume that it must be a man who's responsible for murdering a young girl?' a male detective constable asked. He sounded slightly indignant.

'Because it usually is,' Binita replied shortly.

There was a faint murmur of support for the detective chief inspector's comment.

'We can't assume she was date raped,' Geraldine pointed out. 'It's possible she took the drug knowingly.'

'Kids use ketamine as a recreational drug,' Naomi agreed with Geraldine.

As soon as an image of the second victim was shared, several members of the team recognised her as Cassie's schoolfriend, Ella Robinson. When the identity of the second victim was established it became clear that, despite the differences in the murders, the two crimes must be connected.

'Ella was Cassie Jackson's closest friend,' Binita reminded the team grimly. 'That means the two deaths are almost certainly linked. So, we have someone in York who has taken to killing schoolgirls. We have to find him before he can attack again.'

The fact that Ella had been given ketamine, whereas Cassie had not, suggested that Cassie might have been ready to trust the killer, whereas he had been less confident that he could control Ella.

'It looks as though he may have gained Cassie's trust, but not Ella's,' Geraldine said.

'There's a strong chance Ella was killed because she knew what had happened to Cassie,' Binita added, 'in which case he's unlikely to kill again.'

'Unless any other girls also found out what had happened to Cassie,' Geraldine said. 'If Ella knew about it, or even suspected the truth, then there's a strong chance she might have told at least one other girl.'

Even one murder was disturbing. The prospect of a third was horrific. With a sense of dread, Geraldine drove to the mortuary to see the pathologist. More than ever she missed the cheery approach of Jonah Hetherington, but she forced a smile as she was greeted by his sombre replacement, Catherine. Geraldine had not visited the scene of the discovery before the body had been removed, so she had only seen images of the body lying naked in the mud. Viewing Ella in the mortuary, she felt as though she was seeing the corpse for the first time. Only a week earlier, Geraldine had been questioning her as a potential witness. At the time Geraldine had been focused on what she could learn about Cassie, and had paid attention to Ella only as a potential source of information.

Now she recalled shrewd, knowing eyes glaring suspiciously at her from a thin face with angular features. In spite of her elfin lightness and pale hair, there was a toughness about Ella that made her death seem somehow inappropriate, as though it was an insult to life itself. She had struck Geraldine as a child who had experienced hardship and was determined to survive, even if circumstances prevented her from thriving. And now she was dead. Any opportunity to make even a modest success of her life, any chance of experiencing joy, had all been swept away in one violent swipe of fate. Only it hadn't been fate, but a vicious individual who had to be tracked down and brought to justice. She realised that Catherine was watching her, waiting for her to answer a question.

'I'm sorry?'

'What can you tell me about her?' Catherine repeated impatiently.

Geraldine held back from retorting that she had gone there to find out what Catherine could tell her.

'We know this victim, Ella Robinson, was a friend of Cassie Jackson whom you saw last week,' she said, hiding her own irritation.

'So she was killed because she knew too much?' Catherine enquired.

Geraldine concealed her surprise at finding that Catherine was prepared to indulge in speculation, and gave a noncommittal nod. In a way, she hoped that what Catherine had suggested was true. If Ella's death had been a direct result of Cassie confiding in her, then the killer might stop now that he had removed her as a potential threat. Whatever the reason for Ella's death it was no less of a tragedy, but if she had been murdered solely to silence her, that wasn't as worrying as the prospect of a killer who had developed an appetite for targeting young girls. But it was also possible that another girl had gossiped with Cassie or Ella, before she was murdered. If that was the case, the killer could be planning to silence her too. And he might not stop there because there might be a group of them who had learned his identity from Cassie or Ella before they were killed.

'We don't want to see any more of these murders,' she muttered and Catherine raised her eyebrows.

Geraldine gazed at the body. She wouldn't have known it was Ella straightaway, but looking closely she recognised the pointed nose and chin. Ella's eyes were shut, yet there was nothing peaceful about her scowling features. Usually unmoved by corpses, Geraldine felt slightly queasy looking at this child's body, scarcely matured into adulthood. The dead girl looked as though she could have done with feeding up and Geraldine wondered if she had suffered from an eating disorder, or was naturally very thin.

'How did she die?'

Geraldine was taken aback by Catherine's reply, although the fact that Ella had drowned possibly explained why she had been found naked in the woods.

'She was struck on the back of her head with sufficient force to cause internal haemorrhaging,' Catherine replied in an even tone, 'but the cause of death was water in her lungs. It looks as though she was hit on the back of her head and then her face was held under water. It might have been in a bucket or something similar because there's a light ring of bruising round her neck consistent with pressure against a hard circular ridge. It doesn't appear to have been a full body immersion, although that's impossible to say really because she was lying outside overnight, and it rained. But there's no question that she was knocked out and then drowned.'

'Would she have regained consciousness before she died?'

'That's unlikely, considering she'd ingested a large dose of ketamine before she stopped breathing. The drug would have made her feel woozy and then pretty rapidly put her to sleep. Maybe she would have come round for a matter of a few seconds, between being knocked out, or at least stunned, by the blow, and drowning. Death by drowning happens very quickly,' she added, 'so she wouldn't have suffered for long. But she probably had no awareness of what was happening to her. If she was conscious at all towards the end, she would have rapidly entered fight or flight mode, and struggled briefly, but she would have lost consciousness again quite rapidly and within minutes experienced hypoxic convulsion. She might have struggled without recovering consciousness, before suffering cerebral hypoxia. But either way she would have been dead within minutes, possibly less. She was very light which means the process would have been relatively swift. On balance, I think the likelihood is that she had no idea what was happening to her once she'd been drugged. And the violent blow to the back of her head would have knocked her out and proved fatal even without the immersion.'

'So even before she was hit, she was drugged and might have been completely oblivious to what was going on.'

Geraldine gazed sadly at the small body. Being hit on the head and drowned, possibly in something as mundane as a bucket of water, was a pitiful way to die. To be then dumped, naked, for strangers to find, removed any vestige of dignity from the corpse.

'Yes, it seems our killer wanted to make sure this time,' Catherine said.

Geraldine frowned. 'Do you think it was the same killer?'

Catherine shook her head. 'I'm not the detective here,' she said.

29

GIVEN THE RELATIONSHIP BETWEEN the two victims, Geraldine set up a team to speak to all the girls who were in Cassie's class at school, as well as any other girls with whom she was known to have associated. Cassie's form teacher was a nervous middle-aged woman with a gruff voice. Her short, straight hair was dusted with grey, and her lined face looked set and hard. She supplied Geraldine with a list of around twenty girls she thought might have been friendly with Cassie at some point, after which the head teacher gathered the whole senior school together in the hall so Geraldine could address them en masse.

'The whole country is shocked by what happened to two of your classmates,' Geraldine told the assembled pupils. 'Our priority right now is to find whoever killed them as quickly as we can, so their attacker can be locked up. Any scrap of information we can gather from you could be the final piece of the puzzle for us. Nothing is too small or insignificant to share with us. So we're asking you to do what you can to help us find this killer.' Before continuing, she paused and looked around at a host of young people, their faces pale and tense. 'We have returned here today to appeal for your help in finding who killed these two girls. If any of you have any information at all that might help us to identify this killer, we urge you to speak to one of our officers. Whatever you tell us will be kept confidential. That means that no one outside of the police investigation team will ever know that you told us anything. If you prefer to call and speak to us anonymously, that's fine too. You can use a dedicated phone number and call anonymously. Please don't hold back from telling us anything you know about Cassie's movements in the weeks and months before her death.'

A team of officers trained in questioning teenagers made themselves available. Having set up the questioning, Geraldine returned to the police station to await results. By the end of the day no new information had turned up. The general consensus among the pupils seemed to be that Cassie had been a slut, and no one appeared to have been close to her. Even her supposed best friend, Ella, had referred to her as a 'tart' and a 'cow'. If the pupils at the school knew anything more about Cassie than the police did, they weren't prepared to share their information.

Everyone at the police station knew about Paul Moore. Geraldine had flagged his wife as possibly at risk, so when Laura phoned the station early on Saturday morning to report an incident outside her house, a couple of constables out on patrol were sent to investigate without delay. According to the officer who had spoken to her on the phone, Laura Moore had been hysterical, and Geraldine was afraid her reason for calling might have masked a cry for help. She decided to drive to Laura's house herself, on her way into work, to see if anything had happened that Laura had not chosen to mention on a recorded phone call. Police constables Brown and Nash arrived at the property first. They could see straightaway what the problem was. A word had been scrawled across the front of the Moores' house: PEDO. The message was clear.

The two constables were talking to Paul when Geraldine arrived, while a few curious onlookers were watching from the pavement on the other side of the road. Laura's call to the police had probably been nothing more than a reaction to the ugly graffiti, but Geraldine wanted to talk to her all the same.

Paul looked up as Geraldine approached. Clearly exasperated, he let out a grunt of annoyance.

'Is it really necessary to have so many of you here?' he asked. 'I mean, it's just kids painting offensive graffiti on my house. I can get rid of it in no time. I'm telling you, this isn't the first time we've been targeted like this, and now you're just going to make the situation worse by drawing attention to it. I've done nothing to deserve this harassment.'

It wasn't clear if he was complaining about the graffiti or the police presence at his home.

A young constable stepped forward with an officious air of self-importance. 'We've established that they didn't see or hear anything unusual, and they don't have security cameras,' he told Geraldine.

'Very well,' she replied. 'What about any of the neighbours? Could anyone else have caught a shot of the vandals arriving or leaving? See what you can find out. And one of you had better stay here, to make sure no one contaminates the scene before the wall has been properly examined.'

'You stand guard outside the house,' Bert said to his eager, young colleague. 'I'll speak to the neighbours.'

The two constables set off on their errands, and Geraldine asked to see Laura.

'Fine. I'm sure she'd love to speak to you again,' Paul replied sarcastically. 'I'll be off to get some paint stripper then.'

'What for?'

'To get rid of it, of course. Not that there's much point in trying to hide it now that all the neighbours have had an eyeful.'

He glared balefully at the growing gaggle of people who had gathered over the road to observe what was happening. Geraldine warned him sternly not to touch the graffiti.

'What are you talking about?' he spluttered in sudden indignation, his eyes blazing with anger. 'This is my house.

You have no jurisdiction over what I can or can't do to my own property. This is really too much.' He raised his voice, doubtless for the benefit of his neighbours. 'I've told you, Inspector, I'm an innocent victim of a delusional teenager who got it into her head to deliberately set out to destroy my career. Maybe she really believed in her own fantasy, but her allegation had no grounding in reality, none at all. And now you're telling me I have to submit to this – this persecution by someone who evidently wants to believe the girl's lies. The whole situation is preposterous. What am I supposed to do? Just leave this libellous graffiti on display for the whole world to see? What next? Will you sit back and watch while they lynch me? Why don't you just string me up from the nearest tree yourself, and leave me to die?'

'Mr Moore,' Geraldine replied, 'I can see you're upset. But you have to let us do our job. Right now we're doing everything we can to find out who did this. A forensic team will be here shortly to check for prints, and we're trying to find any CCTV evidence of whoever was trespassing on your property. So I'm sure you understand that the paint on your wall needs to remain uncontaminated until we've had a chance to examine it properly.'

Paul grunted irritably. 'Oh, very well,' he said, 'there's not much point my trying to cover it up now, is there? But as soon as you've finished, that crap is coming off. My wife doesn't want to have to look at it every time she leaves the house, any more than I do. Where's the law that says innocent citizens like us have to be subjected to this kind of abuse?'

'Where is your wife?'

'She's indoors, hiding from the world,' Paul replied bitterly.

'I'd like to speak to her.'

'I don't think she wants to see anyone. Would you believe me if I told you she's very upset? I don't think you appreciate how traumatic all this has been for her. And now, not to be able to escape from it in our own home, where she should feel safe, where I should be protecting her –' His voice cracked suddenly with emotion.

Paul's performance was convincing, but Geraldine wondered if he was only concerned to protect his wife, or if he had another reason for wanting to prevent Geraldine from seeing her.

'I'd still like to speak to her.'

'Does she have a choice?'

Geraldine didn't answer.

Forlornly, Paul led the way into the house. As soon as the front door closed behind them, Laura ran out into the hall and threw herself into Paul's arms, sobbing frantically. He glowered at Geraldine, as if to say, 'Now do you believe me? You can see my wife is beside herself with distress, and you want to hound her with more questions,' while aloud he said, 'For pity's sake, can't you just leave us alone?'

30

GERALDINE ASKED IF SHE could have a few minutes alone with Laura, and Paul gave a resigned shrug.

'If Laura's happy with that,' he said shortly. He turned to his wife and his voice trembled with suppressed emotion. 'They don't trust me. They think you won't dare to speak freely in front of me. They think I'm a monster who abuses children at work and beats his wife at home.'

Laura smiled weakly at him. 'Don't worry,' she whispered. Her voice wobbled and tears spilled from her eyes. 'It's going to be okay, isn't it?' her feeble attempt to comfort her husband changed mid-sentence to a plea for reassurance. 'They won't do anything. They can't, can they?'

'Everything's going to be fine,' he replied mechanically, but clearly he no longer believed that.

Laura led Geraldine to a small dining room at the back of the house. 'I had to call you,' she blurted out as soon as they were alone with the door closed. 'I just knew he'd cover it up again if I didn't.'

'Cover it up again? What do you mean?' Geraldine felt a surge of adrenaline. 'What is Paul hiding?'

Haltingly, Laura explained that four days earlier a message had been painted on the house, at about half past eleven at night. That time the graffiti had been just the same, the one word: 'PEDO.'

'It was the same person – at least I think it was – because

154

Paul said they misspelt paedo both times. He's very good at spelling,' she added, with a nervous hiccup.

On both occasions, the graffiti artist had only stayed long enough to spray one word on the wall. Perhaps the writer had heard someone coming, or had seen a light go on in the house.

'What happened to the first message?' Geraldine asked.

Laura explained that she thought they had scared an intruder away when they had heard a noise outside and had gone outside to investigate. They hadn't seen anyone, only the graffiti on the house. Laura had wanted to call the police straightaway, but on that first occasion Paul had insisted on painting over the graffiti at once, before anyone else could see it.

'He told me it was just kids from his school messing about, but I think he only said that to make me feel better. I think he panicked about the neighbours seeing it. We had an old pot of paint, and he smeared it all over the graffiti to cover up the message before anyone else could see it,' she said. 'Then the next day he bought some paint stripper and removed the whole thing.' She shuddered at the memory. 'He said he couldn't bear to see me so upset, but I was only upset because he was upset.' She raised her head and gazed earnestly at Geraldine, her pale eyes wide apart and glistening with tears. 'How much longer will it be until this is over? Paul didn't do anything to that girl. I know he didn't. Whoever had sex with her, it wasn't him. Surely you can prove it with DNA and that. I don't think anything happened at all. She made it up. Paul says she was a fantasist.'

Geraldine listened sympathetically as Laura repeated what her husband had told her. But the fact that his wife believed him blindly didn't prove anything. Laura hadn't been present when the allegation was made. As for forming an opinion about Cassie's character, she had never even met the girl and had no basis for reaching any conclusions about her. And now it wasn't only Cassie who had been murdered. News about the second victim had not yet been released. Ella's parents would be viewing the body later that afternoon, but that was merely a formality. They had already handed over her hairbrush and the dead girl's DNA had confirmed her identity as Cassie Jackson's closest friend and confidante. It was dreadful to think that Ella might have lost her life because she knew who had killed Cassie. Geraldine knew that grief affected people in many ways, and the way the bereaved reacted couldn't be taken at face value. Sometimes those who initially seemed most shocked turned out to be the least affected by their loss, while others who appeared to be unperturbed were actually suffering deeply. It was by no means rare for family members to rage at her, as though she was responsible for the death of their loved ones, so she steeled herself to withstand whatever the afternoon had in store for her. However it panned out, taking parents to see their daughter's corpse was never going to be easy.

That afternoon, Geraldine met Ella's parents for the first time. Mrs Robinson was a small woman with a weaselly face who stared shrewishly at Geraldine with her dead daughter's mud-coloured eyes. Wrapped in a long khaki raincoat, she seemed irascible rather than sad, and asked when they were going to see Ella. Mr Robinson was a spindly man with ginger hair, whiskery ears, and the stooping gait common in tall men. He opened his mouth as though he was going to speak, and then began rubbing his lips abstractedly with a worried expression.

'We want to get this over with,' his wife said impatiently, as though she was waiting to have a tooth extracted.

The two of them stood gazing at Geraldine, one sharp, the other bemused.

'You don't both have to view the body if one of you would prefer not to,' Geraldine explained gently. 'It's enough for just one of you to see her, if you prefer.'

Mr Robinson hesitated and glanced anxiously at his wife, who answered for both of them. 'We'll do this together.'

Hesitating in the doorway, they went in. Mrs Robinson stared, transfixed, while her husband gave an uneasy nod.

'Yes,' he said hoarsely, 'that's her. That's Ella. We want to know who did this to her, to our little girl.' His voice broke, and he began rubbing his bottom lip in a vain attempt to stop it trembling.

'We don't know yet, but we're going to find out,' Geraldine replied, with more confidence than she was feeling.

'How did it happen?' he asked urgently, as though hearing the circumstances of his daughter's death could somehow lessen the impact.

Geraldine hesitated. 'We're not sure yet, but we're working on several leads.'

'It was that little tart Cassie, wasn't it?' Mrs Robinson blurted out unexpectedly. 'This is because of her, isn't it? I always knew it would end badly. Didn't I say it would end badly? This is her fault. She's been nothing but trouble ever since Ella fell in with her.'

Geraldine noticed Mr Robinson flinched at the mention of Cassie's name, and he glanced at Geraldine with an expression that was almost furtive.

'I understand they were close friends,' Geraldine ventured, hoping to prompt Ella's mother to disclose more about the two girls.

'Friends?' Mrs Robinson repeated in a scathing tone. 'They were more than friends. Ella was besotted with that little tart.'

'Now, Maisie, we don't want the police suspecting there was anything unhealthy about their relationship,' Mr Robinson interrupted. 'They were friends, that's all.'

'It was Cassie this, and Cassie that, all the time with her,'

Mrs Robinson continued, ignoring her husband's interruption. 'And you weren't much better.'

'Inspector, please don't misunderstand what my wife is trying to say.'

'What are you talking about, Mark?' Mrs Robinson snapped. 'Do you always have to find fault with everything I say?'

'It's just that you're making it sound as though the girls were more than friends.'

'More than friends? I don't know what you mean. I'm not suggesting anything,' she retorted angrily. 'You're the one who was always encouraging Ella to bring Cassie home.'

'It was good for Ella.'

'Good for her? How can you say that after everything that's happened?'

'I only meant it was good for Ella to have a friend her own age.'

He glanced at Geraldine and fell to rubbing his lips again. Mrs Robinson also looked round with a scowl, seeming to recall Geraldine's presence. Meanwhile, Geraldine had been growing increasingly uneasy as she listened to them arguing.

All she said to them was that she could see they were both naturally very upset, but she mentioned in her report that she thought Mr Robinson might have been inappropriately interested in Cassie.

'Are you suggesting Ella's father was involved in Cassie's murder?' Ariadne asked, sounding unconvinced. 'Surely you don't think he murdered his own daughter and left her naked body in the woods? I mean, we come across some sick, twisted people, but I find that hard to believe. Of course, that doesn't mean it can't be true,' she added thoughtfully.

Geraldine didn't answer, but she resolved to find out more about Mark Robinson.

31

UNDER INSTRUCTION FROM THE detective chief inspector, the team had been working hard to keep the case out of the media. The murder of a teenage girl was unfortunately something that would interest the tabloid papers, and the police had struggled to keep the investigation out of the spotlight. After the second murder, that proved impossible. Throughout the weekend, headlines had been emblazoned across the front pages of the local papers, and the murders had been reported on local radio and television. Sensationalised details of the crimes, along with pictures of both girls, appeared alongside descriptions of the murders described in language that ranged from restrained to histrionic, depending on the outlet. Images of Cassie looking coy yet provocative were popular, as was the fact that Ella had been found naked.

Geraldine found herself surrounded by reporters when she arrived at work on Monday morning. They swarmed around her as she climbed out of her car and began pestering her with questions.

'Do you have a suspect for the murders of these teenage victims?'

'Has anyone been arrested yet?'

'Are you looking for a serial killer?'

'Is there a sex predator in York?'

'How worried should young women be?'

A particularly strident female reporter in a red coat pushed herself in front of Geraldine, blocking her path, demanding to know if the streets of York were safe for women on their own.

Irritably, Geraldine ordered her out of the way. 'You're preventing me from doing my job, so move on or I'll arrest you for obstructing a police officer.'

Frustrated by the harassment, she made her way past them.

'Don't those reporters realise we're as anxious as they are to find out who killed those girls?' she grumbled to Ariadne as she reached her desk.

'Yes, we really need to do something about them,' her colleague agreed. 'Every time we go in or out, we risk being accosted by some loudmouthed idiot shoving a microphone at our faces. Sooner or later a rookie officer is going to be indiscreet.'

'That's what they're hoping,' Geraldine replied. 'There's always someone who loses their cool and shoots their mouth off. You'd think they'd want to bugger off and leave us to get on with the job, wouldn't you? It's almost like they don't care about wasting our time as long as they get their story. I think some of them would love it if there was another murder.'

'As long as they were first to break the story,' Ariadne agreed. 'One day we'll have a paper orchestrating a crime just so they have the inside track on it.' She laughed.

'If one of us doesn't silence them first,' Geraldine added grimly. 'There should be a law against journalists hounding police officers.'

'They'd say we were trying to hush something up,' Ariadne replied. 'The public have a right to know and all that.'

'The public have a right to walk the streets in safety without worrying about being attacked by a maniac,' Geraldine said. 'We're the ones trying to protect them, not those jackals out there.'

That afternoon, Binita decided it was time to hold a press conference and she instructed Geraldine to arrange it. Geraldine was anxious, knowing that they weren't anywhere close to solving the case. At the same time, she knew that appeals to the public could be effective and she suggested inviting Cassie's mother and Ella's parents to plead with any witnesses to come forward. The conference was set up for the following day. The three parents arrived early, all clearly nervous. After they had greeted one other, Geraldine did her best to reassure them that they had only to ask for anyone who had any information to come forward. Cassie's mother nodded, seemingly too overwhelmed to speak, and the Robinsons mumbled that they understood what was required.

Entering a room filled with news-hungry reporters always made Geraldine nervous. She was uneasily aware that one ill-considered sentence, even a single foolish word, could cause irreparable damage. Most of the reporters she faced were responsible journalists and broadcasters, concerned to uncover what was going on and share that information with the public. But a significant minority seemed happy to twist or even eschew the truth, as long as they could produce a melodramatic story based very loosely on the facts.

After giving her carefully worded statement, Geraldine invited the mothers of the two murder victims to give their equally carefully vetted appeals for help. Cassie's mother spoke surprisingly sensibly. She urged anyone with information concerning her daughter's movements in her final hours to speak to the police.

'We know there's a psychopath out there targeting young women,' she concluded. 'He has to be found and stopped.'

Ella's mother broke down as she started talking. 'Please,' she begged, 'please. This evil monster has to be stopped.' That was all she managed to utter before she became incoherent, sobbing into a tissue.

Mr Robinson cleared his throat. 'This maniac has to be found and punished,' he growled, his eyes glaring.

Uncertain what else he was going to say, Geraldine cut in to thank the three parents, before turning to the reporters. There was only time for a few questions. This was the part of any press conference Geraldine dreaded. She was constantly on her guard, aware that it was easy to make a mistake. She announced that the police were following several promising lines of enquiry adding, slightly optimistically, that they were hoping to have a result soon. She was immediately challenged as to when that might be, and had to respond that she couldn't give a specific date.

'So it could be months before our streets are safe for women again?' the reporter demanded.

'I can't give you a specific date for when we expect to make an arrest,' Geraldine repeated firmly, refusing to be drawn into a discussion about how long the investigation was likely to take.

She was tempted to admit that she had absolutely no idea when a suspect might be found.

'So in the meantime, the streets of York are not safe for young women to walk along?' the reporter persisted, her shrill voice ringing out above the general muted hum of voices.

Patiently Geraldine dealt with the questions, pointing out that no one had actually been attacked on the street, and York was for the most part a very safe place to live and work in.

'Try telling that to the victims,' the reporter snarled.

There was a sudden clamour and Geraldine held up one hand.

'I appreciate you are keen to be given a dramatic headline for your papers,' she said. 'The reality is that we are working extremely hard to find this killer. And make no mistake, we will find him. You can put that on your front pages. We will track down this killer. He will not be able to hide from us forever.' She paused. 'That's all for now. We'll keep you updated with any developments, as far as we can, but obviously most of our work cannot be shared with the public.' And certainly not with you, she was tempted to add.

She rose to her feet and led the parents out of the room, feeling as though she had been mentally abused. She warned them not to speak to the press under any circumstances. The bereaved parents nodded and Geraldine hoped they would take her advice seriously.

'If they get so much as a hint that you're willing to speak to them, they'll hound you twenty-four hours a day, seven days a week,' she insisted. 'Once they understand you're not going to talk to them, the press interest in you will soon fade. But for now, keep a low profile, steer clear of public places as far as possible, and don't say anything at all to anyone. Whatever you do tell them will be distorted and misrepresented and, before you know it, they'll be accusing you of all sorts of things that aren't true, just to provoke a response.'

The journalists had been characteristically strident in their questioning. Although Geraldine appreciated that they were doing their job, and doing it well, she wished they would acknowledge that while they were clamouring for information, she was actively hunting for a killer. Both jobs had their place, but she liked to think her work deserved some respect. Without the police investigation, the killer would never be apprehended, however stridently the reporters demanded an arrest.

32

GERALDINE WOULD HAVE WELCOMED a break. Talking to the press was exhausting, constantly having to watch every word she said and then fending off questions designed to trip her into revealing more than she should. But this was a good opportunity to speak to Mrs Robinson in an apparently informal way.

'Mrs Robinson, we'd like to have a word with you while you're here,' she said, once the press briefing was over. 'It will only take a few minutes. If you could accompany me to an interview room, we won't keep you long.'

'Is this really necessary?' Mr Robinson interjected. He seemed put out when it became clear that Geraldine wanted to talk to his wife on her own. 'We're tired and we'd really like to go home now,' he said. 'This has been very emotional for my wife and I don't think she wants to be questioned right now.'

'Surely you want to co-operate with the investigation?'

Mr Robinson shrugged. He could hardly refuse Geraldine's request after a remark like that.

'PC Nash will look after you,' Geraldine told him.

He scowled at her. 'You mean he's watching me? In case I run off without her, is it?'

Geraldine repeated that it wouldn't take long.

'I suppose I don't have any choice, do I?' Mrs Robinson said, loudly enough for her husband to hear.

Geraldine led her away to an interview room, keen to hear what she had to say when her husband wasn't in earshot.

'You had something to say about Cassie?' she asked when they were both seated.

Mrs Robinson muttered something about Cassie Jackson being a tart. 'I don't like to speak ill of the dead, but that girl was trouble and she led our Ella astray. If you ask me, Ella would still be alive if it wasn't for that girl.' She began to weep softly. 'I'm sorry,' she muttered after a few minutes, blowing her nose noisily on a tissue. 'Please, go on. I'll try to answer if I can.'

'In what way did Cassie cause trouble?' Geraldine pressed on. 'Did she encourage Ella to take drugs? Or to drink?'

'It was nothing like that, although I dare say there was drink and drugs involved. No, the trouble with Cassie was that she was obsessed with sex. Ella never showed any interest in boys until Cassie latched on to her. Then all at once everything changed. And I do mean everything. Ella was like a different child. Cassie was a slut, plain and simple. She ran after boys. Couldn't get enough of them. And she encouraged Ella to do the same, with cheap lipstick and short skirts. It was all done for attention. But Ella never wanted that kind of attention until she fell in with Cassie.'

'Are you sure it was all due to Cassie's influence?'

'Oh yes. I heard Ella talking to her on the phone, and I've got eyes in my head. I could see how Ella changed once she was friends with Cassie. She was like a different girl, all skimpy clothes and make-up and staying out to all hours.'

'Did Cassie stick to boys her own age, or did she see older men as well?'

Mrs Robinson's frown deepened, but she didn't answer.

'Mrs Robinson, we're looking for whoever killed your daughter. Anything you can tell us that will assist us in building an accurate picture of Cassie and Ella's lives might help lead us to their killer. Is there any detail you think might be of use to us? Did Ella mention any boys or men in particular that she or Cassie was spending time with? Can you give us any names?'

All at once Mrs Robinson backtracked, as though something had scared her. 'I didn't really know much about Cassie at all,' she muttered. 'Ella was taken in by her but that's all I can say. That's as much as I know.'

'But you know Cassie was promiscuous?'

'You only had to look at her to see she was a slut.'

Geraldine tried a different approach, frustrated at the way Mrs Robinson had clammed up. 'What about Ella?'

'What about her?' Mrs Robinson was defensive now. After her momentary rush of indiscretion, bitching about Cassie, she had become circumspect.

'Can you think of anyone who might have wanted to hurt your daughter?'

'No.' She sounded indignant. 'It was obviously a maniac, and you need to find him before he harms anyone else.'

Geraldine threw out her next question as casually as she could. 'Would you say your husband has a temper?'

'My husband? A temper? No.' Mrs Robinson seemed bemused, but that might have been an act. Geraldine had a feeling she was frightened.

'Was he as concerned about Ella's friendship with Cassie as you were?'

'I don't think they were friends,' Mrs Robinson replied, deflecting the question. 'They hung out together but I don't think Ella really liked Cassie. I think she was – taken in by her. For an inexperienced girl like Ella, Cassie had a certain sort of vulgar glamour.'

Geraldine paused for a second before asking whether Mrs

Robinson thought her husband had also been 'taken in' by Cassie.

'What do you mean?' she asked, her tone a trifle too sharp. 'He wasn't taken in. But I don't think he took against her either. He didn't see her for what she was. He said it was nice for Ella to have a friend like Cassie.'

'Did she have many friends?'

'Who? Ella or Cassie?'

She was prevaricating, avoiding answering Geraldine's questions.

'Cassie ran after the boys, but Ella was always a bit of a loner. There's nothing wrong with keeping yourself to yourself I told her, and I was right. I mean, look what happened when she started hanging around with Cassie. My husband couldn't see it, of course. He thought it was good for Ella to have friends. He was always encouraging Ella to invite Cassie round.'

'Would you say he showed more interest in Cassie than in Ella's other friends?'

'She didn't have any other friends. If she had, this might not have happened. She wouldn't have been so desperate to tag along with Cassie.'

If Mrs Robinson suspected her husband was implicated in what had happened to Cassie, she wasn't prepared to share her opinions. And then there was Ella. They could be looking for two killers, but the likelihood was that Cassie's killer had wanted to silence Ella because she knew too much. It was even possible she had been blackmailing Cassie's killer. But whatever she knew or suspected, Mrs Robinson wasn't prepared to share her views. With a sigh, Geraldine escorted her back to the entrance of the police station to wait for her husband. Geraldine was on her way to talk to Mr Robinson, when Naomi stopped her in the corridor.

'I need to speak to you.'

'Can it wait?' Geraldine asked. 'I'm about to question Mr Robinson.'

'It's about him,' Naomi replied. 'I've been doing some digging, like you asked.'

Geraldine trusted her judgement, and knew Naomi wouldn't be stopping her without good reason. She couldn't suppress a crazy hope that Naomi had discovered Mr Robinson had been involved in a scandal involving an underage girl. Naomi revealed that Mr Robinson's first wife had divorced him and had since remarried. She and his first daughter had not had any contact with him for years. The reason cited for the divorce was the irreconcilable breakdown of the marriage.

'What's interesting is that his first wife was admitted to hospital with a broken arm and extensive bruising. The doctors suspected she had been physically abused, but that came to nothing,' Naomi added softly. 'His first wife insisted she had sustained her injuries in a fall.'

Geraldine frowned, recalling the brutal attack on Cassie.

33

SCANNING AN ARTICLE IN the local paper, he frowned. He cringed at seeing the squalid details published like that for any stranger to read. In all honesty, he would rather not read about it at all. He hadn't killed them for the notoriety the murders might attract, and it gave him no pleasure to see the details plastered over the front page of the local paper. Obviously the police would have to know what he had done, but it was no one else's business. True, he had killed a second girl, but he had done so to silence her, not to create a whole lot of fuss in the news. It was sick the way reporters wanted to pick at every detail, sensationalising the incidents into some kind of drama. In reality there was no 'serial killer roaming the streets of York searching for his next victim', as one journalist expressed it. They made him sound like Dracula, or Jack the Ripper, which was ridiculous when all he had done was silence two girls who had threatened to become a nuisance. A man had a right to defend himself, which was exactly what he had done.

Still, he shouldn't have been surprised to see reports of his exploits in the news. Now that two girls had been killed, the media were all over the story. It was a pity, but he supposed it was only to be expected. Until the case was resolved, and someone was convicted, journalists would no doubt keep worrying at the story until it grew old or something more newsworthy came along. It would have to be something really sensational to overshadow the murders of not one but two young women. All of the papers already had front page stories about the so-called 'serial killer on the loose' and other such histrionic headlines. As if the deaths of two vacuous girls actually mattered. They had brought it on themselves and, as far as he was concerned, that was the end of the matter.

In some ways, leaving Ella naked had been a masterstroke, giving the papers something salacious to focus on. He had only stripped her as an afterthought, in an attempt to distract attention from his real motive. If he could make it look like a sexual assault, that would hopefully send the police off on the wrong tack altogether. Meanwhile, the media had really gone into a frenzy, and Ella's friendship with Cassie had almost been completely overlooked in a hysterical explosion of speculation about the killer's motive. And not one of them had come anywhere close to the truth. He couldn't help smiling to himself as he read on past the headline.

SERIAL KILLER STRIKES AGAIN
Police Baffled

The police are following several leads in the case of the dual murders of Cassie Jackson and Ella Robinson. The bodies of the two fifteen-year-old schoolgirls were discovered in Fishpond Woods one week apart. As yet no arrest has been made.

He noticed how the reporter had described the girls as fifteen, when he knew for a fact that Cassie, at least, had been sixteen. In a later paragraph, the same reporter decided to interview random women and came up with such gems as:

'I don't feel safe outside' blonde retail assistant Gina Rawlings (22) told us.

'I'm scared to leave my house' dental receptionist Sue James (33) claimed.
'We don't know who is going to be next' Lucy Crawford (29) housewife said.

Whoever the *York Herald* had approached had apparently come back with similar comments. There were several subheadings in bold font:

The women of York are living in fear.
What are the police doing to catch this killer?

He folded the paper as a waitress came over to his table. It was just as well the police were fools he thought, as he ordered a full English breakfast. The waitress gave him a friendly smile, almost winking at him, working hard for her tip. 'What would you like to drink with that, sir?'

She wouldn't be so friendly if she knew what he had done. He tried to picture how she would react if he let it be known, quite casually, that the police were looking for him.

'It was me. I killed those girls,' he imagined saying nonchalantly, as though it wasn't in the least bit important.

And in reality, in the grand scheme of things, it wasn't important. After all, what did it matter if two stupid girls were dead? They were no great loss. There were plenty more to take their place in the world, like this waitress with her gormless grin, waiting to hear whether he wanted tea or coffee with his full English. She would collect her wages at the end of the week, along with her share of the tips, some of which she would no doubt pocket sneakily when the other staff weren't looking. It all seemed so trivial, whereas what he had done was something he would be able to look back on with justifiable pride for the rest of his life. He had killed two girls who deserved to die, and he had got away with it because he was too clever to get caught. He watched the waitress as she hovered, asking if he wanted anything else. If he rewarded her as he had once rewarded Cassie, no doubt she would also do anything he asked. Paid lackeys were easy to recruit.

The papers were wrong, of course. He posed no danger to other young women. He knew he was going to have to stop. He couldn't hope to get away with it too many times. He hadn't actually planned to kill more than once but, like Macbeth, one murder had led to another because of the necessity to cover up what he had done. He had to protect himself. Both murders had been unavoidable, and that was all there was to it. It was a pity for Ella that she had got herself caught up in it, but there was no point in wasting energy on unnecessary regrets. It had happened and that was that. The police were clueless and, as long as no other witness crawled out and ruined everything, his killing spree was over. As far as he knew, no one else suspected him but if anyone did, he knew what to do.

Of course, the waitress brought his drink before his food was ready, so by the time he started eating the tea was nearly cold. That was just typical, but he wasn't about to let it spoil his breakfast. Piercing a fried egg with his knife, he watched the yolk ooze out over a slice of toast and wondered what it would be like to stab a living person. How long would the eyes widen in shock before glazing over? He almost felt sad that he could never find out, but he had no intention of taking any unnecessary risks. He had done what had to be done, and that was the end of it. If he was clever enough to have got away with it so far, he was also clever enough to know when to stop.

34

'I HEAR THEY'RE BRINGING in Cassie Jackson's boyfriend again,' Naomi said as she passed Geraldine's desk on Wednesday morning. 'He's kicking up an awful stink about it.' She chuckled.

'Oh yes, it seems he was busy with his art work again last night, so we're bringing him in for some tough talking.' Geraldine sighed. 'He ought to be charged really, but any defence would argue extenuating circumstances, with him losing his girlfriend like that.'

Geraldine went to speak to Max herself, hoping he would let something slip that was relevant to the murder enquiry in which he was still a suspect. She recognised the sullen youth being dragged into the police station in handcuffs and escorted by a young uniformed constable.

'Get your fucking hands off me,' he was yelling. 'You got no right. Get off me. This ain't right. I'm allowed a phone call. It's the law. You can't do this until I got a lawyer here. I done nothing wrong. Get off me or I'll do you for assault. This is harassment, innit?'

He kept up a stream of complaint, interspersed with foul language and invective against the constable who, he claimed, was victimising him for no reason.

'Back again, Max?' Geraldine greeted him.

'A paint spray can with his prints was found outside Paul Moore's house,' her colleague replied.

'Fuck off, you ain't got nothing on me. It's a fit-up. I'll get you for this, you prick. You don't know what you're on about.'

'Oh we've got plenty on you,' the constable replied breezily. 'How about resisting arrest, for starters? And attempting to assault a police officer?'

'You ain't arrested me,' Max snarled. 'How can I resist what ain't happened?'

Geraldine stepped forward. 'Max, we just need to ask you a few questions to see if you can help us with our enquiry,' she said.

'Yeah right, sure that's all, innit? You ain't gonna fit me up for something I never done?' He made a spitting noise without releasing any saliva.

'We brought him in on a charge of –' the constable began but Geraldine interrupted him with a raised hand.

'That's OK, Constable. Thank you for bringing him in. I just want to talk to him about what's been going on, and then we'll see.' She turned to Max. 'You're here to answer a few questions about the graffiti on Paul Moore's house.'

Max shrugged, suddenly laconic, as though he had expended his fury. 'Weren't me,' he muttered.

'Can you explain how a paint can with your prints on it was found in the street outside Paul Moore's house?'

'I dunno. I never done nothing. Weren't me.'

'Then you won't object to helping us with our enquiry.'

She smiled, and Max gave her a dirty look, muttering obscenities under his breath.

'Hey you, show some respect,' the constable who had brought him in barked.

'You can fuck off an' all,' Max replied.

Geraldine led the youth to an interview room. He was still handcuffed and protesting, but quietly now. Since he had calmed down, his handcuffs were removed while he waited for the duty brief to arrive, and finally Geraldine and Ariadne were able to join him to conduct an interview. They weren't optimistic that he would be very forthcoming, but there was a chance he might shed some light on what had happened to Cassie.

'Max, we know it was you who painted abusive graffiti on Paul Moore's house,' Geraldine began.

'So what? You made up your minds I done it, so what we talking about?'

'Tell us why you wrote "pedo" on the front of his house.'

'No one else was doing fuck all.'

'About what?' Geraldine prompted him.

'About what he done to her, the fucking pervert.'

'To Cassie?'

'Yeah.'

'Max,' Geraldine spoke gently, 'we know you're upset about Cassie. It's understandable. Everyone is desperately sorry about what happened. But we don't yet know for certain that Paul Moore was involved. Until we have proof that he's guilty, there's nothing you or anyone else can do. If you keep painting graffiti on his property, all you'll achieve is to get yourself in trouble.'

Max's frown darkened. 'You just gonna let him get away with what he done?'

'Paul Moore is a suspect,' Geraldine went on. She didn't add that Max was also a suspect. 'If we find out that he's guilty, he'll be tried and sentenced. If it wasn't him, we'll still find Cassie's killer. In the meantime, you have to be patient. You can't condemn a man without knowing for certain that he's guilty, and you can't take the law into your own hands. If it *was* him, we'll catch him and he'll face a trial, just as you will if you break the law again. Trespassing and causing damage is a criminal offence.'

'So she was lying?' Max's voice rose in exasperation.

'Are you talking about Cassie?'

He nodded.

'Tell us what you know.'

His eyes flicked round the room and he licked his lips nervously. 'She told me he done it with her,' he mumbled.

Geraldine watched him closely as he was speaking, but it was impossible to tell if he was embarrassed or lying. It was often difficult to work out whether people were apprehensive because of the situation, facing questioning at a police station, or because they were guilty and afraid of being caught out in a lie. But if Max was really corroborating the allegation against Paul Moore, his statement had to be taken seriously.

'She was dead upset,' he went on. 'She never wanted to do it with that old geezer.'

'By "do it", do you mean have sexual intercourse?'

'Yeah.'

'What did Cassie tell you?'

'He made her do it.'

'Paul Moore forced her to have sexual relations with him?'

He nodded. 'That's what she said, innit?' He stood up. 'Can I go now?'

'Yes, as soon as you sign a written statement confirming what you just told us. And we'll also need your assurance that you will not go to Paul Moore's property again, under any circumstances.'

'Fuck off.'

The lawyer cleared his throat and requested a short break so that he could speak to his client alone.

'Advise him not to be a fool,' Geraldine suggested.

The lawyer was young and seemed eager to help. With a snub nose and blue eyes that actually seemed to twinkle, there was something almost cherubic in his appearance. Geraldine wondered just how useful he was going to be to either his client or the police, but when they reconvened, Max appeared appropriately chastened.

'She was my girl,' he said. 'He's lucky I only done that to his house, after what he done to her.'

He was a picture of dejection, with blinking eyes and slumped shoulders. Geraldine wondered if this onset of misery was genuine, or if it was a pose intended to gain sympathy.

'You must see this is too important to brush off,' Geraldine replied. 'Your testimony could help us to get to the truth about what happened to Cassie.'

'I told you, it was him, innit.'

'Do you have anything further to tell us about what happened between Cassie and Paul Moore?'

'He done it,' Max repeated obstinately. 'She told me he done it.'

What Max had told them was transcribed and they left him to read through it and sign the statement they had recorded on tape.

'He could be lying,' Ariadne said. 'If you ask me, he wants to divert any suspicion away from himself. If anything, he's just made me pretty sure he's guilty.'

'Yes, it could easily have been him,' Geraldine agreed. 'He's got a car with her DNA all over it. If it's true that Cassie told him she had sex with Paul, Max might have lost his temper and killed her himself, and now he's trying to shift the blame on to Paul.'

'Or she might have lied about having sex with Paul in a bid to get attention, inadvertently giving Max the perfect scapegoat to blame when Max himself killed her in a fit of jealousy,' Ariadne said.

Once again it all seemed to come back to the question of what had taken place between Cassie and Paul Moore. Geraldine decided to go back to the school and speak to the staff there again. Meanwhile, Max was released under caution, and Paul was taken into custody.

'We'll let him sit and stew in a cell for a few hours while we question his colleagues,' Geraldine said, and Binita agreed.

Geraldine and Ariadne went back to the school to question the staff.

'Good luck,' Geraldine muttered to her colleague as they pulled up outside the sprawling building.

'I feel like I'm going back to school,' Ariadne replied, laughing.

35

FROM THE OUTSIDE, THE school looked as though it had been extended at various times in the interest of substance rather than style. On her first visit, Geraldine had received an impression of a rundown building, bustling and rowdy, where pupils charged along dusty corridors, swinging their bags at one another. A few of them had stared at her with blatant curiosity, perhaps sizing her up in case she was a new teacher, but most of them were too caught up in their own lives to pay her any attention. A week later, the atmosphere was very different. The school felt hushed and lifeless, as though the deaths of two of its pupils had sucked any vitality from the place. The few children Geraldine passed seemed subdued, and they avoided looking at her.

'How are you all managing in the wake of the double tragedy?' Geraldine asked the head's secretary.

On this occasion the secretary was wearing a navy jumper. Perhaps she considered the dark colour more appropriate in a period of mourning than the turquoise outfit she had been wearing on Geraldine's previous visit.

'Mr Wilson is guiding the school through these difficult times,' the secretary replied primly.

'How well do you know Paul Moore?'

'I know all the teachers here,' she replied frostily, as though she would be neglecting her responsibility if she wasn't personally acquainted with every member of staff.

'Is there anything you can tell me about him that I might not already know?'

'What did you have in mind?' the secretary replied evasively.

'Is he popular?'

'I believe he is well liked by his colleagues, yes.'

'And his pupils? Do they like him?'

'Mr Moore is an excellent teacher, as is every member of staff. Mr Wilson keeps a very close eye on all of them. He doesn't tolerate poor performance.'

There was no doubt that she was being defensive.

'You're not telling me much,' Geraldine said, hiding her irritation.

The woman gave a taut smile and inclined her head, as though accepting a compliment. 'As the head teacher's secretary, I have to be discreet.'

'I'm afraid there is no place for discretion when answering questions in a murder enquiry.'

Before the secretary could respond to Geraldine's thinly veiled reprimand, her phone buzzed.

'The head teacher will see you now,' she announced, with evident relief. 'I'm sure he'll be happy to answer any questions you may have. There isn't really anything I can tell you,' she added apologetically. 'I'm just the head teacher's secretary.'

Accepting that far from being obstructive, the secretary genuinely had nothing useful to add to what the police already knew, Geraldine thanked her and went through to the inner office. The head teacher smiled wearily at her and half rose to his feet, gesturing towards a chair.

'I don't wish to sound as though I'm giving you the brush-off, Inspector, but I really am extremely busy at the moment. Our pupils are understandably upset, their parents are disturbed, and the governors are hectoring me for an explanation of what happened, when there's really nothing more I can tell them, beyond what I've already been able to report. The tragic loss of two of our pupils, in such dreadful circumstances, has completely disrupted the life of the school, and it's proving very difficult to keep the pupils focused on their studies, as you can imagine. The staff are doing their best, but –' He broke off with a shrug. 'I'm at my wits' end and really pushed for time. So I'd be grateful if we could make this brief.'

'Of course. Let's get straight to the point. Is there anything more you can tell me about Paul Moore?'

Mr Wilson sighed. Behind a mask of professional composure his expression was fraught.

'Paul is a conscientious teacher,' he said heavily. 'He's a sensible young man, Inspector, a happily married man whose teaching record is exemplary.'

When Geraldine enquired about Cassie Jackson's character, Mr Wilson looked tense and cleared his throat. When he finally answered the question, it was clear he was hedging.

'Teenage girls can be very volatile,' he said. 'They can be unreliable.'

'Are you saying you think Cassie Jackson lied when she accused Paul Moore of sexually assaulting her?'

Mr Wilson hesitated. 'That is not what I said. I wasn't privy to what went on between them, if indeed there *was* anything going on.' He leaned forward and gazed at her earnestly. 'Inspector, our pupils have been very upset by these two deaths. Many are staying away from school. They are distressed, and naturally their parents are anxious. We need this matter to be resolved as quickly as possible. As long as no arrest is made, rumours are going to continue spreading. The best outcome for the school would be if Paul were exonerated. It is my honest belief that he is completely innocent. But if it turns out that he is guilty, we need to see him convicted as soon as possible. We're already hearing talk of some sort of cover-up, and I cannot allow this delay to affect the reputation of the school. Other than that, I really don't know what to say to you.'

Geraldine told him that she regretted the investigation was still ongoing.

'Until you conclude your investigation, we can't move on from this,' he replied, a note of sharpness in his voice.

'The investigation will be over as soon as possible, but the post mortem on Ella Robinson has only just been completed and we have to wait for the full toxicology report, as well as the results of forensic analysis of the scene. At the moment, we are not even clear whether we are looking for one or two killers. So I'm afraid the investigation will take as long as it takes, and there's nothing we can do to expedite matters, however inconvenient or painful that may be.'

'No, no, of course, of course, I'm sorry. The whole thing has been so stressful, as I'm sure you can imagine.' He leaned back in his chair with a sigh. 'I've been in the teaching profession for twenty-five years, head teacher here for eight, and nothing even remotely similar has ever happened before. Nothing in my training and experience has prepared me for something like this.'

'There is nothing similar to murder,' Geraldine conceded, 'and nothing can prepare you for it.'

The Head of the English department was called Valerie Greenfield. Plump, with short, curly brown hair, she looked easygoing and cheerful, but once she opened her mouth, her domineering manner of speaking dispelled any initial impression of liberality.

'Paul's sound,' she asserted vigorously. 'It's nonsense to suggest he was up to anything. I simply don't believe he's capable of doing anything to harm a pupil. But you never really know with men, do you?' she added, in seeming contradiction of her firmly expressed opinion about her colleague.

'So just to be clear, are you saying you think he could have been guilty of sexual assault and murder?' Geraldine asked.

'Oh good lord, no. I don't believe that for a minute. What I am saying is that, of course, I can't know for certain. But if you ask me if I think he did anything wrong, my answer would have to be no, absolutely not. I don't believe it was him, but then again, I can't be sure, can I? Only someone who actually witnessed the murders with their own eyes could really know for certain what happened to those poor girls. I'm afraid there's not much else I can tell you. Paul's a thoroughly decent guy, and I can't believe he would do anything so idiotic as to jeopardise his whole career, not to mention his marriage, for a girl like Cassie.'

'A girl like Cassie?'

'She attracted a lot of attention from the boys although she wasn't really much to look at, all bleached hair and thick make-up and fake nails. You know the type: a sad child neglected at home, desperate to feel wanted, and mistaking sex for intimacy.' Valerie shook her head. 'Cassie was a very troubled child who used her sexuality to draw attention to herself. Thankfully we don't see this sort of behaviour very often. It sometimes emerges when children have been abused. I've seen it in boys as well as girls,' she added grimly. 'Early abuse doesn't only traumatise a child at the time, it can produce long-term psychological damage. It's sickening. But, of course, by the time anyone becomes aware of what's going on, it's often too late to prevent permanent psychological damage.'

'And you think that's what happened to Cassie? That she was sexually abused as a young child?'

'Oh, no, no, please don't put words in my mouth. I never said she was abused as a child, only that she used to throw herself at boys in a way that a child who had been abused might do. The question was raised a few years ago, as it happens, and social services were called in to investigate, but families can be very adept at covering up the truth. Anyway, like I said, it all came to nothing. If the rumours were true, it would be a miracle if the poor child hadn't become seriously disturbed,' she concluded mournfully.

'But Cassie had a boyfriend?'

'Yes, she's – she was going out with Max Dean.' Valerie scowled. 'Cassie was mixed up and, frankly, Max isn't much better. Neither of them was a stabilising influence, and I don't think they did one another any good. To be fair to Max, if he hadn't distracted Cassie from her studies someone else would have. And he was genuinely attached to her. Her death hit him very hard. It's a terrible thing for a youngster to deal with.'

'Difficult at any age,' Geraldine murmured.

Valerie suggested Geraldine speak to the cricket coach, who was friends with Paul.

'I don't believe a word of it, not for one moment,' the cricket coach said firmly. 'Paul's a good bloke, one of the best, he'd never be stupid enough to risk his whole career for a slutty teenager. It's too ridiculous. Obviously the girl was fantasising, no doubt attention seeking. In any case, Paul's married.'

'Is his marriage happy?'

'Sure. As happy as the next bloke's, yes. Look, if there were any problems there, I'd know. I can tell you, his marriage is solid. The allegation against him is absolute poppycock.'

Everyone Geraldine and Ariadne spoke to came up with the

same response. No one believed Paul Moore could possibly be guilty but, at the same time, no one could be sure he was innocent.

36

As well as questioning Paul Moore's colleagues, the police were keen to pursue all other avenues of enquiry. When Geraldine suggested that they dig further into the family circumstances of both the victims, Binita agreed. It was almost certain the two deaths were linked. They were working on the assumption that Ella had been killed because she had known the identity of Cassie's attacker. Paul Moore was the most obvious suspect, but he continued to insist that he had not touched Cassie Jackson, and without any evidence to back up the arrest, it was going to be difficult to present a watertight case to the Crown Prosecution Service. But even if Paul evaded conviction, his career was over, his reputation shattered.

It was frustrating that there was no trace of his DNA on either of the bodies. All they had against him so far was the unsubstantiated allegation Cassie had made. In the absence of evidence or witnesses, it was really down to the victim's word against her alleged attacker, and she wasn't there to put her case. The only statement from her was what she had told her head teacher, and that report was all but incoherent. She had received no expert questioning, and no legal support, and reliable though the school's report undoubtedly was, there was no question that Cassie's account of what had taken place between her and her teacher was inconsistent. It was frustrating that she had been killed before the process of investigating her claim had really begun in earnest.

Geraldine listened to the statement taken by the school, which had been recorded and subsequently transcribed verbatim. She waited impatiently while the head teacher explained that Cassie had done nothing wrong, and the teacher responsible for safeguarding just wanted to ask her a few questions. If Cassie felt uncomfortable at any time, he said, they would stop. All she had to do was tell the truth. At last they reached the first question.

'You made an allegation against one of your teachers. Did he behave inappropriately towards you?'

'The prick come at me, innit?'

'Just to be clear, are you talking about Mr Moore?' the woman's voice enquired calmly.

Geraldine sighed at the way the questioner was leading Cassie, instead of waiting and letting her speak freely.

'Yeah, him. He come at me. He was always on at me to do it.'

Geraldine wished Cassie's interlocutor had requested clarification at this point. There was more along those lines before the teacher finally asked Cassie to explain exactly what she meant.

'Can you tell me what you mean when you say he wanted you to "do it" with him?'

'He wanted a shag, innit?'

'When did this happen?'

'All the time, innit. He couldn't keep it in his pants. He wanted – he said –'

There was a pause, as though Cassie was thinking. Without seeing her face, it was impossible to form an opinion about what those thoughts might be. She could have been too distressed, or embarrassed, to continue, or she might have been taking time to fabricate her next lie. The teacher who had questioned Cassie was not much help when Geraldine spoke to her.

'What impression did you get of Cassie?'

'We have to take all such allegations very seriously,' the teacher replied earnestly. 'I think I asked her all the right questions. Beyond that, there wasn't much I could do. It's the head teacher's decision how to respond when a complaint is made against a teacher. But, of course, the sexual nature of this allegation meant he had to suspend Paul straightaway.' She smiled nervously.

'Do you think Cassie was telling the truth?'

At that, the teacher merely shrugged and replied that she really couldn't say.

'I'm not expecting a categorical answer, but what was your impression at the time?'

'I really can't remember exactly. The whole thing was shocking. I've no idea if there was any truth to the allegation or not. But you've got the recording and the transcript. There's really nothing I can add to that.'

Geraldine had instructed Naomi to search through public records to see if she could find out anything more about Mr Robinson's first wife, Christina. After spending hours chasing records, Naomi finally discovered an interesting item.

'I brought it straight to you,' she told Geraldine, her eyes alight with excitement. 'I think it might be significant.'

'Go on,' Geraldine said, responding to Naomi's excitement. 'It's time we had a lead.'

'Mark Robinson's first wife was treated in hospital several times for bruising and fractured bones. I managed to track down one of the doctors who treated her injuries. It seems the then Mrs Robinson insisted on each occasion that she had fallen over, but the doctor told me his team were suspicious. She was asked if her husband had assaulted her, and she denied it. But they weren't sure whether to believe her or not.'

'Are there any police records?'

Naomi shook her head. 'The hospital said there was no point in trying to take it any further as the wife was adamant that she was clumsy and often missed her footing. In view of that, it was never taken any further.'

That all sounded plausible. Nevertheless, it was interesting that Ella's father possibly had a history of violence. Geraldine decided to question him again, but first she wanted to speak to his ex-wife. Christina had remarried and was living in Birmingham. Instead of sending a local officer to speak to her, Geraldine decided to make the trip and question Christina herself. She caught the train to Birmingham and arrived at the address she had been given late on Thursday morning. The woman who came to the door was short, with dark hair streaked with silver, and an open, youthful face. She led Geraldine into her front room, and removed a small pile of books from the coffee table.

'Can I offer you a cup of tea or coffee?'

Geraldine declined and assured Christina that she wouldn't keep her long.

'What is this all about, please?' Christina asked, sitting down and picking up a half-finished blanket or shawl she was knitting. 'I mean, I know you told me on the phone you wanted to talk about my ex, but I'd like to know what's going on. Is he in some sort of trouble?'

Her knitting needles clicking, Christina flatly denied that Mark had ever been violent towards her when they were married. 'I mean, he did get very frustrated with the situation. We both did. Struggling to make ends meet when you've just had a baby isn't great. I was quite depressed about it. I think the stress of it all ended our marriage, although maybe we would never have stayed the course anyway. My daughter is still very angry with him, and she hasn't spoken to him since the divorce. She thought he should have stood by me. But I don't think he left me because of our money troubles. I mean, it didn't help matters, but I think we would have split up anyway. Oh, well, it's all water under the bridge now. And I don't think our daughter suffered much. I mean, of course, she lost her father, but she was only two when we separated and she hardly remembers him. Soon after the divorce I met Arthur, my second husband, and he's been wonderful. He's a better father to our children, including my daughter, than Mark would ever have been. Mark wasn't interested in her. Maybe he's changed now and is close to the daughter he had with his second wife. I know they have a fifteen-year-old.'

'Had a fifteen-year-old,' Geraldine said.

Startled, Christina paused in her knitting. 'Oh my goodness, what happened to her?'

Gently, Geraldine explained.

'And you came to see me to ask if Mark was violent?' Christina said. She sounded angry. 'No. Mark had a temper, and he used to shout at me, but he never lifted a finger against me. He wasn't like that. If he had been, I would have packed my things and left straightaway. I could have gone back to my mother at any time. Just because I was young when my first daughter was born, everyone assumes I was helpless, but I'm perfectly capable of looking after myself and my children. I certainly wasn't reliant on Mark to look after me.'

'So just to be absolutely clear, any bruising or other injuries you suffered while you were married to Mark were not his fault?'

Christina sniffed. 'What about the bruises I sustained after we split up? Are you going to blame Arthur for those? My condition hadn't been diagnosed when I was with Mark, but it's different now we know,' she added. 'I have a condition that causes me to black out from time to time. These days I'm on medication so it doesn't happen often, but sometimes things don't go as they should.' She sighed. 'Arthur's very handy and he's put rails everywhere, and he's drilled the kids so they know what to do when I fall. But as far as Mark's concerned, no, I don't believe he would have done what you're suggesting. He might have a temper, but it's all gruffness and raising his voice with him. He's no more likely to have attacked his daughter than – well, than I am, really.'

37

HAVING QUESTIONED MARK ROBINSON'S ex-wife, Geraldine asked him to come to the police station to answer a few further questions. He shuffled into the interview room, his shoulders bowed, his hair sticking out from his head like ginger fluff. Taking a seat, he rubbed his lips nervously with his fingers and waited uneasily.

'How can I help you, Inspector?' he asked at last. 'Have you arrested him yet?'

He looked taken aback when Geraldine told him she had spoken with his first wife that morning. 'You went to see Christina? Well, I'm sure you had your reasons. I haven't seen her in years. I can't imagine why you'd be interested in her.'

'What happened between you and your first wife?'

'We're divorced. It was all a long time ago.'

'Tell me about your first marriage.'

'There's nothing to tell, really. We were both very young. She was only seventeen and I wasn't much older. It was all one big mistake, just a mess from start to finish. I only married her because she was pregnant. I mean, I just assumed the baby was mine when we got married, but then it all kicked off.' He broke off, frowning.

'What happened?' Geraldine prompted him.

'There was a question over who the father was. Something about blood groups. Anyway, the doubt was raised, and in the end I couldn't bear it and insisted we had a paternity test. It turned out the baby was mine after all, but by then our relationship had turned sour.' His face twisted in fleeting bitterness. 'She never forgave me for doubting her. We were too young to cope with each other, let alone a baby. She went back to her mother, and was a lot better off without me.'

'You must have been disappointed.'

'Disappointed? That's an understatement. There I was, all of twenty years old, and I thought my life was over. That woman married me, and for what? Just so she could give her baby a father on the birth certificate.' He gazed miserably at Geraldine. 'I don't think Christina ever wanted to marry me, any more than I wanted to marry her. We never got on. It was a shit relationship right from the start. Acrimonious, the divorce court said, and that just about sums it up. We were always at each other's throats. I was furious with her at the time, but she wasn't to blame. It was no one's fault. We just weren't ready for that kind of responsibility. Anyway, we got divorced, and I haven't seen her or spoken to her since. I did pay child support for a while, which I couldn't afford. Then Chris remarried and that was that, she was well and truly off my hands, and I was free of her at last.' He scowled. 'Like I said, we were very young.'

'Suspecting you weren't the father of your first wife's baby must have upset you very much,' Geraldine said gently.

He grunted. 'What do you think? But looking back on it, you know, we were just kids. The whole thing was stupid. Best forgotten about. All that was twenty years ago. There's no point in raking it up. Of course, it hurt like hell at the time, but I'm well out of it now and we've both moved on. Water under the bridge and all that.'

Geraldine gazed evenly at him. 'Given your experience with Christina, how did you feel when you discovered Ella was interested in boys?'

Mark shrugged. 'I didn't like it, that's for sure. Neither of us did. You want to keep your daughter safe, protect her from trouble.'

'And sex is trouble?'

He frowned, suddenly wary. 'It is for a girl who falls pregnant at fifteen. Or she could have caught a nasty disease. Don't get me wrong. It was only natural Ella would be interested in boys. But I'm not sure she was careful. She always seemed so – desperate. And she became very secretive, wouldn't tell Maisie what she was up to. Anyway, it's too late now. There's nothing more I can do to protect her. But I think about her all the time. I mean, all the time.' A solitary tear dribbled from one of his eyes and trickled down his cheek. 'She was my daughter, mine!' he cried out in a sudden burst of emotion. 'I keep asking myself what more I could have done for her. I thought I was doing my best, but looking back, I never really knew her. I never listened to her. We drifted apart without my even noticing. I thought she'd grow out of it. Her being so distant is just a part of growing up. It's just a phase she's going through, like kids do. But if I could have her back, have my time again, I wouldn't sit and do nothing and wait for her to come to me, I'd – oh, I don't know what, but I'd try a lot harder than I did. And now it's all over and it's too late. There's nothing left but regret. Because I could have stopped it from happening, couldn't I? If I'd spent more time with her, paid her more attention, refused to let her push me away like she did –' He paused, before adding disconsolately, 'Do you think she was looking for a father figure? Was it something she needed from me that I never gave her?'

Geraldine wasn't sure what to say to that. Gently she suggested that the grieving father consult a bereavement counsellor. Loss was difficult to cope with at the best of times and knowing your child had been murdered must be unimaginably painful. She wondered whether his wife would bring him any comfort but recalling the shrewish face and eyes hardened by unbearable grief, somehow she doubted it. She lowered her gaze. She couldn't afford to let herself be blinded by pity. Either one of Ella's parents could have been involved in the murders. Until the case was satisfactorily concluded, no one could be ruled out.

'Is there anything else you can tell us?' Geraldine asked when he appeared to have recovered his composure.

'It wasn't only Cassie Jackson,' he said bitterly. 'Ella talked about that teacher too.'

'Which teacher are you talking about?'

'Mr Moore. Paul Moore.'

Geraldine was instantly alert, wondering if this was an attempt to divert attention from the speaker himself.

'What did Ella say about him?'

He sighed. 'I wish you could ask her that.'

'What did Ella say about Paul Moore?' Geraldine repeated, a hint of urgency in her voice. 'If you know anything at all, please tell me.'

'It's only hearsay,' he replied. 'She can't tell you herself.'

'It might still help us. Please, what did she say?'

'She said he was a pervert.'

'What else did she say?'

He shrugged. 'Just that Cassie told her.'

'Told her what?'

'That Paul Moore was a pervert.'

'What did she mean by that?'

But Ella's father shook his head. 'I don't know,' he replied. 'I wish you could ask her.'

Geraldine wondered whether there was more to the rumour than anyone now knew. Like Mark Robinson, she wished she could question Ella and find out what she knew about Paul Moore.

Geraldine had just returned to her desk when Binita called the investigation team together and instructed them to focus their attention on Cassie's movements up to the time of her death. All of her contacts were to be investigated. They were all fairly confident that one person was responsible for both Cassie and Ella's murders. Ella must have been in possession of information that would incriminate whoever had murdered her friend, and she had been killed to prevent her from revealing what she knew.

'If Ella were still alive, it seems pretty certain she'd be able to tell us who killed Cassie,' Binita concluded. 'Now it's down to us to discover the truth.'

Geraldine found herself hoping that no one else knew who had killed Cassie Jackson. Such knowledge could be dangerous. On the other hand, if no one but the killer now knew the truth, it might be impossible to track him down.

38

LAURA HADN'T TOLD PAUL that she had the day off on Thursday. She hadn't intended to keep it a secret, but somehow the subject had never come up. Normally, when he was at home in the school holidays, he would make a point of finding out when she was free, and they would plan what to do with their time together. But lately nothing had been normal in their life. When she woke up at the usual time on Wednesday, she decided to leave the house early as though she was going to work. Paul would never know. He rarely went out now and, if he did, he went no further than the nearest parade of shops, and hurried home again as quickly as he could.

The episode with the graffiti had made him more nervous than ever about leaving the house, so there was very little risk of her bumping into him if she went window shopping. Even so, she decided to take the bus out to the shops at Monks Cross, just to be certain she couldn't run into him. After all, she only had his word for it that he was home all day. He might actually be roaming the streets while she was at work.

Monks Cross shopping centre was surprisingly busy. Laura wondered where all the people came from, and why they weren't at work in the middle of the week. There were children too, who should surely have been at school. She made her way through noisy hordes of people to reach her favourite store, where rails of colourful clothes offered a welcome distraction from her troubles. She had always enjoyed trying on new clothes. When they fitted well, she felt like a different person: attractive, happy and successful. As a child she had loved clothes shopping with her mother, and then when she was a little older she had graduated to shopping with friends. It was not as much fun trying on clothes on her own. Not only that, but studying herself in a full-length mirror, she was dismayed by the change in her appearance. Her hair had lost its lustre and hung limply around a face that looked worn out and lined, as though she had physically aged since Paul had been suspended from work. Far from cheering herself up, she was becoming even more miserable than before.

Desperately she threw herself into the task of choosing clothes to try on, and before long was busy transforming herself with blouses, trousers and dresses. But anxiety for the future wrapped itself around her like a vast web. The thought that she and Paul might soon be struggling financially made her reluctant to spend any money, which rather spoiled her outing. There was not much point in going window shopping to lift her spirits, when she knew that before long she might be destitute. She was miserable and lonely, but it was too early to go home. She had to stay out for the day or admit to Paul that she hadn't been at work. This time when her phone rang she answered straightaway.

'John! It's so great to hear from you.'

'Can I take you out for lunch?' he asked, clearly pleased by her enthusiastic greeting.

'Why not?' she thought, as she replied that it would be lovely. 'I'm in Monks Cross at the moment. Why don't you join me here?'

If he wanted to meet in York, she would have to make an excuse and decline his offer. She couldn't risk an encounter with Paul, especially not if she was with John. To her relief, he agreed to meet her in the shopping centre straightaway. There wasn't time to get her hair done, but she bought herself a new jumper, which was reduced, and retouched her make-up to mask the tiredness in her eyes before he arrived. Sitting at a table in Pizza Hut, he ordered a bottle of red wine.

'I shouldn't really,' Laura giggled.

But it was lovely being taken out, and for a while they chatted happily about innocuous subjects. She was never sure whether it was best to raise the matter and get it out in the open, or gloss over it and pretend it wasn't happening. Eventually the conversation flagged, and she felt impelled to ask. 'How's mum?' She washed away the salty taste of the pizza with a sip of wine and waited for him to reply.

John sighed. 'I see her as often as I can, but she doesn't recognise me.'

Laura reached out and put her hand on his. After the first stroke, the doctors had been optimistic about her mother's chances of making a recovery to something approaching normal, but somehow that had never happened. By the third stroke, no one mentioned recovery any more. Her brain was too severely damaged and vascular dementia had developed more rapidly than anyone had anticipated.

'I ought to go and see her,' Laura muttered fatuously.

They both knew she would never see her mother again. The silent creature lying motionless in bed, clinging to a meaningless existence, wasn't the same woman whose spirits had brimmed over with the joy of being alive. Fiercely, Laura blinked away the memory of her mother's infectious giggle and the warmth of her embrace. It didn't help to dwell on the past. 'Smile,' her mother used to urge her whenever Laura was upset. 'It will pass. Everything will seem better tomorrow.' Only now there was never going to be a better tomorrow for her mother. She would continue to breathe until her heart stopped beating one day. That was all she had left of life. Laura wondered if John had actually visited her recently, or was only saying that to make her feel better. It made no difference either way. His wife no longer recognised him, and she didn't respond to her daughter. Not by so much as the flicker of an eyelid had she acknowledged Laura's greeting on her last visit.

'There's no need for you to feel obliged to see her, not any more,' he said kindly, as though he could tell what she was thinking. 'You'll only upset yourself, and it won't help her.'

'But what if she senses when we're there? It might comfort her to know we still visit her.'

He shook his head. 'She's past any help either of us can possibly give her. But she's well looked after,' he added with a lopsided smile. 'You did what you could for her.'

'We both did,' she replied softly. 'It wasn't fair.'

'It wasn't fair on any of us,' he agreed mournfully. 'But life goes on and you mustn't go upsetting yourself about something you can't do anything about.'

She nodded. He was right. The same was true of her marriage. There was nothing she could do about Paul's troubles either. He was her husband, but she couldn't help him.

'You're not to blame for what's happened,' she murmured, but she was talking to herself.

'No one's to blame,' he replied, still talking about Laura's mother.

As they were ordering dessert, at John's insistence, she felt her phone vibrate in her pocket. Glancing at it, she saw that Paul was calling her and declined the call, unable to face hearing any more bad news. She was trying to enjoy herself for once. She had spent enough time stressing about what was happening at home. She had scarcely slept for a week and had lost nearly half a stone in weight. Now that she was out having a good time, she didn't want the interlude to end. Paul could

200

wait. Ignoring the rush of guilt that threatened to overwhelm her, she smiled at John.

'Is everything all right?' he enquired with his usual solicitude.

'Everything's fine,' she lied.

She hadn't even spoken to Paul, but all the joy had gone out of her day, swept away by his call.

39

GERALDINE WAS INTERESTED TO hear that Paul had resisted coming to the police station to talk to her. The constable who had gone to collect him reported that the suspect had flatly refused to accompany him to the police station, and had demanded to speak to his lawyer before leaving the house. When the constable had informed him that he could call his lawyer from the police station, Paul had made a run for it.

'What do you mean, he made a run for it?' Geraldine asked.

'He barged past me and made a run for it, straight into my partner's arms.' The constable replied. 'If he'd run out the back and over the fence, he might have slipped past us, but he hadn't thought it through. If you ask me, he panicked. He was most apologetic once we actually had him in the car. We cuffed him, of course, just to make sure, but I don't think he was going to try any more funny business.'

At last Paul had been settled in a room to face a formal interview. There were grey smudges under his eyes, and he gazed at Geraldine with a haunted expression. It would hardly be surprising to learn he hadn't been sleeping well over the past few weeks. An allegation of paedophilia and an impending murder charge were more than enough to disturb anyone's rest. His lawyer was seated at his side, poker faced, his yellow hair temporarily brushed back off his face, making his eyes seem to protrude even more than the last time Geraldine had seen him.

'My client has already answered all your questions.' The lawyer began the interview in his clipped tones. 'Unless you have some new evidence to implicate him in this unfortunate affair, there is no justification for this harassment. I suggest you release him at once.'

He spoke of the 'unfortunate affair' as though the tragic death of two young women was somehow distasteful, like a nasty stench.

'I'm sure Paul is as keen as we are to get to the bottom of all this,' Geraldine replied smoothly. She turned to Paul. 'Did you ever approach a pupil demanding sex?'

'What?' He started at the abrupt question but she was interested to see he made no attempt to deny the suggestion.

'Did you ever make any reference to sexual acts in the presence of a pupil?'

'Oh, for fuck's sake,' Paul cried out. 'Yes, of course, I made references to sex. You try teaching literature without mentioning it. We usually discuss how old Romeo and Juliet are in the play, and I always point out that teenagers are not ready for the emotions that can accompany a physical relationship, although most of the pupils laugh when they hear that. As for Lady Macbeth giving suck, perhaps you've never read that line with a class of horny teenage boys? Take it from me, they don't interpret it as evidence that Lady Macbeth had given birth. But I can assure you any reference I made to sex was minimal. Believe me, I have no wish to discuss sex with teenagers of any gender or orientation. I spent most of my time in class trying to persuade the boys to think about something other than sex.'

Geraldine wasn't sure whether to believe him.

'Did you ever discuss literature with pupils individually?'

'Absolutely not. Anything I discussed was with a class of pupils. I didn't give private one-to-one tuition. Very few teachers would dare do that these days in case, well, in case of some trumped-up allegation being made against them.' He raised his eyebrows and shrugged. 'And if a pupil ever had to stay behind, I made sure to keep more than one of them back, and left the door open. I did everything any sensible adult would do to protect themselves from this kind of nonsense. I was careful and vigilant. It's not just common sense. We're trained to guard against inviting problems. And where has that got me? Up against you lot who wouldn't recognise the truth if it came up and hit you in the face. Oh, this whole thing really is preposterous, and how anyone can give any credence at all to a deluded and damaged young girl like Cassie Jackson is frankly beyond me. Have you bothered to read her school record? You should take a look. She was repeatedly absent without parental permission, and she was involved in a number of physical altercations with other girls. Cassie Jackson was a messed-up, damaged teenager with a clear agenda to do everything she could to gain as much attention as possible, no matter who she wrecked along the way. This unfounded allegation against me is just a pathetic effort on her part to gain some kind of notoriety. Considering her history so far, something like this was bound to happen sooner or later. It just happened to be me she targeted.'

'How do you know about her school record?'

'I take time to look up all my pupils and read anything that's not strictly confidential. Because I'm conscientious.'

However hard she pushed and cajoled, Geraldine couldn't persuade him to admit that he had seen Cassie anywhere but in class, and he insisted she had crept up on him uninvited on the last occasion he had seen her.

'I didn't hear her come in. I was waiting for my next class and suddenly she was there, talking to me.' He screwed up his eyes. 'I can't even remember what she said. All I can remember is that she was chewing this filthy grey gum and her breath stank. She started talking about feelings, and saying I had feelings for her.' He shook his head, disbelieving. 'So I told her to leave. I said she had to go away or she could get me in serious trouble. I've always been so careful but she ambushed me, caught me on my own. Then she started accusing me of looking at her, and said I found her irresistible, something along those lines. It's all a bit of a blur really. I was so shocked, I could hardly take in what she was saying.'

'But you didn't leave the room?'

'Naturally I wanted to get out of there, but she had positioned herself right in my way. I couldn't get past her without touching her to move her aside, and I thought that would be more risky than talking to her. So I kept repeating that I wanted her to leave. I remember thinking that she could ruin my career if I didn't get rid of her.' He broke off, realising what he had just said. 'If I couldn't get her to leave me alone, that is. But she didn't move. She just kept talking.'

'Can you remember anything more of what she said?' Geraldine asked.

'She told me she knew what I wanted. Can you believe it? A precocious child like that having the faintest idea what goes through my mind.'

'What was going through your mind at that moment?'

'What do you think? I was terrified.'

'Terrified of your impulses?'

'The only impulse I had was to bellow at her to get away from me with her stinking breath and disgusting grey gum she was chewing. I held it together, and told her my next class was due and she had to leave. She just stood there grinning. I didn't realise it at the time but, of course, that was what she was waiting for; she was waiting for her audience to arrive. I even tried appealing to her not to put me in this compromising position. She just kept on grinning and chewing her foul gum.' He paused, shuddering at the recollection.

'And then? What happened next?' Geraldine prompted him.

'After that it's all a bit of a blur. I think the bell went. As the door opened, she threw herself at me, trying to force her lips against mine. I turned away and tried to retreat but she shoved me backwards, right up against the wall. If it hadn't been for that, I think I would have fallen over. She was really pushing me, pressing herself against me. Next minute she was shrieking and screaming, and the pupils who had just entered were yelling, and my colleague arrived to see what all the noise was about. And that's as much as I can remember about what happened. Next thing I knew, I was hurrying from the room and speaking to the head, who suspended me immediately. Of course, he was following procedure, but I'd done nothing that warranted suspension from my duties. Nothing! She just picked on me, for no reason.'

He sat back in his chair, arms folded, and glared at Geraldine.

'There's always a reason,' she murmured.

The problem was, they didn't know what the reason was in this case. There remained the question of why Cassie Jackson had selected Paul Moore as her victim, if what he was telling them was true. Whatever had really happened between him and Cassie, he wasn't deviating from his story, so Geraldine abandoned that line of questioning.

'Why did you resist my colleague's invitation to accompany him here?'

'That was stupid, I admit, but I panicked. Wouldn't you if the police suddenly turned up on your doorstep wanting to drag you off to the police station when you had nothing more to tell them? I didn't do anything to that girl.'

'So you say. What can you tell me about Ella Robinson?'

Paul gave a despairing sigh and shook his head. 'She was another girl in my year eleven set. Very quiet. I had the impression she looked up to Cassie, who was a far more flamboyant character. But you know what? I didn't kill Ella either. Someone must have sent Cassie to set me up and then killed her, God knows why. Ella came across the same killer, or else she found out about it and the killer found a way to stop her from talking.' He groaned. 'I can't make head nor tail of it. Believe me, I'd help you if I could, but I have no idea what it's all about.'

Geraldine was inclined to believe Paul. At least he seemed plausible. Binita was not convinced.

'Of course, he's going to deny having done anything wrong,' she growled. 'Unless he's prepared to confess and go down for a very long time, he has no other option but to claim that she set him up. Everything points to him. We just need to find the proof. And we will. There's going to be something somewhere on someone's CCTV or phone that places them together. We just need something that confounds his claim that he never saw her out of school, and the whole tissue of his lies will begin to unravel. We have to keep searching to find out more about both Paul and Cassie, and in the meantime, we'll arrest him. Hopefully a few nights in a cell will convince him he's not just going to walk away from this. And then I'm sure we'll be able to persuade him that it's in his best interests to work with us. The prospect of a reduced sentence if he shows enough remorse is always compelling. And it sounds as though he can at least claim the girl was a willing participant, although whether or not a jury is going to believe that is out of our hands.' She sniffed. 'You did your best, Geraldine, and I'm sure no one could have tried harder to persuade him to confess. But now we need to put pressure on him. He has to realise that he can't talk his way out of this.'

'You're assuming he's guilty,' Geraldine said.

'He tried to scarper, Geraldine. That seems pretty conclusive to me. Or do you have another suspect in mind?' Binita asked.

'Well, no, not really.'

'Let's start applying pressure on Paul then. Hopefully he'll confess before too long, and we can get this wrapped up.'

40

GERALDINE SIGHED WHEN SHE heard that Max had been brought into the police station again, this time for being drunk and disorderly. He had been picked up in the town centre late at night, shouting at the top of his voice, swearing at the world in general and Paul Moore in particular, and crying for Cassie, yelling that he just wanted her back. Once he had sobered up overnight in the custody suite, Geraldine decided to speak to him herself.

'Max, you can't go on like this,' she began, speaking as kindly as she could. 'Cassie wouldn't have wanted you to go to pieces. She cared about you, didn't she? And she would have wanted you to pick yourself up and carry on with your life. I'm not saying it won't be hard, of course it will, but there are people who can help you.'

'And there's some fucker walking around what done her in, and what the fuck are you doing about that? What the fuck are you doing talking to me when you could be out there –'

'We've arrested someone,' Geraldine said quietly.

Max's eyebrows rose and his anger appeared to subside suddenly on hearing that. He let out a long breath and his shoulders slumped, so that he resembled a punctured balloon.

'Wicked,' he said, with a vicious grin. 'That old fucker needs to get what's coming to him or I'll do for him myself.'

'Do for him?' Geraldine queried gently.

'Too fucking right.'

Geraldine frowned. 'Are you threatening to kill the suspect if he's not convicted?'

'Don't you go twisting what I said,' he replied. 'I want my lawyer here.'

He refused to say another word until the duty brief was present. The duty brief who had attended the previous interview arrived, looking just as alert and angelic as the last time Geraldine had seen him. After he had conferred in private with his client, the interview resumed.

'My client was expressing his anger against the man he believes killed Cassie Jackson,' the lawyer explained.

'By threatening to kill him?'

'My client did no such thing. To suggest he did is a gross misrepresentation of what he said.'

'He said he would "do for him",' Geraldine said.

'Which is merely a manner of speaking.'

'Meaning what, exactly?'

'Meaning that my client would appeal to the suspect's conscience and exhort him to confess, as should any law-abiding citizen who's convinced they're speaking with a murderer.'

Geraldine couldn't help smiling at the equivocation. The idea that Max might sit down with Paul and make such an appeal was ludicrous.

Max grinned. 'That's it,' he said. 'In a nutshell. That's what I meant. I never threatened to kill no one, not even some old geezer who deserves to rot in hell.'

Geraldine considered what Max was saying very carefully. His conviction that Paul was responsible for Cassie's death seemed genuine. She wondered why he was sure, or if he was actually protesting so fervently to cover up his own guilt.

'Max, what are you not telling me?'

He shook his head. 'Plenty,' he said. 'What I do ain't your

210

business, innit. There's plenty I don't tell to no one. I bet you got your private thoughts. Well, so do I.'

Geraldine sighed. Max was so woolly in his use of language, and so pedantic in his expectations of her.

'All right, let's make this question more specific. Of course, I'm not interested in every private detail of your life. What I want to know is why you're so convinced Paul Moore killed Cassie and Ella. Why him?'

'He's a teacher, innit. And a paedo.'

'We only have Cassie's word on that.'

He bristled. 'You calling her a liar?'

'No, no, it's not that. It's just that if he is guilty, we're as keen as you are to see him convicted. We're on the same side, Max. We both want whoever killed Cassie and Ella to be locked up for life. It's what they deserve. But in order to convict Paul Moore, we need to build a case against him.'

'Don't talk to me like I'm a retard. I understand what's going down. But you got your evidence. Cassie told you. She told us all. Ask anyone. They'll tell you. We all heard her.'

'I know, and I believe her,' Geraldine fibbed. 'But a judge is going to need more than that.'

'More than what she said?'

'Yes. We need proof. And so far, we've found nothing that ties Paul Moore to either of the bodies. He must have been very careful to avoid leaving any trace of DNA, or fingerprints, or shoe prints, or anything at all that would prove he was there. You see our problem? We haven't found anything. That doesn't mean he didn't do it, but it does mean that we're struggling to prove his guilt. And if we can't prove it, then a jury might let him off.'

'They can't. He done it and you got him.'

'If there's the slightest doubt about his guilt, a jury might decide not to convict him, and no one wants that to happen, not if he killed those two girls. So you have to help us, Max. Tell us why you believe he killed them. Is there anything you're not telling us?'

Max frowned. He appeared to be thinking. 'You mean, like a photo with them having it off?'

'Yes, exactly. That would more or less clinch it. He's going to argue strenuously that he's done nothing wrong, and he'll have clever lawyers putting his case as strongly as possible. Their arguments are going to be very compelling. But however hard he argues, a photo of him in a compromising position with Cassie or Ella is going to blow his defence out of the water.'

She waited anxiously but Max didn't answer. If Max could supply a picture of Cassie and Paul Moore together, the case might be as good as tied up.

'Well?' she prompted him, controlling her impatience. 'Have you got any images of Paul Moore being intimate with one of the victims?'

Max shook his head. 'I ain't got one. That's your job, innit?'

'Then what makes you so sure he's guilty?'

'I seen them out together, innit. But I got no picture. You think I'm a perv, taking pictures of them?'

'Are you telling me you saw Cassie and Paul Moore together?'

He nodded, his face twisted in anger. 'Yeah, I seen them. I told her, innit. She was mad at me for following her, but I only done it because I wanted to protect her. It wasn't her fault,' he added, red-faced. 'We had a bust-up so we weren't an item, not then. The bitch said she only done it to make me jealous. But she done it and I seen them both. He put his arm round her and then they was getting in a car. Not his car. It was an old one. He must've got it so no one would know it was him.'

Geraldine listened with growing excitement. If she could find out exactly when and where Max had seen Cassie and Paul

Moore getting in a car together, there was an outside chance they might have been caught on CCTV somewhere.

'Max, I want you to think very carefully. Can you remember when and where you saw Cassie and Paul Moore together? This is very important.'

He nodded. 'You might get them on CCTV, innit.'

Max could only actually recall seeing them together on one occasion, but once could be enough. He told Geraldine he had followed them from the corner of Cassie's street to a pub outside York, always leaving at least one vehicle between them so he wouldn't risk being spotted.

'She'd have done her nut if she'd seen me creeping on her,' he explained.

According to Max's testimony, Cassie and Paul had left the car in a pub car park and hurried off into a densely wooded area. By the time Max parked, they had disappeared. He couldn't remember exactly where the pub was located, but he remembered its name. What was more, he was sure he had seen them on a Saturday evening, three weeks earlier, because that was when he and Cassie had split up. Max and Cassie had reconciled two days later, the same day Cassie had accused Paul Moore of molesting her at school.

'That's why he was so frectic,' Max explained. 'She'd bailed on him, and he was crushed.'

41

ARMED WITH THE INFORMATION Max had given her, Geraldine phoned to speak to the manager of the pub he had mentioned. In explaining the situation, she made no mention of the murder enquiry, but stressed that data on his CCTV could be instrumental in assisting the police with an investigation into a serious crime. When she enquired how far back film of the car park was kept, he told her it was stored electronically, which meant that film from three weeks ago should still be accessible.

'I'd like to know what this is all about,' the pub manager said.

'I'm afraid I can't share that information with you at this point, but I assure you the evidence is needed for an urgent enquiry we're conducting. It's very important we are able to access data recorded by your security camera.'

'I'm not sure I'm prepared to share any information if I don't know what it's needed for.'

'It's nothing you should be concerned about. Our enquiry has nothing to do with the pub itself, unless you choose to obstruct us, in which case I'll have no option but to close the pub and seize all security devices. But that really shouldn't be necessary.'

'Close the pub? You can't do that,' he replied indignantly.

'I'm afraid I'm going to have to if you obstruct us in the course of our enquiry by withholding information.'

'What information?' he spluttered. 'I never said I was withholding anything.'

'My colleagues will be with you shortly. What's it to be? I really don't want to threaten to have to close the pub. It's in no one's interest to disrupt a local business but I need access to that CCTV footage. It's a top priority for the police right now.'

'Wait a minute.' There was a pause before the pub manager came on the line again, sounding curiously animated. 'You said you're Detective Inspector Steel. Steel?'

'That's right.'

'You're working on that murder enquiry, aren't you? I saw you on the news. You're investigating those two kids who were murdered.'

Geraldine suppressed a sigh. 'I'm not at liberty to discuss that, sir. We just need that data, and I hope I can count on your absolute discretion,' she added hopelessly.

'Of course,' he lied. 'You can rely on me.'

They both knew that as soon as the conversation ended, the manager would be telling his staff, and anyone else who would listen, that he was working with the police to catch a killer. There was nothing else for it but to thank the man for his co-operation.

'Of course, of course,' he repeated distractedly. 'Anything to help put that filthy paedo away.'

It wasn't long before the video footage was downloaded at the police station.

Geraldine instructed a VIIDO team to scrutinise every shot of the car park recorded on the Saturday evening when Max claimed to have seen Cassie with Paul Moore.

'They apparently turned up in an old banger, left the car at the pub and walked off into the trees. See if you can spot them arriving and leaving. What we want is a clear shot of their faces so we can be sure who they are. We need to identify both Cassie

Jackson and Paul Moore. We don't know the exact time of arrival and departure, but it was some time on Saturday evening. Start at four o'clock and keep going until you find them.'

'It hopefully shouldn't take too long,' one of the VIIDO team assured her. The officer who had spoken was a stocky woman who seemed to be permanently smiling. With red hair and green eyes and a face smothered in freckles, she grinned affably at Geraldine. 'It's a reasonably short time period to observe and as we're looking for two people getting out of a car, with any luck we should be able to get through fairly quickly.'

'Depending on how busy the car park was that evening,' one of her colleagues added.

The red-haired woman's grin broadened, creasing her chubby cheeks until her eyes all but disappeared. 'Thanks for that,' she called out adding, under her breath, 'Cheerful Charlie.'

'I heard that,' he growled.

The female officer winked at Geraldine who smiled back at her. After that there was nothing for Geraldine to do but wait impatiently to hear confirmation that Paul Moore had been captured on film driving Cassie Jackson to the pub car park and taking her for a walk. It didn't take much imagination to speculate about what they had done in the woods. Later that morning, a member of the VIIDO team summoned Geraldine. Abandoning her search of Cassie's contacts, she hurried to join her red-haired colleague. The image displayed on the screen was grey and blurred. All that could be discerned with any confidence was that two figures emerged from a car.

'Is that Cassie?' Geraldine asked.

She watched as the film was replayed, this time focusing on the back of the girl who climbed out of the obscured car and looked round once. There was only a fleeting glimpse of her face, but it was enough.

'Can we enhance that frame?'

'We can do better than that,' her colleague replied. 'Never mind relying on your eyes, we've matched this frame with the image we have of Cassie Jackson's face. The technology has confirmed beyond any doubt that this is Cassie Jackson. We suspected as much, and now we know. It's watertight.'

They sat watching a film of Cassie in the company of a man who had most probably killed her. They studied the whole sequence, but the man had his back to the camera the whole time.

'What about later? When they return?' Geraldine demanded, fighting to control her frustration at having come so close to proof of Paul Moore's guilt.

He had insisted that he had never seen Cassie out of school. If they could prove that was a lie, they were halfway to a conviction. But the VIIDO officer shook her head.

'No, I'm afraid not.'

'What do you mean?' Geraldine couldn't hide her dismay. 'They must have come back and then he would have been facing towards the camera.'

'They approached from the road. They must have walked in a circle. It was starting to rain, so maybe they didn't want to keep to the muddy paths in the trees.'

She fast forwarded to another sequence. This time, Cassie and her companion approached the car from the opposite direction, both with their backs to the camera. Geraldine swore.

'And this was the only camera?'

Her colleague added. 'We have no image of the man's face. Not even in the rear mirror of his car,' she added, 'or the wing mirrors as he approached. We checked everything. And whatever angle we try, we can't see the registration number.'

They watched the film again. From the back, they could see the edge of what looked like a tartan scarf showing above his coat collar, but even that was unclear when enhanced. Geraldine insisted on viewing the film repeatedly, focusing on a different area each time.

'What's that?' she asked, finally, indicating a mark on the back of the man's coat. 'Could that be on the coat?'

The VIIDO officer confirmed it could be a mark on the coat, a smear of mud or a stain. It was visible both when he was arriving and departing.

'If it's a stain....' Geraldine said softly.

It wasn't much, but it could be enough.

42

It CAME AS NO surprise when Paul denied ever having driven Cassie to a pub in his car.

'What kind of man do you think I am?' he fumed. 'An imbecile as well as a paedophile? Why not call me a rapist as well? Oh, wait, you already have. And a murderer. But seriously, do you really think I'm a complete moron?'

'Don't worry, the police are just eliminating you from their enquiries,' the lawyer said quietly, although they all knew Paul was the main suspect in two murders.

'No, they're not. They want to confuse me into contradicting myself, so they can make me sound unreliable in court.' He turned to face Geraldine. 'That's what's going on here, isn't it? I'm not stupid. I can see perfectly well what you're doing. You think you can push me into making a confession, just to make this stop. Well, you won't pressurise me into confessing because I've done nothing wrong. And you're not going to bamboozle me into changing my account of what happened. I've told you the truth.'

'No one wants you to confess to something you didn't do,' Geraldine replied gently. 'But we need you to be sure you're telling us the whole truth. So I'll ask you again. Did you take Cassie Jackson out in your car? There's no point in lying because we have this on film.'

'If you had incriminating evidence of me on film, you wouldn't need me to say anything. But you can't have proof of something that never happened. Have you found DNA of the murdered girl in my car? You say I drove her to a pub, but have you searched my car for evidence she was a passenger in it? No, you haven't, because you know damn well you're not going to find any proof Cassie was ever in my car. You're just trying to pin this on me because I'm a convenient suspect. But I'm telling you, I never touched that girl, and I never saw her outside school.'

Geraldine displayed an image of the back of a man's beige coat with a small dark patch. Paul glanced at it without reacting.

'For the tape can you describe what you can see in this picture?'

'It's a coat, probably a man's coat, light coloured, long, possibly waterproof. I don't know what you want me to say. It's a coat.'

'Can you confirm that this is an image of your coat?'

'No, I can't confirm that this is an image of my coat because it's not my coat. I haven't got a coat like that.'

'Have you ever worn a coat like this?'

'No. I've never worn a coat like that. I've never bought one, I've never borrowed one, and I've never stolen one.'

'Have you ever worn a coat that looked like this one?'

'No. I just told you. Why would I wear a coat that's not mine?' He screwed his eyes up, peering closely at the image, before adding, 'I've never worn that coat or a coat like it before in my life. I'm sorry if that ruins your attempt to set me up, but that coat isn't mine.'

Waiting until the hair salon where Laura worked had closed, Geraldine went to see her at home and showed her the same image. Laura's response was less convincing than Paul's. Shaking her head vehemently, she muttered that she had never seen that coat before, but she fidgeted in her chair and looked uneasy as she spoke. When she looked down, her fair hair fell forward over her face, casting a shadow over her eyes. Pale and set wide apart, they usually gave her the air of an ingénue. Now they seemed to be concealing a secret in their hidden depths.

Geraldine had brought two constables with her to search the house; they found no trace of a similar coat.

'There's no man's coat at all here,' one of the constables reported after they had looked everywhere, including the garden shed.

That in itself was possibly suspicious, since it suggested that Paul might have thrown his coat away. Laura denied that suggestion fiercely.

'So you're telling me Paul doesn't own a coat at all?' Geraldine asked.

'He wears jackets,' Laura replied. 'He doesn't have a coat. He never seems to feel the cold.'

Geraldine was tempted to reply that he probably felt cold in his cell.

'Are you positive you've never seen the coat in this picture before?' she asked once again.

When Geraldine had first held the image up, Laura had flinched and looked startled in a way that would have been unlikely if she had never seen the coat before. Watching her closely, Geraldine was convinced Paul's wife was lying, but by now Laura had regained her composure and merely shook her head.

'It's just a coat,' she replied. 'I don't ever remember seeing it before but, of course, it's possible someone came to the hair salon in a coat like that one. I can't be expected to recall everyone who comes to the salon, and everything they wear. Clients take their coats off as soon as they come in, and we hang them up. But I sometimes spend time making coffee – we have a coffee machine in a little kitchen in the back – and

221

I'm often occupied with clients and may not have noticed a coat someone took off. That's not to say I've never seen it. I mean, it's just a coat. I might have seen it, or one like it. Probably more than one because it looks like a fairly ordinary coat. It's hardly something I can be expected to recognise after just seeing it once, is it?'

She shrugged, as though remembering a particular coat would be unlikely. But she was talking a lot, and Geraldine had the distinct impression she knew more than she was admitting.

'Do many men visit the hair salon where you work?' she asked.

Laura mumbled that clients were sometimes accompanied by their partners.

'What about outside of work?'

Laura shrugged. 'We haven't been out much lately.'

'And before that?'

'No, I mean I may have seen a coat like that before. Who hasn't? But not so that I'd remember. It looks like a perfectly ordinary coat.' She frowned. 'What's this about, anyway?'

Geraldine made one last attempt to persuade Laura to confide in her. 'Are you absolutely sure you haven't seen Paul in this coat?'

Laura gazed across the table, her eyes stretched wide open in her habitual look of surprise. Geraldine wondered what dark secrets lay concealed behind her innocent expression.

43

As soon as the front door closed behind the detective, Laura burst into tears. She didn't even care that the police might return, like Columbo, to ask just one more question. They probably did that routinely, to see how people reacted after they had gone. But it didn't matter. With a husband in prison, it was only natural that she might cry as soon as she was on her own. That in itself was no admission of guilt. Besides, it was stressful being grilled by the police, even when she had done nothing wrong and had nothing to hide. And on this occasion, she had deliberately concealed a worrying truth. She had been given no choice. If it turned out that she had made a terrible mistake, she could always call the police and claim she had just remembered seeing that coat before. But first she had to talk to someone and there was only one person she could trust absolutely. The man she loved most in all the world had been arrested on a murder charge. She was a mess, outwardly and inwardly. Confused and distressed, she decided it was time to do a little investigating of her own. Whatever the outcome, she would have to deal with it, but she couldn't manage this alone, and she knew only one person to whom she could turn for help.

Having washed her face, and reapplied her eye make-up, she appraised herself in the bathroom mirror. Her eyes, which were her most attractive feature, were puffy from crying. Blue and limpid, they gazed mournfully back at her, glistening with yet more tears. Her skin had taken on an unhealthy pale tinge, and she was afraid she was developing wrinkles on her forehead from frowning so much. Still, considering what she was going through, she didn't look too bad. If anything, she looked more than usually delicate and vulnerable, which wasn't necessarily a disadvantage. She gave a little grimace at her reflection because now, more than ever, she needed to be strong and resourceful, however fragile she appeared. Paul was no longer there to look after her and take care of everything. Thinking about him made her cry again, and she had to force herself to remain calm. She didn't want to have to reapply her make-up. Apart from the time it took, she used expensive brands. The idea that she might have to economise in future almost reduced her to tears yet again, but she forced herself to remain calm.

Grabbing her bag on her way out, she drove to Turnberry Drive, only a mile or so from the care home where her mother now lived – if her mother's near vegetative state could be called living. Pulling up outside the house, she hesitated. It was almost impossible to believe she had been deceived by her husband, but the police were keeping him in custody, which must mean they suspected him of killing those girls. They hadn't seen one another for days, but she was too upset to visit him. By contrast, she had known her stepfather virtually all her life, and didn't doubt his integrity. She felt embarrassed to have entertained a fleeting suspicion of him, even though he would never know what had been going through her mind. But after what had happened with Paul, she wasn't convinced she could trust her own judgement.

There had to be a simple explanation for the picture the detective had shown her, and she had to know what it meant. Taking a deep breath, she marched up to the front door and rang the bell. Hearing it chime, she had a sudden urge to turn and run away. What if her stepfather refused to help her? She would be alone in the world. She clutched her bag close to her chest, as though it could protect her from the future, and shuffled back a few steps. The allegation against Paul, and the subsequent arrest for murder, had unbalanced her. She had to stop allowing her thoughts to wander so fitfully. Since Paul had been arrested, she had honestly believed she might be losing her grip on reality. She had to find something to hold on to in the whirling madness that was threatening to overwhelm her. She would start right now, by turning to her stepfather. He had never let her down before and there was no reason why he should now.

The door opened slowly. John's wary expression lifted into a smile of welcome on seeing her and he greeted her warmly.

'Come in, come in,' he said, as she entered the hall. As soon as he closed the door behind her, she blurted out that Paul had been taken away by the police.

'Well, here I am all on my own now that your mother's gone, and there's you, all on your own, with Paul out of the way, so it's high time you came back home. There's no point in both of us being lonely, when we could be together, is there?'

'Maybe,' she murmured, 'just until Paul comes home.'

'Oh, my poor child.' His smile switched to an expression of concern and she had to struggle to hold back her tears. 'I don't think Paul will be coming home any time soon.'

Involuntarily, she took a step back. 'What makes you say that?'

'Come on, don't be cross with Pappy,' he coaxed her.

She hadn't used that nickname for him since she was a child. When she was twelve, she had decided that 'Pappy' sounded babyish, and so they had discussed what she would like to call him. Her friends called their fathers 'Dad' but she had pointed out that he wasn't actually her father, but her stepfather.

'You can't call your father "Stepdad",' her mother had objected. 'You can call him "Dad", like everyone else does. He's your father, legally and in every other way that matters. He's just not your biological father. That doesn't matter. We're not animals.'

Laura had stuck to her opinion and her stepfather had agreed with her that 'Dad' didn't seem to suit him. In the end, the two of them had agreed that she would call him John because that was his name, and her mother had grudgingly accepted their decision. After all, as Laura had pointed out, it was for her and John to agree on what she should call him.

'I'm not cross with you, John,' she said now, making a point of using his name. 'But there's no point in my moving back here because Paul could be released at any time and I have to be there when he comes home.'

John invited her to share a bottle of wine with him while he made them some supper. Not wanting to put him to any trouble, Laura suggested they go out to eat, but he told her he was planning to cook that evening and it would be just as easy to cook for two as for one.

'I've already got the salmon out,' he explained, as though that somehow decided the matter. 'I can defrost another piece in the microwave. It won't take long. Now, before we do anything else, let's go and sit down and have a glass of wine. You look as though you could do with something to help you relax and I've got a beautiful bottle of white in the fridge which should be nicely chilled. Come on, not another word until we've opened that wine.'

There was no reason to resist, and she was too tired to argue, so she followed him into the living room and accepted a glass of wine without demur.

'Come along, drink up,' he urged her.

He smiled at her and for a moment she completely forgot why she had gone to see him.

'Now,' he said, still smiling, 'you know there's no need for you to go back to that empty house all on your own.'

'Don't be daft,' she replied, returning his smile. 'I mean, that's very kind of you but I can't possibly move in here. It would be far too much upheaval, for both of us, and it would be very temporary. It's really not worth it. I'm sure Paul will be home soon. I only popped round to ask you about something.' She frowned, trying to remember what she had wanted to ask him, but her mind felt foggy.

'No,' he replied, 'you're staying here, with me. I insist.'

She took a gulp of wine and reminded him she was no longer a child. She was a married woman. Perhaps wine on an empty stomach had been reckless in her current emotional state because she suddenly started shaking and felt almost unbearably apprehensive.

'You can't know Paul won't be home soon,' she blurted out. 'That's a horrible thing to say. He's my husband.'

'Not a very good one,' John replied drily. 'Where is he right now? He's left you all on your own in the house.'

She was suddenly so angry she wanted to leave, but when she tried to stand up her legs felt weak. Indignation was making her head spin. She went to put her glass down and missed the table. Seeing wine soaking into the sofa, she began to cry.

'I'm sorry,' she stammered. 'I'm not well. I need to go home. It's the wine. I shouldn't have drunk so much.'

'It's out of the question for you to go home while you're feeling like this,' he replied gently. 'Let me take you upstairs and you can sleep it off. Your room's ready for you.'

She nodded gratefully. John was always there for her when she needed him.

'Thank you,' she murmured. 'Yes, that would be nice.'

All she wanted to do was sleep. John led her across the hallway, and she noticed his beige coat had a small stain on the back. There was something she had wanted to ask him about that coat, but she couldn't recall what it was. She remembered only that it was important. As she struggled to think clearly, the carpet came rushing towards her. Strong hands grabbed her, preventing her from falling. At the same time, she was dimly aware of a voice telling her not to worry.

'You'll be safe here with me,' John said. 'I've been waiting for you.'

She wanted to ask him why he had been waiting for her, but her lips wouldn't move to form the question.

And then she was being carried up the stairs into darkness.

44

GERALDINE WAS FEELING FRUSTRATED and that made her irritable. Unused to having someone on whom to offload her exasperation at home, she snapped at Ian, who grinned. That incensed her even more.

'Whoa,' he laughed, 'if I was a cat I'd be getting a right kicking.'

'Don't exaggerate,' she replied. But she knew he was right. 'I'm sorry, I just lost it for a moment.' She gave a hollow laugh. 'It's not you, it's me.'

'I know, I understand, it's the case. But you mustn't let it get to you.'

She nodded.

'I thought you'd made an arrest?'

'Yes, we have, but what if we've got the wrong man?'

Ian looked faintly concerned. 'Is that likely?'

She didn't answer. Two young girls had been killed and her fear was that there could be more, if it turned out that Paul wasn't guilty after all. No one else seemed to share her misgivings but somehow she wasn't convinced Paul had murdered Cassie and Ella.

'Geraldine, if you've got reservations, you need to follow them up. I don't know how you manage it, but somehow your instincts seem to be virtually infallible.'

'Virtually,' she repeated dully. 'I could be wrong.'

She didn't add that she hoped desperately that she was wrong, and Paul was indeed guilty.

'Are you telling me you're reluctant to stick your head above the parapet? You? Seriously?'

'It's not that I'm nervous about my reputation,' she replied. 'If I was certain we'd arrested the wrong man, of course I'd be yelling it from the rooftops, or at least I'd be arguing the case with the DCI. But I just don't know. It's all such a muddle. And I'm sure Laura Moore was lying when she denied recognising the man who was with Cassie in the pub car park,' she added. 'Which points to Paul being guilty.'

Ian nodded. 'If Paul's wife recognised Cassie's companion, that as good as proves Paul's guilt.'

'But she insists it wasn't Paul.'

'It seems pretty obvious Laura is lying to protect Paul, but if you've got qualms, you need to follow them up,' Ian repeated doggedly.

'I just don't know. I don't really have anything to take to Binita. The thing is, I'm sure Laura recognised the man's coat; that is, I think she did. I don't know. She denied knowing whose it was, and seemed quite convincing, but she definitely reacted when she first saw the picture.'

'There's only one way to find out.'

'I don't think she's going to talk.'

'If she's protecting someone, it has to be Paul, and he's already locked up. And if she didn't actually recognise that coat, then you've just been wasting time on futile speculation.'

Geraldine nodded. 'We've got a team trawling through social media and photograph albums, looking for an image of Paul wearing that coat. That should sort it.'

'Good. Now, let's forget about work for a while, shall we? I don't know about you, but I'm starving. What are we going to eat this evening?'

Geraldine was quiet throughout supper. Several times Ian was forced to repeat what he had said, and in the end he gave up and they ate in silence. When they had finished, she began clearing the table, but Ian reached out and put his hand on hers to stop her.

'I'll do all that,' he said. 'You go.'

'What? Go where?'

Ian smiled at her. 'You know you're not going to rest until you've questioned Laura about her husband's coat. There's not much traffic around at this time, and it's not too late to call on her, so why don't you go now? If nothing else, it will put your mind at rest that you've done all you can.'

Geraldine hesitated, but she could see the sense in what Ian was proposing. 'All right, I'll go and speak to her again, and thank you.'

She kissed him distractedly and hurried off.

As she drove along the Holgate Road to the Moores' house, she rehearsed what she was going to say. Somehow she had to persuade Laura to confide in her, but it was difficult to see how she was going to do that. Arriving outside the house, she still wasn't quite sure how she was going to broach the topic. Geraldine was pretty sure Laura had recognised the coat. That meant she was lying about it to cover up for Paul. If Laura's priority in all this was to protect Paul, then claiming to be concerned for his wellbeing seemed to be the most pragmatic approach to adopt. A direct question like: 'Why did you lie to me?' might possibly startle her into letting something slip, but it was more likely to make her clam up in fright. Appealing to her conscience would probably prove pointless if she was already lying to protect Paul. On balance, Geraldine concluded that saying something along the lines of: 'Whoever committed these murders is sick and needs help,' would be the most helpful approach. By now Laura must realise that her husband had a problem. Offering to help resolve it might be the only way to persuade her to open up.

Primed with what she was going to say, Geraldine approached the front door with a sense of excitement. It was unlikely but just possible that she might be on the brink of cracking this case. She rang the bell and waited, but no one came to the door. She rang again, and again she waited, but still the door remained stubbornly shut. Staring at the peeling paintwork on the door frame, her eyes shifted to the window. Old-fashioned net curtains were closed and there was no light on inside, so when she peered in she couldn't see much. Beside the window was an area of white paint, so faint that it was only visible at close range. Someone had scrubbed the wall until only a palimpsest of the graffiti remained on the brickwork. She rang the bell one last time, although the house had an empty feeling, and she no longer expected the door to open.

The street was motionless under a cloudy night sky, the menacing sense of endless darkness relieved only by the cheering orange glow cast by the street lights. Without them, only the occasional dim gleam from a window was visible, illuminating the interior of a house but shedding no light on the street outside. She shivered, and strode quickly back to her car where she pulled out her phone and called Laura's mobile. Somehow she wasn't surprised that there was no answer. She had a chilling sense that something was amiss, although she couldn't have said what was giving her that feeling. Resolving to return early the next morning, before Laura could have left for work, she went home.

'How did you get on?' Ian asked.

He had finished clearing up and was seated in the living room, his long legs outstretched, his slippered feet resting on a footstool. Geraldine smiled, suppressing her vexation at her wasted trip.

'She wasn't there.'

'Oh well, you tried. There's no need to look so downhearted. It was only a hunch.'

'I'll go back first thing and catch her before she leaves for work.'

'Good idea,' Ian said, but she could tell he wasn't really listening. 'Come here and put your feet up, you look all in,' he said kindly.

In that moment, Geraldine wanted nothing else but to sit on the sofa and snuggle up next to Ian.

'I think something's wrong,' she whispered.

'With two unsolved murders on your hands, I'd say that's a certainty, but I'm sure you'll sort it out tomorrow,' he replied cheerfully.

She closed her eyes, and the warmth of his presence beside her dissipated her tension.

'Yes, tomorrow,' she murmured.

There was always tomorrow. Until there wasn't. There would be no tomorrow for Cassie, or Ella. But Geraldine had tomorrow, and she was going to use it to bring their killer to justice.

'If it's the last thing I do,' she muttered.

'What are you mumbling about?' Ian asked as he bent down to kiss her.

45

GERALDINE LEFT THE FLAT before Ian was stirring the next morning. Kissing him lightly on the top of his head so as not to wake him, she tiptoed from the bedroom and left without stopping for breakfast or even a cup of tea. She would grab something when she arrived at work, but for now she was focused on reaching Laura while she was still at home. Even that early in the day the traffic was building up in the narrow city streets, not helped by interminable roadworks that seemed to proliferate everywhere so that whatever route she took, there were delays. Even so, she reached Laura's house before seven thirty. If she had missed her, Geraldine would have to fight her way through yet more traffic to find her at the hair salon.

Geraldine rang the bell and swore under her breath when the house remained impenetrable. After waiting for longer than seemed reasonable, she went back to the car and phoned Laura. There was no answer. With a sigh, Geraldine set off for the salon. It didn't open until ten. Instead of spending yet more time stuck in traffic, driving to the police station and back again, she went and sat in a nearby café. Breathing deeply to calm her vexation, she attempted to relax with a large decaf full fat latte and a croissant which was slightly stale even at that time in the morning. It must have been left over from the day before, but she didn't mind. She was hungry enough to enjoy it, fresh or stale. Feeling invigorated after her unexpectedly enjoyable breakfast, she made her way along the street to the salon and arrived just after ten. It was still closed. She could see movement inside and banged on the door. After a moment, a woman scurried over to let her in. She had luxurious, long blonde curls and her flawless make-up was thick, with obviously fake eyelashes and lips that looked unnaturally full.

'Hello, Madam,' she greeted Geraldine with an ingratiating smile. 'I don't think we've seen you in here before.' As she was speaking, she introduced herself as Gina and gave Geraldine's hair an appraising glance. 'A trim, is it? Or do you fancy highlights? They can be so effective on black hair, you'd be surprised.'

Just for a moment, Geraldine allowed herself to be seduced by the stylist's easy professional patter. She wished she had the time to slouch in a comfortable chair for an hour or more, sipping coffee and glancing through magazines while someone else washed her hair and snipped and styled it for her. She was even tempted by the idea of having highlights. There wasn't much else a stylist could do with her cropped hair. Breathing in an enticing hint of a sweet scent, she sighed. But she wasn't there to be pampered. She had a job to do. With a start, she pulled herself back from the luxury of even a moment's relaxation.

'I'm not here about my hair,' she said bluntly.

Deciding against revealing her identity straightaway, for fear of frightening Laura off, she asked to speak to her.

'Laura?' the woman replied, her expression momentarily twisting into a scowl. 'I'm afraid Laura's not in today,' she went on, resuming her professional smile. 'But I've got Sam, one of our most experienced stylists. She's an absolute wizard with short hair.' She turned to summon the girl, but Geraldine stopped her.

'No, it's Laura I need to see, not anyone else. I'm not here to have my hair done,' she reiterated. 'I'm not a customer.'

'Not a client?' Gina replied, placing deliberate emphasis on the word 'client'. Her smile had gone altogether now and her voice was cold. 'Thank you for calling by, but we're not interested in anything you're offering. Now, if you don't mind, we have a very busy day ahead of us. We're snowed under with bookings. I was going to try and fit you in, as a favour, as you haven't been here before, but we couldn't necessarily have seen you today. As I said, we're very busy.'

Geraldine doubted they were very busy at ten o'clock, but as Gina was speaking, a client came in. Perhaps Saturday was a busy day for the hair salon after all. The stylist turned to greet the newcomer.

'I'm sorry,' Geraldine said, 'but I need to speak to Laura.'

Gina gave a disapproving sniff. 'You can wait,' she said grudgingly. 'But I can't offer you a seat.'

'Thank you. I'll come back. I've got a car outside.'

The other woman's scowl deepened. 'You can't park along here. It's restricted parking during the week. You'll get a ticket.'

Ignoring the warning, Geraldine went and sat in her car. As she waited, she trawled through Laura's social media pages, looking for contacts they hadn't yet approached, but she didn't seem to have many local friends. She was in touch with some schoolfriends but none of them lived nearby and several had moved abroad. After five minutes, she returned to the salon where Gina glared warily at her.

'What time are you expecting Laura?'

Gina shook her head. 'She should have been here by ten. She hasn't called.' She frowned. 'It's not like her, but she's been flaky recently.'

'Do you know where she might be?'

Gina leaned forward and spoke softly. 'Now I get it. You're with the police, aren't you? Only we heard there was trouble with her husband.' She glanced around to see if anyone was listening. 'He's been arrested, hasn't he? Poor lamb. What it must be like for her, finding out her husband is a monster. I'm not surprised she hasn't shown her face in here. When you speak to her, tell her to come back to work. We're all on her side and she's going to need our support. We won't ask her about what happened and if she doesn't want to talk about it, that's fine. We just want to know she's all right. And we don't want to lose her. She's very popular with our regulars. Tell her, won't you?'

Geraldine nodded. 'If she comes in, please ask her to contact me at once.' She handed over a card with her number on it. 'Or you can call me yourself and let me know she's back. I really need to speak to her as soon as possible. It's very important.'

The manager of the salon nodded anxiously. Walking out of the salon, Geraldine was more convinced than ever that something wasn't right. She had to find Laura.

46

GERALDINE DECIDED TO SPEAK to Laura's mother, who was in a care home. Her records suggested she might not be much help, but it was worth visiting her in case she was able to tell Geraldine where her daughter might be. The care home wasn't far from the city centre, in the Acomb district, just off the A59. Geraldine drew up in the car park of a purpose-built square redbrick building with rows of small windows on the first and second floors, and large picture windows on the ground floor. Geraldine just gave her name without mentioning the purpose of her visit. She was buzzed in by a small woman with tightly curled fair hair, who asked her to sign in and enquired whom she had come to see. Geraldine explained she was there to have a word with Angela Walters. The receptionist looked faintly puzzled.

'Angela Walters?' she repeated. 'What relationship are you to her?'

Geraldine explained that although she didn't actually know the woman in question, it was nevertheless important that she speak with her.

'I just want to ask her a few questions. It's about her daughter, Laura Moore.'

The receptionist interrupted her. 'I'm afraid there's no point,' she said with an air of finality.

'If you don't mind, I'd like to see her and assess that for myself.'

The receptionist hesitated and her hair twitched, although her head didn't appear to move. It seemed she took her sentry duties very seriously, and was unused to being challenged. Her tone suddenly brusque, she repeated that she wasn't authorised to let Geraldine see Angela.

'I'm afraid you're not on the list,' she said. 'Here at the Golden Years Care Home we take good care of every individual, and make sure we protect our residents from anyone they or their next of kin haven't put on our list. I'm very sorry, Miss Steel, but your name doesn't appear on the visitors' list for Angela Walters. If her husband consents to you visiting her, that's another matter.'

'Couldn't you ask Angela for me? I'll only take a minute of her time.'

'I'm afraid that's not possible.'

Concealing her annoyance, Geraldine showed her identity card and asked to speak to the manager of the home.

'I'm afraid the answer's still the same, whoever you are. You can speak to anyone on the staff, but there's no way you can talk to Angela. There's really no point.'

'I'd like a word with the manager,' Geraldine repeated.

The manager of the home was a cheery woman with an Irish accent. Behind a façade of ebullience, Geraldine detected a sense of frustration as though the woman was subject to constant harassment.

'And how can we help you, Inspector?' she asked, leading Geraldine into her office.

An untidy pile of papers lay strewn across the desk, along with a mug of coffee and a half-eaten egg sandwich. Although the wrapper had been folded back over the top of it, the redolence of boiled egg pervaded the room. The manager didn't seem to notice the smell. Taking the proffered seat, Geraldine explained the reason for her visit.

The manager nodded. 'I see. I think you misunderstood what Lily was trying to tell you. The fact is, there really is no point in your speaking to Angela. She won't be able to reply and we don't think she understands anything we say.' She sighed. 'She suffered a series of paralysing strokes. Even if she had any inkling about what you said to her, she wouldn't be able to answer your questions. We look after her as well as we can, but all we can really do is try to make her comfortable. Not all of our residents require such constant care,' she added brightly. 'We lay on plenty of activities for them, to keep them occupied and happy. But it's all wasted on Angela, I'm afraid. She's in a permanent vegetative state and the chance of recovery is slim.'

Geraldine had read the report on Angela, but had not realised the extent of the damage caused by her strokes.

'It's actually her daughter I want to talk to, but we're having difficulty locating her.'

The manager shook her head. 'Lorna?'

'Laura,' Geraldine corrected her gently.

'Yes, of course, Laura. We haven't seen Laura for a while, I'm afraid. Not for a few months, at least. We'd love her to come and see her mother, of course, but that's up to the individual relatives, and some people find it too distressing when close family members don't recognise them.' She paused. 'We don't judge them for it, but it's a pity for everyone concerned. I'm so sorry we can't help you. I hope Laura's not in any trouble?' she added, without much curiosity.

'No, no,' Geraldine hurried to reassure her. 'It's just a routine enquiry. Something she might be able to help us with.'

The manager frowned. 'Well, perhaps Mr Walters can help you. He's very close to his daughter. He used to come and visit Angela regularly. He's a lovely lovely man.' She sighed. 'He came every day when she was first admitted here, and he used to sit talking to her. He did everything he could for her, but nothing he did made any difference. In the end I think he just couldn't bear to see her like that. We haven't seen him for a while either.' She shook her head and sighed. 'I always think it's a pity when family members can't face seeing what their loved ones have become, but it's understandable and, like I said, we don't judge them for it. I'm sure everyone does their best and these are trying circumstances, very trying. And poor Mr Walters did what he could for her. He was a family minded man but he couldn't take the pain of seeing what she'd become. It takes a very special kind of person to care for people in Angela's condition. We have a marvellous team here, shouldering burdens that even the most dedicated of families can't bear. Our carers are the unsung heroes of society, and I can assure you the care our residents receive here is second to none.'

Geraldine knew that Laura had a stepfather who had married her mother before Laura was two, her biological father having died a few months before she was born. Her stepfather having adopted her, he was now technically her father. She thanked the manager, and departed after looking in on Angela briefly. As the manager had told her, there was no point in trying to have a conversation with Laura's mother, but hopefully her father would be able to help Geraldine find his daughter.

47

AT FIRST LAURA DIDN'T know where she was. Coming out of a deep sleep, she opened her eyes several times, blinking to make sure they were actually open in the darkness. Gradually she became aware of a faint patch of light that seemed to coruscate in the distance, making her feel queasy. It reminded her of the feeling she once had on a ferry across the Channel on a turbulent sea. She closed her eyes and an afterimage of the square patch of light faded slowly.

'What is it?' she wondered. Her voice hovered in her mind. It seemed to echo in a vast empty space inside her head, as though her thoughts had a physical presence inside her brain. She wondered what would happen to them if they escaped. Outside her head, where would they go? 'Where am I?' she asked and again her voice sounded distant and incorporeal. The words slid indistinguishably into each other, making no sound. She realised that she wasn't uttering words at all, but emitting a muffled groaning that started in her chest and spread upwards to her head.

Overwhelmed by the effort it had cost her to try and speak, she closed her eyes and began to drift away. She wanted to surrender to sleep, but felt too sick to let go. All at once, she thought she was going to vomit. She sat up abruptly and felt something dragging on her, holding her down. Surprised, she stared down at her hands. In the darkness she felt, rather than saw, bands enclosing her wrists, pressing against the bony excrescences and digging into her flesh. Bewildered, she stared into darkness, straining to see. Then she opened her mouth and released a thin frail sound that spun round and round inside her brain sending sparks of light into the blackness. She understood that she was dreadfully ill and possibly dying, but it didn't seem important. Nothing mattered any more as she lay back and waited for darkness to engulf her.

With a click, a light came on, startling her awake. Raising herself up on her elbows, she saw a light bulb suspended from the wooden rafters on the ceiling, its brightness searing her brain. Screwing up her eyes against the glare, she looked around. Below wooden slats overhead, the walls looked rough and uneven, scored by marks left by a trowel that had slapped on plaster carelessly. Cobwebs hung from the rafters, thick with dust and swinging slightly in the current of air from the opening door. There was one small window, through which she had seen light shimmering when she had first woken. It seemed like hours ago. She wondered how long she had been lying there, only half conscious. Outside the single square pane of the window, everything now looked black.

Swivelling her eyes, she saw John standing by the light switch he had just flicked on. His outline was fuzzy but she could vaguely make out his smile, solicitous as ever.

'How are you feeling?' he asked, moving closer and looking down at her.

She swallowed a taste of bile but it persisted, stinging her throat and making her gag. 'What's happening?' she asked. Her voice came out in a mumble and she thought of her mother and suspected she was similarly afflicted. 'Have I had a stroke?' Her tongue felt as though it was clamped to her bottom jaw.

Her arms had been secured, but she could move them as far as the restraining bands would allow, and she could move her legs. That had never happened to her mother, who had been rendered immobile by her first stroke. Her head was throbbing painfully, and she felt confused. Gradually she became aware of her surroundings and felt, rather than saw, that she was lying on a bare mattress on a dusty wooden floor.

'Where am I? What's happening to me?' she asked but her tongue was like a lump of jelly and wouldn't move to form the words. 'Why can't I speak?' A slurred sound issued from her lips.

'Don't try to talk,' her stepfather said gently, squatting down on the floor next to her mattress. 'And don't worry. You're safe now. I'm here to look after you. I'll take care of everything. Just rest.'

She wanted to cry out that she didn't feel safe. She didn't want John to look after her. She wanted to go home. But he stood up and walked over to the door.

'I'll come back soon,' he said. 'Do you want anything?'

'Yes, I want to go home,' she cried out, desperately struggling to form the words clearly, but all that she could manage was a weird strangled cry.

The light clicked off, flooding the room with darkness once more. A few seconds later she heard the door close and the key turn in the lock. A memory flashed into her head from when she was a teenager. She had begged her parents to let her have a lock on her bedroom door, insisting that she wanted some privacy in her own room. She knew that her mother snooped in there while she was at school. She had set up a little trap, fixing a hair from the door to the frame each morning, to discover whether the door had been opened in her absence. She had returned from school one day to find the hair broken. Her mother had fiercely denied it, of course, but they had both known Laura's accusations were justified. Eventually, against her mother's wishes, her father had installed a lock on her door. Laura's delight had been short lived. Her mother had continued to spy on her, and Laura had realised there was more than one key to the lock on her bedroom door. Of course, her mother had denied that too. Laura hadn't gained herself any privacy at all, despite having won the argument.

More than four years had passed since she had moved out of her parents' home and she hadn't given the lock on her door there another thought, until now. Helplessly, she began to cry. She wanted to ask John what was going on, but he had disappeared. All she could think was that he must have tied her wrists together to stop her from falling over, but why had she been so unsteady on her feet that he couldn't trust she would be safe on her own? And how would tying her hands together help her, anyway? Perhaps she had been horribly drunk. She struggled to remember what she had been doing before she fell asleep, and to work out where she was, and why John was there with her. But he had vanished and she was no longer sure he had ever been there.

Still trying to work out what had happened, she felt a wave of exhaustion wash over her and closed her eyes. John had told her to rest and that was good advice. She would feel better after a long sleep, and then she would insist he untie her and explain exactly what was going on. Her worst fear had always been that, like her mother, she would suffer a stroke. She hoped that hadn't happened to her. Not yet. She was too young. But something was wrong. When she woke up, she would find out what was going on, but for now she just wanted to sleep.

48

HAVING LEARNED NOTHING FROM Laura's mother, Geraldine decided to visit her stepfather and see if he had any ideas about where his daughter might be. Although he had given up visiting his wife, he lived only just over a mile from the home where she was living. It was a sunny day, and Geraldine was tempted to leave the car at the care home, but she decided against it because she couldn't really afford the time. It was a pity, she thought, as she drove slowly away from the home. It really would have been a lovely day for a walk. She sighed. She had given up so much to pursue her career, and where had all the little sacrifices actually got her? True, she had helped to track down quite a number of vicious criminals and, in her own small way, had helped to make the world a safer place. But if she wasn't doing it, the job would still be done. She was one tiny cog in the machinery of the police force.

Binita had taken the place of Geraldine's former detective chief inspector, who had taken early retirement due to stress. At the time, Geraldine had greeted the news of her senior officer's departure with dismay, but the investigation they were working on had carried on regardless. No one was indispensable. Geraldine wondered if she had been misguided in dedicating herself to her career. Dismissing her depressing thoughts, she parked in Turnberry Drive where John Walters lived, and turned her attention to finding Laura.

People rarely vanished without leaving a trace; someone must know where Laura had gone. Her father had to be a likely candidate to help in the search. Effectively a widower with a wife, John Walters was also trapped by Angela's condition. Unable to mourn her loss, he was probably struggling to cope with his situation, even though he was free to carry on with his life, should he ever wish to do so. He lived in a narrow detached house in a pleasant street just across the A59 from the care home. Geraldine parked nearby and approached the house, hoping this visit wouldn't prove as futile as her previous one. There was no reason why Laura's father would have any idea where she might be at any time. But given the problems Laura was currently experiencing, it was possible she had confided in her father, especially since she obviously couldn't talk to her mother.

She rang the bell, and a few moments later a deep voice called out, wanting to know who was there.

'Hang on a moment,' the voice replied when Geraldine had announced herself.

A few minutes later, the door was opened by a middle-aged man. He had clearly taken good care of himself, and looked as though he worked out. His dark hair was neatly cut and he was clean shaven. Geraldine knew that he worked as a financial advisor, and her initial impression was that he was probably very good at his job. Something about his neat bespectacled appearance inspired confidence. But she hadn't come to see him for financial advice.

'Yes?' he enquired with a faintly puzzled smile. 'Can I help you?'

'I'm looking for your daughter,' Geraldine replied.

'My daughter? Laura?' he repeated, looking startled. 'What do you mean? What do you want?'

'Please, this is nothing to worry about and I'm sure she's fine. But we'd like to ask her a few questions about an investigation we think she might be able to help us with, and we haven't been able to locate her.'

'This is about that husband of hers, isn't it? He's got himself in trouble, I hear.'

Geraldine decided to pursue this point as Paul's father-in-law had broached the subject. 'What have you heard about it?'

John shook his head. 'Only that he was in a spot of bother with an underage girl. But, of course, I don't need to tell you that.' He laughed mirthlessly. 'Between you and me, I wasn't that surprised,' he went on, more seriously.

'Why not?'

He hesitated and then continued in a low voice, as though he were sharing a secret. 'I never really took to him. I didn't trust him the very first time I met him, and I'm a good judge of character. Not that I ever suspected him of doing anything criminal. Nothing like that. I never tried to dissuade my daughter from marrying him, but he wouldn't have been my choice for her. I just hoped she would be happy with him, and I believe she actually was. Until now, of course. Poor Laura. She must be devastated.'

'Do you know where your daughter is?'

John glanced at his watch. 'At work, I should imagine,' he replied. 'She has a job at a hairdresser's in the city centre. She's a stylist,' he added with a touch of paternal pride. 'They tell me she's very good.'

Geraldine told him that Laura had not turned up at work that day. 'We wondered if you know of any friends she might be visiting?'

'No one that I can think of. She seemed to think Paul was enough for her.' He smiled sourly. 'Of course, she has her colleagues at work, but she's rather drifted away from her schoolfriends. Most of them have moved away from the area. Once they get married, it's never the same, is it? They all go off and live their own lives. She doesn't confide in me any more, not like when she was younger.' He scowled and gave an apologetic shrug. 'I don't keep tabs on her.'

'So you have no idea where she is right now?'

'Well, I would imagine she's upset about all the trouble Paul's in,' he replied. 'I suppose she's probably at home, feeling sorry for herself. Would you like me to give you her number?'

'Thank you, but we have her contact details.'

'Yes, yes, of course, I'm sure you do. You knew where to find me, didn't you?' He smiled. 'It's reassuring to know the police are so efficient, especially these days.'

'These days?'

'Yes, there is so much of it about. All this crime, I mean. We could do with seeing more of you on the streets, you know. A visible presence. It would make everyone feel safer, except the criminals, of course, and hopefully enough of them would be deterred by seeing more police out on patrol to lower the crime figures.'

A faint mewling sound reached them from inside the house.

'Oh, that cat,' John said, taking a step back and reaching for the door. 'I was about to feed her when you rang the bell and now she's growing impatient. I'd better go and see to her.'

'Yes, well, thank you very much for your time, Mr Walters. And if you do hear from Laura, please tell her I'm trying to contact her. Here's my direct number.' She handed him a card. 'I really would like to speak to her as soon as possible.'

'Yes, of course, although frankly you're more likely to speak to her before I do,' he replied as he closed the door.

A team were tasked with tracing all of Laura's friends from school, but so far no one had given them any indication as to where the missing woman might be found. It was a lengthy process that made Geraldine frantic with impatience, but there was nothing she or anyone else could do to speed up the process. Eventually she went home but she slept badly that night, constantly alert for a phone call that never came, bringing her news of Laura. When she did manage to doze off, she had strange dreams of wading through knee-high mud, searching for a body no one could find. She woke up feeling, if anything, more tired than she had been before she fell asleep.

49

WHILE SHE WAS WAITING for the result of the interviews with Laura's friends, colleagues and acquaintances, which had so far yielded no helpful information at all, Geraldine decided to question Paul again, and went along to the custody suite. The custody sergeant was a stocky officer with a broad face like a bulldog. With the insouciance of an officer close to retirement, he smiled easily at Geraldine and made an unoriginal quip about how they couldn't keep meeting like that, to which she gave an equally lighthearted response.

'You know there's nothing I'd like better than to stand here chatting, but I need to talk to one of your guests.'

'Lucky man,' the sergeant replied.

Geraldine laughed. 'Not that lucky.'

She found Paul lying on his bunk, staring at the ceiling. He sat up as she entered the cell and gazed at her with a mournful expression. He hadn't shaved and his eyes looked dull, as though he had been sedated. His shoulders drooped, his back was bowed, and all his energy seemed to have drained away. It seemed almost inconceivable that he had ever been capable of facing a class of teenagers.

'We don't want to worry you,' Geraldine said, 'but we can't find Laura.'

'What do you mean, you can't find her?' he asked in a flat voice, showing no sign of interest.

'She didn't go to work yesterday, and she's not at home. Her

251

father has no idea where she is, and her mother –' Geraldine broke off with a shrug. 'I take it you've seen her mother?'

'Angela has no idea about anything,' Paul said. 'There's no point in trying to get anything out of her.'

'We think Laura has probably just run away from all the pressure, but we haven't been able to find her. Where do you suppose she might have gone? Only I'd really like to speak to her.'

'I don't believe Laura's run off. That's not her style. If anything, she'd lock herself in the house and refuse to come out. She wouldn't go away anywhere by herself. That's not something she would do.'

Geraldine went through a list of Laura's friends and acquaintances with Paul to make sure they hadn't missed anyone out, but he had no new suggestions to give her. He claimed to be as baffled as Geraldine was concerning Laura's whereabouts.

'You don't suppose –' he began, and broke off with a grimace. 'Do you think something's happened to her?'

'She's probably fine. It would hardly be surprising if she wanted to escape from all the media attention. I know you said that's not something she'd normally do, but these are not normal circumstances.'

'With her husband accused of rape and murder, you mean?' he replied, with a flash of bitterness.

Geraldine didn't answer and he subsided back into apathy.

'Well, either Paul doesn't know his wife as well as he thinks he does, or she's been at home all this time and not answering the door,' Binita said, when Geraldine went to her to share her concerns.

'Is it time we took a look inside their house?' Geraldine suggested, and the detective chief inspector agreed.

It was easy to find the key in Paul's personal effects and before long Geraldine was on her way to his house, with a search team on alert in case they were needed. Once again there was no response when she rang the bell. While she was waiting, a next-door neighbour called out from her front step. She was a stout woman in late middle age, with a ruddy face and frizzy grey hair.

'He's not there,' she said, crossing her fleshy arms and staring at Geraldine with a truculent air. 'He's been arrested for murdering them two girls. It's been on the news.' She paused, screwing up her eyes and peering at Geraldine to see the effect her words produced. 'All these years we've been living here, and we had no idea we were living right next door to a murderer!'

There was little point in trying to remain anonymous. Pulling out her identity card, Geraldine explained that she was looking for Laura.

'She was in on it too, was she?' the woman asked, making a tutting sound. She shook her head. 'Well, I always thought there was something funny about her. All hoity toity she was. I never thought her hair was natural blonde. Well, good riddance to the pair of them, that's what I say.'

There was little point in asking if the neighbour knew where Laura was, but Geraldine tried anyway.

'Done a runner, has she?' the woman asked. 'Well, I hope you catch her.'

'She's not a suspect,' Geraldine said, but the woman would have none of it.

On balance, Geraldine decided there was no point in asking the neighbour to contact her if Laura returned. She was as likely to rush over and tell Laura the police were after her to charge her with murder. She turned away and rang the bell one last time before letting herself into the Moores' house.

'Hello!' she shouted from the hall. 'Police! I just want to talk to you, Laura. Can you come here, please?' She waited but there was no response. 'I've been to see Paul,' she called out.

Still there was no sign of Laura in the house. She appeared to have gone out in a hurry because when Geraldine walked around she saw dirty plates in the sink, and the curtains had been left open. Possibly Laura had just popped out intending to return soon. But whatever the reason for her disappearance, there was nothing obvious to suggest where she might have gone. Having completed a circuit of the house and checked outside in the garden, Geraldine summoned the search team. She waited while they went through the house looking for evidence of where Laura might have gone, and a technical officer checked her laptop. They drew a blank. It looked as though Laura had just gone out and not returned.

So now they were faced with looking for two people: they were no closer to identifying the man who had driven Cassie to the pub, and they couldn't find Laura. Geraldine had a feeling the two issues were somehow linked, but she couldn't work out the connection.

'She must have a friend we don't know about,' Binita said.

But Laura's social media accounts had been thoroughly searched without throwing up any new leads. All her contacts had been visited by local officers and no one was able to tell the police where Laura had gone.

'We'll have to speak to them all again,' Geraldine said. 'Someone must know what's happened to her. Someone's lying.'

Binita wanted an appeal made to the public, and Geraldine set that up immediately. 'It's important we find Laura,' she announced via the media who were broadcasting the petition. 'We think she may be in danger.'

'Let's hope she's just run away from all the pressure and turns up safe and sound soon,' Ariadne said.

'Yes,' Geraldine agreed. 'Wouldn't it be great if she just walked through the door of the police station and said she'd taken a trip to the coast to look at the sea and gather her thoughts?'

'I can't see there's anything to worry about. I mean, she must have just gone off somewhere because we haven't been able to find her car,' Ariadne pointed out.

Geraldine did her best to share Ariadne's optimism. Details of Laura's car had been circulated to every police station in the country, but so far there had been no sighting of it. Geraldine suspected Laura wouldn't be easy to trace, and wondered what secrets she was hiding that had led her to run away.

'My guess is she's freaked out by having to lie to give Paul an alibi, and she's done a runner,' Ariadne said.

Geraldine pondered that for a moment before agreeing that Ariadne was probably right.

'But you think there's more to it, don't you?' Ariadne asked, looking shrewdly at Geraldine, who shrugged.

'People don't just vanish overnight without careful planning.'

'So you think her disappearance was premeditated?'

'I don't know what to think,' Geraldine admitted.

50

SOMETHING WAS BOTHERING GERALDINE. She scrolled through all her notes yet again, but couldn't find anything she had missed previously. Casting her mind back to her pointless visit to the care home, she remembered what the manager had told her. According to John, he hadn't seen much of his daughter since her marriage, yet Geraldine distinctly recalled the manager saying that Laura and her father were close. She decided it might be worth speaking to John again, but first she went to question Paul, hoping he could clear up her confusion about his father-in-law.

Paul was taciturn and barely glanced at Geraldine when she entered his cell, but he looked up when she told him her reason for wanting to speak to him.

'John?' he repeated. 'I wondered when you'd cotton on to him.'

'What do you mean? Is there anything we ought to know about him?'

'Oh, it's nothing really. Nothing you'd be interested in.'

'Tell me anyway.'

'He's just a bit of a creep, that's all. In a way it's understandable, given that his wife's as good as dead.' He grunted.

'What's understandable?'

'That he'd be so protective of Laura. It was like getting past Fort Knox seeing her to begin with. But she made up her mind and that was that. There wasn't anything he could do to stop us getting married. To be fair, he gave her up with good grace, in the end.'

'You'd describe him as overprotective of her?' Geraldine repeated.

Paul nodded. 'A lot of fathers are like that,' he said.

Thoughtfully, Geraldine went to find Binita.

'He told me I was likely to speak to her before he did,' she told Binita. 'He implied that he didn't see his daughter very often. He said the relationship was never the same after she was married and living her own life independently of her parents.' She paused and consulted her notes. 'She doesn't confide in me any more and I don't keep tabs on her,' she read aloud. 'That's how he put it, which sounds a bit odd, doesn't it? Him telling me he doesn't keep tabs on her. But the manager of Angela's care home told me Laura and John are still very close, which is also odd, given that he claims he hardly ever sees her now she's married.'

'I don't see anything odd about it,' Binita replied. 'In fact it all sounds fairly normal to me. I dare say the manager was trying to be nice about Angela's family, that's all. It's not her place to complain about relatives who don't visit. It sounds to me as though he and Laura grew apart once her mother went into care. Who knows how that affected both of them? That's probably very common, don't you think? In any case he's not Laura's real father, is he?'

'He adopted her as a baby so yes, I'd say he absolutely is her real father.'

Geraldine kept her tone level, and Binita nodded, perhaps recalling that Geraldine herself had been adopted at birth.

'Yes, of course,' Binita said. 'But it's not unusual for fathers and daughters to grow apart once a woman gets married.'

'Yes, that's true,' Geraldine agreed. 'But Paul told me John was overprotective of Laura –'

'Well, we have Paul Moore safely in custody, and hopefully he'll soon get as fed up as we are, and be prepared to co-operate with us. He's a stubborn man, but he'll break in the end. They all do. And once we've got a confession from him, that'll be that. The sooner he caves in the better, in my opinion. I start to get nervous when things drag on like this. We can't hold him any longer, but I'm sure if we put pressure on him he'll tell us what happened, and we can get this over with. I'll let you lead the interview.' She smiled at Geraldine. 'You've done good work on this case, and you should be feeling very pleased with yourself. We're nearly there, Geraldine, and that's partly thanks to your efforts.'

Geraldine wracked her brains, but could find nothing to convince Binita that they might have arrested the wrong man. She wasn't even sure about it herself. That evening she went home, still feeling uneasy.

'You look like you've lost a pound and found a penny,' Ian said. 'What's up? Maybe egg and chips will cheer you up? What's it to be? Fried or scrambled?'

After supper, Ian asked her what was on her mind. 'I can see you're bothered about something. It might help to talk about it. If I've done something to upset you, I'd rather you spit it out.'

'What?' she replied in surprise. 'No, no, it's nothing like that. It's nothing to do with you. I mean, you haven't done anything wrong. Quite the opposite, you've been wonderful.'

'Why are you so distant with me, then? Come on, tell me what's on your mind.'

With a sigh, Geraldine caved in and admitted that she couldn't stop thinking about the case she was working on. She was relieved when Ian seemed pleased to hear that she had been thinking about work.

'I was afraid you were punishing me for something I'd done, or forgotten to do,' he admitted.

Geraldine almost retorted that she wasn't his ex-wife, but she held the words back. Clearly it would take time for Ian to learn that she would never play games with his emotions, whether out of pique or resentment.

'No, no, if I was upset with you, I'd tell you,' was all she said about that. 'No, it's just this case.'

'Do you want to talk about it? You know I'm a good listener.' He smiled kindly.

Geraldine explained the contradiction between what the manager of the care home had told her and John's claim about his relationship with his daughter.

'It just doesn't seem to fit. The manager was clear that they were close, but he said they weren't. Something about it doesn't feel right. And then Paul told me that John used to be overprotective of Laura. Binita thinks it's all perfectly normal, and I suppose she's right, but –' She sighed. 'Why do I get a bad feeling about all this?'

'It's shocking when teachers turn out to be corrupt,' Ian said. 'But perhaps your suspect isn't the man everyone expected him to be, given his career. We want people who work with vulnerable youngsters to be honest and moral.'

Geraldine thought about this. Not everyone had held a high opinion of Paul. His father-in-law hadn't seemed surprised by Cassie's allegation of serious misconduct. She told Ian what Laura's father had said about distrusting Paul right from the start.

'He told me he's a good judge of character, not that that means anything. But it's understandable he might not have got on too well with Paul. Fathers-in-law and sons-in-law can have an emotionally tricky relationship.'

'Why don't you press him to tell you more about his relationship with his son-in-law? He might let something slip that will help you to nail Paul.'

'Yes. Actually, that's not a bad idea.'

Ian's smile broadened.

The following morning, Geraldine rang John's bell early.

'Wait a minute. I'm just getting dressed,' he called out when she gave him her name.

She seemed to be waiting for a long time, but at last the door opened. To her surprise, John seemed genuinely pleased to see her. He invited her in but she told him she couldn't stay.

'No, of course, you must be busy. So, how can I help you? I take it you've found Laura? That's good to know. I hope she's all right. Poor thing, she must be very disturbed by everything that's happened.'

'I wanted to ask you about your relationship with her husband,' she replied curtly.

He looked surprised. 'My relationship with him?' He hesitated. 'I never thought he was right for Laura, but that's all I've got to say about him, really.'

Geraldine suspected he was just a stereotypically possessive father, uneasy with his daughter's choice of partner, but she prompted him to tell her more.

'Frankly, the man's a narcissist,' John said. 'Maybe it's something to do with his being a teacher, but I always felt he spoke down to Laura. He's big headed and bombastic, the kind of person who can never be wrong. You know the type. But as for his being a paedophile, and a murderer, of course that's absolutely shocking. I've been reading up on the case online and it beggars belief what that man got up to. How is Laura? I tried to phone her to ask her how she's coping but she didn't want to speak to me.' He sighed. 'I really wish we'd been closer but somehow, when her mother fell ill, everything in my life fell apart. It must have been hard for Laura as well, but she had Paul to support her. I was struggling to come to terms with what happened to Angela, and I'm afraid I didn't think about anyone else. But I must tell you, I had a bad feeling about Paul all along.' He shook his head sadly. 'I always felt there was something off about him. Turns out I was right.'

'Did he ever say or do anything that made you suspect he might be, as you put it, "off"?' Geraldine asked.

John shook his head and a curious expression crossed his face.

If Geraldine had blinked at that precise moment she would have missed an expression of triumph.

'Nothing specific,' he replied. 'I wish I could be more helpful. And I wish I'd spoken out sooner. I should have tried to stop her marrying him, but what could I do?'

Geraldine suspected he knew more than he was telling her. There was nothing she could do but thank him and leave, feeling worried. As soon as she could, she spoke to Binita, who seemed irritated by her request.

'I understand you want to investigate John but so far, other than being Laura's father, we have nothing to suggest he's involved in anything of interest. We need something more definite than that before I can request a search warrant. Think about it, Geraldine,' she added more kindly. 'The manager of the care home was just trying to reassure you. Her focus would be on convincing you that the care home are doing a good job with Angela. That's all. I suggest you focus your attention on finding evidence that will help us convict Paul Moore. That's where we need to be putting our energies, so let's get on with that, shall we?' she concluded slightly brusquely.

Geraldine nodded and withdrew. She wasn't sure enough of her position to stand up to her senior officer, but she was privately resolved to find sufficient evidence to persuade the detective chief inspector to look into John Walters.

51

THE NEXT MORNING, GERALDINE returned to Turnberry Drive. In the daylight, her unease had settled, and she no longer suspected John of hiding anything. Everyone she had spoken to seemed to think it was natural for a father to be concerned about losing his daughter to a son-in-law, and to resent being ousted by a younger man. Ariadne had been quite forthcoming on the subject.

'And it wasn't only my father,' she concluded. 'My mother treated him with blatant suspicion. More than suspicion, she told him outright he wasn't good enough for me. Nico laughed about it, but I was furious with her. She came round when we had a traditional wedding, mainly to appease her, but I still don't think my father has accepted him, even though my parents both hated the idea of my staying single. You know Nico, and I couldn't be happier, or luckier, but no one was ever going to be good enough for my parents.'

Accepting the general opinion that her suspicions of John were unfounded, Geraldine still hoped he might be able to help them find Laura, so she went back to Turnberry Drive to question him again. As before, when she announced herself, he didn't open the door straightaway but called out from inside the house. This time he sounded annoyed.

'What do you want this time?' he shouted through the closed door.

'I just want to talk to you.'

'I've got nothing more to say to you.'

Geraldine rang the bell again.

At last the door opened a crack, and John peered out at her. 'You again,' he grumbled. 'What is it with you people? This is the third time you've come here, pestering me for information I don't have. Well, you can go back to your boss and tell them that if this continues I'm going to have to make a formal complaint. They've got no business sending you to harass me like this.'

He began to close the door, but Geraldine stopped him by putting her foot in the gap.

'No one sent me here,' she told him, hoping to placate him.

'Then what are you doing here?'

'There are a few more questions I'd like to ask you. I'm hoping you can help me find Laura. Of course, you don't have to talk to me if you don't want to. But if it helps to put your mind at rest, I'm here unofficially.'

John pulled the door fully open, his eyes narrowed in suspicion. 'You're saying it was your idea to come here?' he asked. 'No one else sent you?'

'Exactly. You're not a suspect,' Geraldine assured him.

That was technically true. She was alone in harbouring suspicions about him.

'I'm just concerned about Laura,' she went on. 'I'm trying to find her and I think you might be able to tell me the names of one or two of her local childhood friends we don't know about.'

He hesitated before inclining his head. 'Oh very well, you'd better come in then. I'm as keen as you are to see Laura safe, and if there's anything I can do to help, of course, I'll co-operate. This way, please.'

He led Geraldine along the hall to a small study at the side of the house. It was a poky room, furnished with a narrow wooden desk and two upright wooden chairs. A wooden filing cabinet stood beneath one small window that looked out on a brick wall. The room smelt faintly of mould and Geraldine spotted what looked like mouse droppings in a corner.

John gestured to one of the chairs and she sat down.

'Now,' he said, with a benign smile that lit up his face. 'What is it exactly you want from me?'

Something about his unexpected cordiality warned Geraldine to be on her guard, although John had said nothing to alarm her. Carefully she explained that her team had spoken to every contact of Laura's they had been able to trace: former schoolfriends and current associates, work colleagues and neighbours, but they still hadn't managed to find her.

'We've checked all her online friends on social media, everyone we can trace. I'm wondering if you might know of any contacts – schoolfriends or perhaps neighbours – who might not appear on her social media sites. She can't have just disappeared. She must be somewhere, and we think the likelihood is that she's staying with a friend as we can't find any trace of her in any local hostels or other paying accommodation.'

'I see.' John nodded. 'You've been very thorough.'

'But without any success.'

'That's a pity, but I don't really see how I can help you. I tell you what. Leave it with me and I'll see if I can remember anything. If I do, you'll be the first to know. So, is that all? Only I have somewhere to be.' He glanced at his watch, as though to illustrate his point.

As they left the room, Geraldine thought she heard a faint scuffling sound.

John heard it too and swore under his breath. 'Bloody mice,' he said, with an apologetic shrug. 'I had the council in only six weeks ago. They said they'd got rid of them all, but the pests keep coming back.'

'Mice?'

He nodded. 'It's not an infestation,' he added smoothly, 'just a few stray mice that wander in from time to time. I'll have to get on to the pest control people again.'

'Your cat isn't much of a mouser then?'

For an instant, John looked puzzled. He recovered his outward composure quickly, but his momentary perplexity had been enough to convince Geraldine that he had lied about having a cat when she had first called at his house. He had told her he needed to feed his cat in response to a noise that could have been made by a cat. But the mewling Geraldine had heard could equally well have been made by a different creature – perhaps a woman who was tied up and gagged.

Geraldine thought quickly. Her wild speculation suddenly seemed horribly plausible. She needed to act without delay. Laura could be in immediate danger. On the other hand, she would only make matters worse if she attempted to deal with the situation by herself and failed. The only sensible course of action was for her to leave as quickly as possible, without alerting John to her suspicion that Laura might be somewhere in the house. Once she had left, she could summon urgent back-up and have a team surround the house and restrain John, before searching the property.

She had told no one where she was, and needed to leave the house immediately. In all probability she was mistaken in her suspicions, and had misunderstood the situation with the cat. John could have been taking care of a neighbour's pet when Geraldine was last there, or perhaps he had owned a cat that had just died. But there was a chance that Laura was in the house and in danger. If she was wrong, it would be embarrassing, and Binita would be furious, but Geraldine figured it was worth the risk. Her theory might be far-fetched, but it would explain Laura's disappearance, and fitted the impression she had formed of John as a possessive father.

Smiling as convincingly as she could, she thanked John for his co-operation and apologised once again for disturbing him at home. When he led her out of the room, she couldn't tell if he was deliberately positioning himself between her and the front door. As she was speaking, she was weighing up her chances of barging past him and reaching the door, but she wasn't sure that would work. She might physically restrain him, but she wasn't confident of her position. She could imagine what Binita would say were it to transpire that Geraldine had assaulted an innocent member of the public because he didn't own a cat. Binita already seemed to have the impression that Geraldine was pursuing some irrational vendetta against John, and she still had no actual grounds for suspecting him. He could deny ever having mentioned owning a cat. Geraldine hadn't made a note of it in her report. She had possibly made an error of judgement in omitting to mention it, but at the time it had seemed to have no bearing on the case.

'We share a common objective,' she said, taking a step forward. 'We both want to see Laura safely back home.'

John made no move to allow her to reach the front door. 'You can stop fretting about Laura,' he replied quietly. 'She's perfectly safe. Unless you decide to do something stupid that is.' His eyes glittered. 'You said you want to keep her safe. So you need to be careful. It's up to you now. You see, if anything happens to me, no one will ever find her. And neither of us wants that, do we? You're going to have to play by my rules from now on, if you don't want anyone else to die.'

52

DESPITE HIS EFFORTS TO reassure himself that everything was fine, Ian's irritation had slowly turned to apprehension when Geraldine failed to answer her phone for the third time that evening. She had never before stayed out so late at night without calling him, but that was no reason for him to be alarmed. She knew how to take care of herself. Now the case was over, she might have decided to go and see her sister, on a whim. It was even possible she had told him about the visit, and he had forgotten. But he knew that Geraldine thought the wrong man had been arrested and was upset that her reservations had been dismissed by her senior officer, however much she protested that she wasn't rattled. If she was right in thinking the killer remained at liberty, she might have been pursuing a lead of her own, and there was a possibility she could be in danger.

Eventually he had fallen asleep, resigned to the fact that she wasn't going to answer her phone or call him back, but he had slept fitfully. Driving to the police station the next morning, he told himself she would be at her desk, buried in work. It wouldn't be the first time she had worked through the night. But she wasn't at her desk; nor could he find her anywhere on the premises. He even went and checked in the custody suite, in case she was down there talking to the prisoner on her case.

The custody sergeant greeted him with a smile. 'Who are

you here to visit? I've heard they're throwing a party in one of the cells. Got your invitation?'

Ian explained that he hadn't come to talk to a prisoner. He was looking for Geraldine. 'Is she here?'

The sergeant shook his head. 'She was here a couple of days ago, to see Paul Moore, but she's not been here since. Do you want me to look it up?'

'No, that's okay,' Ian said. 'I think I'll go and have a word with Paul Moore after all.'

The prisoner looked up with lacklustre eyes, and hauled himself wearily into a sitting position on his bunk. When Ian enquired about Geraldine, Paul nodded and said she had been to see him recently. He couldn't recall exactly when.

'Days don't have much meaning in here,' he added miserably.

All he could tell Ian was that Geraldine had gone to see him to complain that she couldn't find his wife. He spread his arms out in a gesture of helplessness.

'How the hell am I supposed to know where my wife is? She could be anywhere, and I'd be the last to know.'

When Geraldine had still neither reappeared nor contacted him by mid-morning, Ian went back to speak to Ariadne. Not only was she Geraldine's colleague working on the case with her, but they were close friends. If anyone knew where Geraldine had gone, she might. Glancing around, he leaned towards Ariadne and asked her where Geraldine was.

Ariadne shook her head, and her long black curls swung and rippled with the movement.

'She was talking about going to see Paul Moore,' Ariadne said in answer to Ian's enquiry. 'I expect she's gone to talk to him again.'

Ian frowned. 'Is there a reason why she might want to question the suspect informally?'

'I don't know.' Ariadne shrugged, looking despondent. 'She

seems to think there might be something his wife's not telling us. I honestly don't know what gave her that impression. And now his wife's gone off the radar.'

'Is there something going on that I should know about?'

Ariadne shrugged. 'All I can tell you is that Geraldine wasn't happy about the arrest, but I've no idea why. I'm not sure she knew herself. She said she just had a feeling something was wrong.'

Ian nodded. He was accustomed to Geraldine's inclination to explore her own theories. Senior officers were sometimes irked by her independent working, but they all had to admit that Geraldine's instincts were uncannily accurate.

'I can't tell you what she's got in mind because she didn't say, but she was definitely preoccupied the last time I saw her.'

Ian gave a rueful smile. 'When isn't she?'

They agreed that Ariadne should try and find Laura in case she had any idea where Geraldine was. They knew Laura hadn't been to work for several days now, but it was possible she had returned and had spoken to Geraldine. There was nothing more Ian could do for the time being so, leaving the question of Geraldine's whereabouts to Ariadne, he returned to his desk and did his best to occupy himself with his own work. At lunchtime he caught sight of Ariadne in the canteen and hurried to join her.

'Well?' he blurted out impatiently.

Ariadne raised her eyebrows, her mouth full of cheese omelette. Swallowing her mouthful, she shook her head.

'I couldn't find Laura,' she admitted.

Ian questioned her and she explained that there was no answer at Laura's house, and she hadn't showed up for work that day.

'The manager of the hair salon where she works said Laura's not been seen there since Friday and she hasn't been in touch to say where she is or why she's failed to turn up. The manager said that she knows Laura's had problems lately, but unless she's too ill to pick up the phone, like in a coma or something, she's going to be in serious trouble. Basically, I suspect Laura's lost her job.'

She frowned and Ian returned her worried gaze.

'We can't find Laura and now Geraldine seems to have disappeared as well,' Ian said.

'As far as we know, Laura's been missing since Friday.'

'Geraldine was around on Saturday –'

'Yes, I saw her here,' Ariadne concurred.

'And she was with me on Monday night. So she seems to have disappeared on Tuesday, which is four days after Laura was last seen at the hair salon.'

Ariadne nodded. 'They could be connected. I know Geraldine was looking for Laura.'

'Perhaps she found her,' Ian said. 'But where are they? What's going on, Ariadne?'

As they were discussing their next move, Ian made a decision.

'You know Geraldine and you know what she's been working on, even if she's been looking at something unofficially,' he added quietly. 'I want you to drop anything else you're doing right now and draw up a list of anywhere Geraldine might be. Get someone to produce a comprehensive list of all Laura's contacts from the year she was born to now. This is a priority. I'll get a message out to everyone. We need to find Geraldine's car.'

Ariadne nodded.

'I'll be back with you as soon as I can. This is a priority, Ariadne. If anyone approaches you about anything else, refer them to me. Go.'

Ariadne cast a regretful glance at the remnants of her lunch and rose to her feet.

'We'll keep in touch,' Ian said. 'This is a priority.'

'I understand,' Ariadne said. 'Finding Geraldine is a priority.' She reached out and put her hand on Ian's arm. 'We'll find her, Ian.'

He nodded. Neither of them voiced the concern that by the time they discovered where Geraldine was, they might be too late to save her life.

53

GERALDINE REMEMBERED EXACTLY WHAT had happened. She could replay the incident in her mind, minute by minute, as though she was watching a film playing in slow motion, frame by frame. Her concern for Laura's safety had prevented her from resisting when John had tied her hands together behind her back with a length of rough cord, and gagged her, after which he had propelled her up two flights of stairs. He had pushed her through a door and down on to a mattress on the floor, where he left her securely tied up, gagged and scarcely able to move her arms. The door had slammed shut and she had distinctly heard the key turn in the lock. For a few moments, terror had threatened to overwhelm her; a dizzying rush of adrenaline made her heart pound and she began to sweat. Controlling her fear with an effort, she had decided to explore her prison. The challenge of moving around in darkness was preferable to lying there, surrendering to the grip of pointless panic. It might even prove useful in some way.

Doing her best to ignore the pain that had started to plague her neck and shoulders, she shuffled off the mattress. It was difficult to move easily with her hands tied behind her back, pulling her shoulders painfully, but she felt her way along the walls with the side of her arm, rattled the one locked door, and finally sank to the floor and stared out at the sky through one small window. Even if she had been able to reach it, the single pane looked too small for her to crawl through, and she had no idea what the drop was like on the other side. From the bare rafters of the ceiling, and the small skylight, she had the impression she was in an attic. If she managed to squeeze through the window, any attempt to drop to the ground from there was likely to prove fatal. That kind of gamble might work out in films, but she wasn't about to risk her life by jumping off a roof with her wrists tied together.

She leaned back against the wall, and refused to entertain the idea that John might never come back. While she waited, she struggled to work her hands free but succeeded only in tightening the knot in the cord. She decided to turn her attention to her gag. It was made of some kind of fabric, and tasted salty. It was probably filthy. By biting against it, and moving her lower jaw and bottom lip furiously, she finally managed to work it downwards on to her chin so she could speak. She wondered if anyone would hear her if she screamed, but decided to save her energy and use that as a last resort. Her hands were still tied. She would have to find a sharp ridge of some kind to rub against the cord. It was too dark to see much, but she picked her way slowly across the floor, until her foot collided with something. Crouching down, she felt the corner of another mattress. She pulled herself on to it and her fingers touched a hand. At the same time, there was a muffled whimper and the hand moved away.

With a sickening lurch, Geraldine understood that she was not alone.

'Laura?' she whispered. 'Is that you, Laura?'

Whoever was imprisoned with her began to moan softly.

'Laura,' Geraldine repeated, 'is that you?'

The moaning stopped abruptly and a muffled voice made an incoherent sound.

'Are you gagged?' Geraldine asked. 'Laura, can you talk?'

There was another faint moan.

'If you are Laura, can you reach out and touch my hand again?' Geraldine said.

For a moment there was no response, and then a hand tapped Geraldine's arm three times, very deliberately. There was no mistaking the sign.

'Tap twice if you are Laura,' Geraldine whispered.

She waited and after a few moments her fellow captive tapped her arm, twice. Geraldine had found Laura concealed in John's house, where she had presumably been held captive since she had disappeared several days earlier. Geraldine had found her, but was unable to do anything to help her. She tried to think calmly about the situation. If Laura had indeed been in captivity for four days since she had gone missing then John must have been giving her water and probably food as well, which meant he had no intention of killing her, at least not yet. That didn't mean his intentions towards Geraldine were equally benign. He might have some feelings for his stepdaughter but, as a stranger, Geraldine meant nothing to him. On the contrary, he viewed her as a troublesome pest. Now that she knew what he had done to Laura, her own life must be in danger. On the other hand, if John killed her, he would never be able to release Laura. As things stood, he might still harbour some idea of convincing Laura that he had put her in the attic to protect her.

'I'm going to try and free my hands so I can untie you,' she said, and Laura moaned in response.

Before Geraldine had a chance to feel around for something to help her break the cord that bound her wrists, she heard the door open. She spun round. In the light coming through the door, a man's figure stood silhouetted on the threshold. For an insane instant, Geraldine thought it was Ian come to rescue her, and she heard a moan escape from her own lips. Then the shadowy figure took a step forwards into the room and a voice reached her.

'You see,' John said, as though they were in the middle of a conversation, 'it never does any good in the long run, meddling in other people's business. You brought this on yourself, you know. And now I'm going to have to decide what to do with you.' He sighed. 'You are a real nuisance. Why couldn't you have stayed in your police station, where you belong, instead of poking your nose into my affairs? This is my house. You should never have come here.'

'What about Laura?' Geraldine asked. 'Should she have stayed away?'

'Laura's back here with me, where she belongs,' John replied, seeming not to notice that Geraldine was no longer gagged. 'I'm quite capable of looking after her. You know, she grew up here, in this house, with me, and now she's back. Of course, she should never have left. She understands that now. Her mother's abandoned me, but Laura isn't going to leave me as well. That would be too cruel. I know why you're here, but I won't let anyone take her away again.'

Beside Geraldine, Laura moaned.

Geraldine turned back to John and spoke as firmly as she could. 'You need to untie us both, right now. I'm a police officer and my colleagues have this building surrounded.'

John laughed. 'Of course they don't. That's just another one of your lies. They'd have been breaking the door down by now if they knew you were here. You came here all by yourself, looking for Laura, and your colleagues probably haven't even noticed you're missing. And when they do, how do you think they're going to find you here? I know, you think they'll see your car parked outside and put two and two together. But your car keys were in your bag, you stupid bitch. Do you really think your car is still there, out in the street for everyone to see?' He laughed again. 'You think you're clever, but believe me, you're no match for me.'

'You care about Laura, don't you?' Geraldine said gently. 'You need to consider what's going to happen to her when you're arrested and convicted of holding a police officer against her will. Because my colleagues will catch up with you. Even as we're speaking now, they'll have realised I'm missing and they'll be searching for me. And that means they're going to hunt you down. Listen, if you let me go right now, we can write this off as a temporary error of judgement, a drunken escapade that went wrong, whatever you like. We can say you crumbled under all the pressure your family's been under lately. That way, we can make sure you stay out of prison and you'll be able to look after Laura. But if you continue with this insanity, you will be convicted, and you'll be locked up for a very long time. The only way you'll ever see Laura again will be for brief meetings in a prison visiting room, across a table, with no physical contact, and guards watching your every move. It's not conducive to maintaining a good relationship. Laura will return to her husband and after a while she'll stop visiting you, and there won't be anything you can do about it because you'll be behind bars. You won't be able to go and see her. Possibly you'll never see her again. In any case, by the time you get out you'll be a very old man, and she'll have forgotten all about you. Probably she and Paul will have moved and you won't even be able to find them. Her only memory will be of a maniac who kept her tied up against her will.'

'Shut up,' John snapped. 'We've heard more than enough from you. You won't be in a position to tell anyone about this, I'll make sure of that.'

Geraldine forced herself to laugh. 'You might be clever, but you won't get away with murdering a police officer.'

Despite her bold words she was trembling because it was clear that John intended to kill her. He approached her, and held out his hand. In the darkness, she could barely make out the water bottle he was holding.

'You must be thirsty,' he said, and his voice sounded surprisingly gentle.

With a start, Geraldine realised that he was not planning to kill her, not yet at least. And as long as she was still alive, there was a chance she would survive. Ian would have noticed her absence, and by now Binita would have set up an extensive search for her. All she had to do was manage to stay alive long enough for them to find her.

'Drink,' John urged her.

If she had the use of her hands, she could have overpowered him, but with only her legs free she wasn't sure that it would be sensible to launch herself at him. In the meantime, she was suddenly aware of a terrible thirst. Her throat felt as though it would close up, it was so dry. She nodded and opened her mouth. As the cold liquid slid along her tongue, it occurred to her that John might be poisoning her, but she was too thirsty to care. Greedily she gulped the water and was only half aware of a bitter taste as it reached her throat. In the darkness beside her, Laura moaned. Then Geraldine felt her eyes closing and her body sagged. Her gag was pulled across her mouth again and tightened around her head, but she was too sleepy to remonstrate.

She knew only that she had lost.

54

THAT AFTERNOON, NAOMI WENT along to the canteen, hoping to bump into Geraldine. She was disappointed not to see her, but she did spot Ariadne walking in. They had all been working on the same investigation, and Naomi knew that Geraldine and Ariadne were close, so she went over and joined Ariadne in the queue. There were a couple of people ahead of them, one of whom was taking an inordinately long time to make her selection.

'What's the latest?' Naomi enquired cheerily. 'I thought Geraldine would have turned the conviction on its head and nailed another suspect by now.' Seeing Ariadne scowl, Naomi felt uncomfortable. 'Sorry, sorry, it was just a silly joke,' she said hurriedly, afraid she had spoken out of turn. 'I didn't intend any disrespect to a senior officer.'

Ariadne grunted.

'Say, what's up?' Naomi asked. 'We've cracked it, haven't we? We've got the killer behind bars. Don't tell me new evidence has come up and we've had to let him go?'

'No,' Ariadne replied tersely.

'I've been trying to find Geraldine,' Naomi added, 'but she doesn't seem to be around today. Have you seen her at all?'

Ariadne hesitated before admitting that she didn't know where Geraldine was.

'To be honest,' Ariadne went on, lowering her voice, 'we're a bit concerned. She's been off the radar for a couple of days now, and no one seems to have any idea where she is.'

'Ask Ian,' Naomi replied promptly. 'If anyone knows where she is, he'll know.'

'It's not that simple,' Ariadne replied and she shared her concerns about Geraldine's disappearance. 'Ian's as worried as I am,' she concluded. 'We're starting a search because it's beginning to look as though something might have happened to her.'

Hearing that Ian had no idea where Geraldine was, Naomi felt a cold chill that made her voice tremble. 'Does the DCI know? Can't she do something?'

'She doesn't know yet.'

'Someone should tell her.'

They reached the front of the queue and Ariadne ordered a takeaway coffee.

'I haven't got time to sit around,' she muttered to Naomi. 'We have to focus on finding her.'

'This is terrible,' Naomi replied. 'How can Ian not know where she is? They live together.'

Ariadne sighed. 'I know. But he hasn't seen her since Tuesday morning.'

'We have to find her,' Naomi said.

Naomi had a particularly close bond with Geraldine, who had always been kind to her, and had once saved her life. Taking their coffees, the two of them went to find Ian. After a brief discussion, they all agreed it was time to share their concern with the detective chief inspector

Binita glanced up as they knocked and entered her office without waiting to be invited in.

'Whatever it is, it will have to wait,' she said, turning back to her screen. 'I've got a budget meeting in half an hour –'

'Your budget meeting will have to wait,' Ian blurted out, momentarily allowing his feelings to supplant protocol.

The detective chief inspector sat back in her chair and

glared at Ian, drumming the manicured fingers of one hand impatiently on her desk.

'Go on then,' she said, making no attempt to conceal her annoyance, 'but you'd better not have interrupted me for nothing.'

Binita was as concerned as her colleagues on hearing that they had been unable to contact Geraldine. Ian and Ariadne had done what they could to initiate a search, and Binita listened to them with a solemn expression. Naomi thought the key to finding Geraldine lay with the investigation.

'It's certainly true that when Geraldine's working on a case, nothing else exists for her,' Ian said.

No one contradicted him.

'So we need to pinpoint where Geraldine was in terms of the investigation, before she disappeared,' Binita said. 'What was she planning? Do any of you know? Because there's nothing in her decision log to suggest she was going off on her own. Was she pursuing a particular lead?'

'She suspected Paul might have been wrongly arrested,' Ariadne said.

Binita nodded. 'Yes, I know, she made no secret of the fact that she had a theory about that, but without any evidence it was no more than a hunch.'

'But if her hunch was right, that means someone else was responsible for killing Cassie and Ella,' Ian pointed out.

'If she had a theory about who had really killed them, she might have gone to question her suspect, and if he was the killer –' Naomi began and broke off, momentarily overwhelmed. 'She could have got herself into hot water,' she concluded lamely.

'Geraldine's not foolhardy,' Ian objected. 'She would never go and speak to a potential suspect without back-up. But she might have gone to see someone who she thought might know more than they were telling us.' He turned to Binita. 'Do you know where she might have been going on Tuesday?'

'Tuesday?'

Ian nodded. 'She didn't come home on Tuesday night.'

'You mean she's been missing for two days?' Binita sat forward, looking alarmed. 'Why wasn't I told before now? Was she working on her own? What was she up to, Ian?'

'She was looking for Laura,' Ian replied. 'I didn't think she'd appreciate my coming to you,' he added lamely.

They were all aware of the tension that had followed Paul's arrest, but that was trifling compared to the potential crisis they were now facing.

'Surely she doesn't suspect Laura killed Cassie and Ella?' Binita said, momentarily nonplussed.

'We know Cassie was in the pub car park with a man,' Ian replied, 'so no, Laura's not a suspect. But we haven't been able to find her.'

'Laura disappeared before Geraldine,' Ariadne interrupted.

'Then we need to speak to everyone who knows Laura and might be able to tell us where she could be,' Binita snapped. 'Presumably that's what Geraldine was doing. And we need to get on to this as a matter of urgency.'

Ariadne was tasked with taking a team to the hair salon to speak to all of Laura's colleagues and find out if anyone there had any idea where she might be. Ian went to speak to Paul, who was probably the person most likely to know where his wife had gone. After that, Ian was going to arrange for any friends of Laura's they knew of to be questioned, no matter where in the world they were. Keen to do something, Naomi volunteered to question Laura's father about any friends she might have that the police had not yet come across. Confident that they were doing everything possible to find Geraldine, they all set off.

'We'll find her,' Ariadne said, clearly concerned to reassure Ian.

'We have to,' he replied tersely.

Naomi nodded and they dispersed. As she drove away, she struggled not to break down in tears. She couldn't imagine life at the police station without Geraldine. It had been hard enough losing the previous detective chief inspector without any warning, but at least they knew she was recuperating in safe hands. They had no idea where Geraldine had gone, or if she was even still alive. Naomi knew the situation must be unbearable for Ian.

'Don't worry,' she muttered fiercely to herself, 'wherever she is, we'll find her. We have to find her.'

55

IAN ENTERED THE CELL, and Paul looked up listlessly, merely grunting in response to his greeting. When Ian enquired where Laura might be, Paul shrugged.

'I asked you where you think your wife might be,' Ian repeated impatiently. 'Don't play games with me. This is serious. Answer me!'

'All right, all right, I heard you the first time. I'm sitting right here, aren't I? I can hardly not hear you.'

'Then tell me where your wife is,' Ian repeated, anxiety making him short tempered.

'How the hell should I know? I haven't heard from her in a week.' Paul's shoulders slumped. 'Even my wife's given up on me.' He dropped his head in his hands, clearly overwhelmed by self-pity.

His annoyance under control, Ian chose his next words with care. 'We think Laura might be able to help us, but it seems she's not really coping very well with all this.'

Paul burst out laughing, but his expression remained bitter. '*She's* not coping very well? How does she think *I* feel? I hate to complain, seeing as I'm being accommodated and fed, and all at the taxpayer's expense, and not costing me a penny, but it would be nice to feel that I had *some* support from my wife. But no, the first sign of trouble and she's dumped me.'

'What do you mean, she's dumped you?'

'I don't know what's going on with her. I tried calling her

again yesterday, but she didn't even do me the courtesy of answering the phone. To me, her husband. I can't even talk to my wife!'

'The thing is,' Ian went on, choosing his words cautiously, 'we haven't been able to locate her.'

'So she's done a runner, has she? Walked out on me. Well, I suppose I can't blame her. I'm not much of a catch now, am I?' He gestured towards the walls of his cell.

'We're worried something might have happened to her,' Ian said quietly.

He wasn't sure how much of Geraldine's suspicions it would be wise to share with Paul, who remained their main suspect in a double murder enquiry.

'What's that supposed to mean?'

Ian hesitated. 'Just that, if it turns out you weren't responsible for the deaths of your pupils –'

'If!' Paul snapped.

'And someone else was,' Ian went on, 'we're wondering whether that might have anything to do with your wife's disappearance.'

Paul pulled his knees up on the bunk, shaking his head. 'You can't think Laura did it?' he gasped, clearly horrified by the suggestion. 'That's – that's just – that's crazy.'

'No, no, that's not it at all. The thing is, we were just wondering whether she might be privy to information that could help us to find out who *is* responsible. Assuming it wasn't you, of course, which we haven't yet established.'

Paul scowled. 'So you think Laura might have information that would exonerate me, her husband, and she's chosen not to come forward and share that with you?'

'There is another possibility, always assuming for a moment that someone other than you killed Cassie and Ella. Think carefully, Paul. Maybe Laura's in hiding because she knows the truth and she's convinced her own life is in danger. Where might she be hiding? If we can find her, we can ask her what she knows, and we can keep her safe. And possibly even clear your name.'

Paul shook his head. 'I've no idea what you want me to say,' he replied. 'I don't know what you're talking about. But if my wife's life is in danger, you need to find her and protect her from whoever you think might be threatening her. That would be your priority, if what you're saying is actually true. I'm struggling to get my head around this. To be honest, nothing makes sense any more. When you find her, tell her I want to speak to her.'

'We would, if we knew where she was.'

'Find her, can't you?'

'That's what we're trying to do. Believe me, we're doing our best to find her, but we need your help. Can you tell us where to look?'

Paul glared at Ian. 'If anything happens to my wife, I'll see you rot in hell.'

'There's no point in threatening me,' Ian said mildly. 'What you need to do is help us work out where your wife might have gone. That way, if she is in hiding because she's afraid she's in danger, we can protect her.'

But Paul shook his head. 'You probably know better than I do where she might be. You know how to trace people's contacts. All I can tell you is where she worked and who our friends are. There's nothing I can tell you that you don't already know.'

There was one more lead with which Paul might be able to help. Ian went to see the VIIDO team to enquire about the CCTV footage they had of Cassie outside the pub. Having studied it carefully, he asked whether it was possible to enhance the image of the man's face. A young ginger-haired VIIDO officer shook her head. Ian noticed she had unusually green eyes, and wondered if she was wearing coloured contact lenses. He sighed. Lately every officer he came in contact with seemed to be much younger than him.

'We've done everything we can to make the image clearer,' she replied, 'and I'm afraid this is the very best we can come up with. If you had an image of the person you suspect it might be, we might be able to match his physique and his gait, but I don't think we have a clear enough shot of his face to do anything with that. I'm sorry.'

Ian asked her to send it to him anyway, and returned to the custody suite.

'Back again,' the cheerful custody sergeant greeted him. 'This is becoming a habit. If it goes on much longer you'll have me thinking you're after my job.' He laughed. 'There's plenty of perks. There's never any shortage of company down here.' As he spoke, they heard someone, probably drunk, calling out incoherently. 'See what I mean?' the custody sergeant said. 'They even sing to me sometimes. How many people can say they're serenaded at work?'

Ian nodded and made his way back to the cells, where he showed Paul a short grainy video on his iPad.

'This was captured on CCTV at a pub near Fishponds Wood,' he explained.

'Your colleague has already shown me that,' Paul said wearily.

He and Ian studied the footage, but it was impossible to see the man's face clearly. Paul squinted at the film. He stared at it closely and asked for it to be rerun several times while Ian waited, watching Paul's face closely. Eventually Paul shook his head. Ian closed his laptop and was about to leave, when Paul cleared his throat.

'Well?' Ian prompted him. 'You were going to say something?'

'I can't be sure,' Paul replied. 'I mean, it's not exactly clear, is it?'

'No, unfortunately it's not. But does it remind you of anyone?'

'It looks a bit like John,' Paul said, with a puzzled frown. 'I mean, he's got a coat like that. But it can't be him. I mean, how could he know Cassie?'

'John?'

Paul nodded. 'John Walters. Laura's stepfather.'

For an instant Ian stood, transfixed. Then he spoke, attempting to keep his voice level, but he couldn't completely hide his excitement.

'Tell me about John.'

'Like I said, he's Laura's stepfather. Her mother's in a home, well, you probably know all about that.'

'What can you tell me about Laura's relationship with her stepfather?'

'She never complained about him and he was always kind to her, from what I could see. But if you ask me, he was more than a bit possessive.'

'Unnaturally so?' Ian asked, his excitement growing.

Paul shrugged. 'I really couldn't say. But Laura did complain that he changed after her mother had a stroke.'

'Changed how?'

'I don't know. Like I said, he struck me as possessive. And pedantic. The kind of bloke who always has to be right about everything, you know. I saw enough of them on the staff at school,' he added with a sniff. 'You get to recognise the type even when they do their best to hide it. It was never made explicit, but I know he resented me for taking his daughter away. I suppose all fathers are like that when their daughters get married. Anyway, I didn't like the guy and he didn't like me so we didn't see much of him. I don't think Laura minded.

"I've made my choice," she said when I asked her about her father.' He smiled sadly. 'It looks like she's made another choice now. "Look to her, Moor, if thou hast eyes to see, She has deceived her father and may thee." Not that she deceived him, but she did leave him, and now it seems she's left me.' He dropped his head in his hands again and sighed.

Ian had heard enough. He turned and ran back along the corridor, barely pausing to acknowledge the custody sergeant's greeting as he hurried past.

'Do you really think John Walters could have overpowered Geraldine?' Binita asked thoughtfully when Ian reported his suspicions.

Ian shrugged. 'If he caught her off guard,' he suggested uncertainly.

'Or if he had a gun,' Binita added. 'I'm summoning an armed response unit, just in case.'

'Won't that take time to set up?' Ian asked. 'If he has got Geraldine, we need to get her out of there fast.'

Binita nodded. 'We'll get there as quickly as possible, but we can't take any chances. If you're right, and Geraldine is in there, we want to make sure we come out of this without any avoidable fatalities.'

'And before Naomi gets there,' Ian added with a sudden tremor of fear. 'We need to warn Naomi.'

Binita was already picking up her phone.

56

GERALDINE WOKE UP IN darkness. For an instant she thought she was at home lying in her own bed, and she reached out for Ian's reassuring presence beside her. But as soon as she shifted position she realised she was lying on a mattress on the floor, with her hands tied behind her back. She felt as though a heavy weight was pressing down on her head, making it difficult to move, and there was an excruciating pain in her shoulders when she tried to change position. Tentatively she tried to rotate her shoulders, and winced, but she knew it was important to keep them mobile.

Through a sickening fog of confusion and pain, she remembered how Laura's father had bound her hands and forced her upstairs. With a lurch she recalled why she had allowed him to subdue her without putting up a fight. He had warned her that were she to resist him, she would be responsible for putting Laura's life at risk. His words seemed to echo in her mind: 'You're going to have to play by my rules from now on, if you don't want anyone else to die.' She had complied with his wishes, thinking that would be the best way to protect Laura. Now, she wasn't convinced that had been a sensible choice. Her acquiescence had only resulted in her own captivity, rendering her more powerless than before to help Laura.

She had no idea how long she had been lying there, unconscious. When she tried to call out to her fellow prisoner, she found she was unable to talk. Her tongue felt like a large ball of lead, filling her mouth with its weight. For a moment she was afraid her captor had injured her, but making a deliberate effort to speak she realised her mouth was intact and she was gagged. Her fleeting relief at discovering she still had her tongue was almost immediately ousted by the sickening knowledge that her gag had been put back. A length of fabric was pressing across her open mouth, tied tightly around the back of her head, preventing her from speaking. The gag tasted foul and stank of vomit. She fought to control her fear, knowing that were she to throw up again, she would probably choke. On the other hand, if the vomit wasn't hers, that could be even more dangerous. Just the thought of it made her feel nauseous.

She let out a muffled sob and immediately someone moaned, like a ghostly echo. Geraldine blinked furiously, trying to clear her mind, but her thoughts were so muddled she was convinced she had been drugged. A faint memory came back to her of someone pouring water into her mouth. She shook her head, and an agonising throbbing started up at the back of her skull. The feeble moaning came again, and all at once Geraldine knew exactly what she had to do. To begin with, she needed to remain strong and cling on to her determination to survive. She had been in dangerous situations before, and besides, her captor hadn't killed her yet. As long as she was careful, there was every chance she would come out of this ordeal alive.

Her immediate undertaking was to free herself from her bonds. Frantically she worked at her gag, at the same time struggling to release her hands from the cord tied tightly around her wrists. There was a little room for her to wriggle her hands, so that eventually she thought she might be able to free them, but it was going to take a long time. While she was twisting her hands, scraping her skin until it stung, she set to work trying to chew through her gag. Her efforts with both the rope and the gag didn't seem to be making any impact, other than to graze her wrists until they bled, but she persisted. She had to keep going in spite of the pain which was making her whimper involuntarily.

After what felt like a very long time, she managed to manoeuvre her gag down over her chin. For a moment she lay still, panting through her unobstructed mouth. Her lips were sore from rubbing against the rough fabric, and her lower jaw ached from moving. Cautiously she moved her tongue and licked her dry and cracked lips.

'Laura?' she whispered into the darkness, feeling the word roll around her aching tongue.

She was answered by a low moan.

'Laura, listen to me,' Geraldine went on, talking fast now that she knew her tongue was uninjured. Words tumbled out of her mouth in a barely coherent stream. 'We don't have much time, so you're going to have to trust me, and you need to listen very carefully. I'm a police officer and I'm going to get us out of here. It's important that you don't panic, and you mustn't give up hope. There are two of us here now, and we're in this together. I'm going to help you. My colleagues will be here soon, and they're going to rescue us, but in the meantime, we need to do everything we can to free ourselves from our bonds. Between the two of us we'll be able to overpower John and get away from this house. And that's what we're going to do. But first we have to get our hands free. So can you try? It's going to hurt, but don't worry about that. The important thing is to get out of here before your stepfather comes back. Laura, we have to escape from him. Listen, if I stand with my back to you, do you think you could try to untie my wrists?'

She had no way of knowing whether Laura was injured, and couldn't tell how much she had understood. All the time she was talking, Geraldine kept trying to free her hands, but the rope was scraping her skin so severely, she could hardly tolerate the stinging pain. Her legs were not shackled, so she clambered to her feet. Shuffling cautiously to the wall, she was able to feel her way along it in the darkness. With her back to the door, she tried to turn the handle but, as she had suspected, the door was locked. Standing beside the hinged edge, so she would be hidden behind it when it opened, she continued working on the rope that bound her wrists together.

All at once there was a loud shuffling noise which reached her through the door. It didn't sound like footsteps and she wondered whether there was a wild animal on the other side of the door, guarding them. The noise increased in volume until, without any warning, the door was flung open and a grotesque figure burst into the room. It looked like a hunchbacked ogre, black against the light behind it. As Geraldine stared in horror, it broke apart and she saw that it was in fact two people. John was bent over, dragging another figure behind him. The unknown person was resisting the pressure and dragging their heels, which had given rise to the shuffling sound.

With a sudden burst of energy, Geraldine darted at John, shouldered the other figure out of the way, and brought her knee up with a ferocious jab at his genitals. He let out a screech, and crashed to the floor, dragging his new captive with him. Geraldine struggled to keep her balance as a head struck her chest, and a woman's voice yelped right by her ear. Geraldine hoped John's new victim had escaped any serious damage. A bruise on her own chest was a minor inconvenience compared to what she might yet have to face. Fleetingly, she hoped John had suffered a fatal injury in falling, but in the semi-darkness she saw him scramble to his feet, and heard him growling with rage like a savage beast. While she hesitated, poised to spring, he leapt at her and she felt something sting her arm.

She tried to scream but, even though she had removed her gag, she seemed to have no voice. Her legs felt so weak they could no longer support her weight. She sank to her knees and was unconscious before her head hit the floor.

57

AT LAST EVERYTHING WAS in place. Shielded by police vehicles, an experienced negotiator was waiting, while an armed response unit stood by in case the suspect tried to use a gun before he was arrested. A host of police officers had cleared the street of civilians and set up cordons at either end, while overhead a helicopter hovered, watching for any sign of movement from the house. Nearby, an ambulance had drawn up with a medical team ready in case they were needed. Ian waited impatiently while all the necessary preparations were put in place. He could scarcely keep still, he was so frantic with worry. He appreciated that the necessary protocols had to be followed, and the correct safeguards put in place, but while all that was being set up, time was ticking by and Geraldine might be in danger. Naomi's disappearance had clinched the matter for the detective chief inspector. Two of her officers had gone to see John Walters and both had failed to return.

'Come on, come on,' he muttered. 'We need to get her out of there.'

He refused to contemplate the possibility that his sense of desperate urgency might be misplaced, and they might already be too late to save Geraldine. Furiously, he paced up and down the pavement, fretting at the enforced waiting. He had always known there was an element of danger to his work. That recognition was concealed in the back of his mind. Occasionally it surfaced. Being practical, he and Geraldine had discussed what they might do if either of them was injured, or killed, in carrying out their duty, but they had never arrived at a conclusion. He tried to recall what they had said, as he waited to find out whether she was still alive.

Finally, they were ready to commence proceedings. Binita gave Ian a tense nod as a uniformed constable stepped forward and rang the bell, shouting for the householder to open the door.

'Police!' he yelled. 'Open the door! Police!'

There was no response from inside the house.

The officer rang the bell again, and knocked, shouting for the door to be opened, but it remained closed. After a few tense moments, the negotiator stepped forward, and raised the tannoy.

'John, we know you're in there.' He spoke lightly, his voice blaring out unnaturally loudly through the tannoy. 'We just want to talk to you, John.' There was a warmth to his tone of voice that must have been fake, but somehow it drew Ian in.

Still there was no response.

'John, let's work this out together,' the negotiator continued in his pleasant tones. 'We want to resolve the situation to everyone's satisfaction. That means we need to have a conversation with you so you can tell us what it is you want.' He paused for a moment before resuming. 'John, you can't stay holed up in there indefinitely. It will be easier for all of us if we get this resolved soon, before you run out of supplies.' The negotiator pressed on, remorselessly encouraging, his voice impossibly loud yet reassuring. 'John, you have to tell me what you want from us. Whatever it takes to sort this out, I can help. But you have to talk to me. If I don't know what it is you want, I won't be able to help you.' He waited a moment before resuming his one-sided conversation. 'John, we know you're in there. We just want to talk.'

Ian knew the negotiator was doing his job, but the friendly voice was beginning to grate on his nerves. At any rate, it evidently wasn't having the desired effect on John because he still hadn't shown himself. For the first time, it occurred to Ian that John might not actually be at home. Or perhaps they were all in there, Geraldine, Naomi, Laura and John, and they were all dead. He shivered and approached the detective chief inspector.

'How long are we going to stand around out here?' he hissed.

'As long as we have to.'

'What if he's not in there? What if he's taken them somewhere else?'

Binita frowned. 'This is a waiting game,' she replied, but he could tell she was troubled by his suggestion, which must have occurred to her as well.

Hours seemed to pass without any sign from inside the house. At last the sun rose, and the order came through to break in, since John wasn't responding to the negotiator's increasingly extravagant offers of help. Ian felt as though a weight had lifted from his shoulders when he heard the decision.

'Move away from the door!' an armed officer yelled. 'We're going to break it down!'

The negotiator repeated the instructions, as calmly as if he was ordering tea and cakes. There was a loud crash as the back door gave way, and armed officers ran into the house. Outside, everyone watched anxiously for John and his captives to be brought out. Instead, only armed officers emerged and trotted lightly down the path. The house was unoccupied. Ian strode over to the leading officer who had searched inside the house.

'Did you look everywhere? What about the loft? Or under the floor?'

The uniformed officer nodded. 'Yes, sir. We looked everywhere.' He reported signs that the abductees had been locked in the attic.

'Signs? What signs?' Ian demanded. 'What are you telling us?'

'There's a couple of mattresses on the floor of the attic,' the officer replied. 'And we detected what appear to be urine and blood stains on the mattress and the floor, along with signs of human defecation. There's also a discarded syringe, so it looks like they were drugged.'

'We need to have everything tested immediately,' Binita said.

Another officer nodded at her. 'Samples are already on their way to the lab,' he said.

'What else? What else?' Ian demanded.

'The place stank,' the officer said, 'but whoever was in there has gone. The house is deserted.'

'They must be there, they must,' Ian said. He could hear the desperation in his own voice.

'Come on, Ian,' Ariadne said, taking his arm. 'There's nothing we can do here. Let's get back to the police station and try and find out where he could have taken them. A man and three women can't just vanish into thin air. He's taken them somewhere. We're going to find them.'

Ian allowed her to lead him over to her car and drive him back to the police station.

Neither of them asked the question they were both thinking: would Geraldine, Naomi and Laura be found alive? The chances were it was already too late.

'I don't think I could bear it,' Ian began and faltered. 'It can't end. Not like this.'

'It's going to be all right,' Ariadne replied.

They both knew that was unlikely.

58

WHEN GERALDINE CAME TO, she was no longer lying on a mattress, but on a bare wooden floor. The pounding in her head had intensified, as had her nausea. A quick investigation of her circumstances revealed that her wrists were still secured behind her back, and her gag was in place again. She let out an interrogative moan and heard an answering whimper, followed by a second one that seemed to reach her from a different direction. She remembered John dragging a third captive into the room, and realised there must now be three of them tied up in captivity. Even if she hadn't been lying on bare floorboards instead of a mattress, she would have known straightaway that she had been moved to a different location. This place had a very different atmosphere to the room where she had first been imprisoned. It wasn't as dark, and she was aware of a damp smell of moist soil and mildew. The only sound was a distant hum of cars passing, from time to time, too far away for anyone to hear her muffled screaming. Something tiny crawled across her neck and she tensed, momentarily terrified, but there was nothing she could do about it with her hands secured behind her back.

After a few moments, she decided to shift her position before her legs seized up. In moving, her foot hit an obstruction. At the same time, someone groaned. Moving with difficulty, Geraldine scrambled on to her knees and managed to clamber to her feet. Once she was upright, she began shuffling around, taking care to avoid the two mounds of bodies dimly discernible on the floor. The place where they were now being held appeared to be some kind of wooden construction. Slivers of light penetrated the interior through narrow gaps between the panels of the walls and ceiling. She tried kicking one of the wooden slats, but it was sturdier than she expected, and her efforts succeeded only in jarring her shoulders. Meanwhile, both her companions let her know they were still alive, as they moaned and whimpered through their gags.

As her eyes grew accustomed to the semi-darkness, Geraldine's heart seemed to beat faster when she peered around. They were in what appeared to be a garden shed. She couldn't see any tools, but several terracotta plant pots were stacked on a shelf. Turning her back on them, she swung her hands wildly. On the third attempt, she knocked the pots off the shelf. There was a crack as they hit the ground. Only one of them had broken, but that was enough. Crouching down, she felt around behind her back, very slowly, so as not to cut herself on a broken shard. At last she found what she was searching for. Twisting her right hand she tried to saw through the rope holding her wrists. It was difficult. A couple of times she scraped her skin. Unwilling to risk severing an artery, she moved into a narrow shaft of light and turned so that she could see her hands. Then she reached out with her foot and nudged one of the figures lying on the ground. The figure moaned but didn't move. She tried the other one and this figure stirred and hauled herself to her feet. With a stab of dismay, Geraldine recognised her colleague, Naomi Arthur. Quickly she turned her back to show her colleague the shard of pot she was clutching. Hesitantly, Naomi took it and Geraldine thrust her wrists towards her. With a despairing grunt, Naomi began to work on the rope around Geraldine's wrists, twisting her head round and watching her own bound hands over her shoulder. They both knew there was a risk that Naomi would lacerate Geraldine with the sharp edge of the fragment of pottery.

In the cold silence, Geraldine tried not to shiver as she listened to the faint scraping sound of Naomi sawing at her bonds. It seemed like an impossible task, but suddenly there was a faint snap and Geraldine's hands fell to her sides, unbound. She let out a sob of relief. The pain in her shoulders was almost unbearable as her arms swung free, and her hands were seized by cramp, but she forced herself to scrabble at the rope binding Naomi's hands. Snatching her gag from her mouth she spoke, and her voice sounded hoarse and unfamiliar.

'We need to get out of here,' she said. 'We can't wait any longer. It's going to take too long to cut through your bonds. I'm sorry, but I can barely move my fingers.' She pulled Naomi's gag from her mouth.

'Yes, we need to go,' Naomi replied urgently. 'Don't worry about untying my hands. Let's get out of here.'

On the floor, Laura moaned.

Geraldine kicked the door as violently as she could. It trembled but held firm. She tried again.

'Let's do this together,' Naomi said.

'On the count of three.'

Geraldine counted and she and Naomi both kicked as hard as they could. At their third attempt, the door shuddered and flew open. A gust of night air blew into the shed, and Geraldine felt tears in her eyes.

She turned to Laura. 'Get up,' she urged her.

Laura didn't move. Geraldine looked at Naomi.

'I'll stay with her, you get help.' Geraldine said. 'Go!'

'I'm not leaving you here. No way.'

'Just go! That's an order, Sergeant.'

With a sharp intake of breath, Naomi turned and stumbled through the open door. Meanwhile Laura struggled to her feet but she seemed incapable of walking, and Geraldine had no strength to carry her. Only then did she realise that it might have been a mistake to let Naomi go for assistance, instead of leaving her to take care of Laura. Barely able to move her own hands, there was little Geraldine could do. She used her voice to try and reassure Laura as she dragged her slowly out of the shed. In the moonlight she could see other sheds in neighbouring allotments, but she didn't think she could haul Laura that far, and in any case the doors were probably padlocked. Even if she managed to break one of them open, John would spot the break-in and find them. All she could do was drag Laura around the back of the shed they had just vacated, hide in the grass, and hope that Naomi would be back before John returned.

She didn't hear him arrive. She had no inkling he was there until she heard him swearing on discovering they had escaped.

'I know you're here somewhere,' he snarled. 'You can't have gone far. I'm going to find you and this time I'll make sure you never get away. Laura –' His voice changed to a wheedling tone. 'I know those bloody policewomen have got hold of you, but it's all right. I'm here now. I'll save you. We don't need them interfering in our lives. We don't need anyone. I'll look after you. We'll go back to how we were before.'

Lying on the grass beside Laura, Geraldine held her breath. And then Laura whimpered, unable to control her fear. Geraldine lifted her head to look up as John appeared around the corner of the shed.

'Ha! Gotcha!' he crowed.

Desperately Geraldine clambered to her knees and prepared to crouch, tensed to rush at him, when she heard the roar of a helicopter. A dazzling beam of light swept across the allotments from the night sky. With a sob, Geraldine collapsed, burying her face in the wet grass. Naomi had succeeded in summoning help, and the terrifying ordeal was over.

59

THE FOLLOWING MORNING, GERALDINE slept late. She had been taken straight to hospital from the allotments for a thorough check-up. Having hit her head, she was given a full brain scan and was more relieved than she would admit when the result came back and she learned that she had suffered no internal head injury. She was lucky to escape with no broken bones, but her wrists had both been rubbed raw and were smarting painfully. Nevertheless, she insisted on being discharged the following day. After going home to shower and change, she was confident that she was fit enough to question John, and Binita yielded to her importunity, on the understanding that Ian would be there to conduct the interview.

John looked very different to the debonair man Geraldine had first encountered. He had dropped his easygoing manner. His mask removed, he glared across the table at his interlocutors, making no attempt to control his anger. His lips twisted as he spoke.

'This is an outrage!' he fumed. 'I demand to be released at once. You have no right to keep me cooped up in a stinking cell. I won't stand for it. You can't do this to me. I've done nothing wrong.'

Geraldine sat patiently listening to his diatribe. He must have known there was nothing he could do to persuade the police to release him. At last, Ian interrupted John's ranting to read out the charges against him. It was a long and damning list. John's lawyer was a nervous-looking young man who seemed to be overawed by the situation. Geraldine wondered whether this was the first time he had worked with a client accused of murder. The lawyer glanced anxiously at John before responding in a curiously high-pitched voice.

'My client denies all the charges.' He adjusted his metal-rimmed glasses with long, pale fingers, and stared into the space between Geraldine and Ian as he spoke.

'He can't deny abducting my colleagues, tying them up, gagging them and locking them in his attic, before drugging them and transporting them to the shed on his allotment where he again imprisoned them,' Ian pointed out quietly. 'DI Steel present here, and DS Naomi Arthur, were both held captive, along with the accused's stepdaughter, Laura Moore. We have statements from all three of them.'

John shook his head irascibly, but had the sense to keep quiet and allow his lawyer to reply.

'My client says that was a misunderstanding.'

'A misunderstanding?' Geraldine retorted, provoked into responding.

She held up her hands, displaying her bandaged wrists.

'For the tape, DI Steel is showing the accused her arms, injured from the rope he bound her hands with.' Ian paused, his face contorted with emotion, and Geraldine took over.

'The medical reports relating to my injuries, sustained while being held under duress, are a matter of record. The same is true of my colleague, DS Arthur, and of Laura Moore, a civilian and the accused's stepdaughter.'

'My client denies all charges,' the lawyer responded in a flat voice.

'He thinks he can argue against three women, including two police officers, who all confirm he assaulted them, tied them up, and locked them in,' Ian said, with a disbelieving smile.

'My client denies all charges,' the lawyer repeated in a flat voice.

'Good luck with that,' Ian scoffed. He continued to speak in an even tone, but his eyes glared fiercely at the suspect. 'We have evidence that's going to put you away for a very long time, John. You're going to be locked up for the rest of your life. And we haven't even got to the murder charges yet,' he added with relish he was unable to conceal.

Geraldine intervened in a low voice. 'John, you must see this is madness. You can't possibly convince anyone that this didn't happen. You can't argue against the statements given by Laura and two police officers. Tell us why you did it. If you confess, you'll make it easier for yourself.'

'Easier for you, you mean,' he muttered.

He leaned sideways and whispered to his lawyer who nodded, but looked concerned.

'My client says he has been set up. He is an innocent party in this.'

'Unless he has an identical twin living in his house, who drugged me and tied me up and drove me to the allotment, then his claim is nonsense,' Geraldine replied, with a barely concealed sneer.

'Your client is understandably desperate to deny the accusation,' Ian resumed. 'Assaulting police officers in the course of their duty is a serious offence. But you must know your client is clutching at straws. We have a civilian witness and two police officers who can confirm that he committed these offences.'

'There's no wriggle room,' Geraldine added, smiling coldly at John.

She flexed her fingers under the table, remembering how tightly her wrists had been bound.

'This is a clear case of victimisation,' the lawyer replied.

'She always had it in for me,' John added. 'That bloody policewoman. Yes, you.' He turned from Geraldine to Ian. 'You know what happened? She got it into her head that I was guilty of killing those two girls. Me! And when it turned out to be someone else all along – someone you've already arrested – she just couldn't let it drop.' He turned to address Geraldine again. 'You can't bear to be proved wrong, can you?' He spoke finally to his lawyer. 'She's a crazy bitch who had it in for me right from the start. She's determined to see me convicted for a crime I didn't commit. She set this whole thing up. She wanted me to confess to killing those girls, and now she wants to blame me for what she did to Laura and that other policewoman, when it was her fault all along. And, of course, her cronies here are backing her up. But they won't make it stick in court. Any jury is going to see through their lies straightaway. Everyone knows you can't trust a word the police say. They're corrupt, through and through. As for trying to pin those murders on me, that's ridiculous when they've already arrested Paul for killing those girls. It's obvious they're just trying to scare me. I'm being victimised, and as soon as I get out of here I'm going to sue the arses off all of you.' He leered angrily at Geraldine. 'You won't get away with harassing me. My wife tried that, and you know where she ended up.'

'What happened to your wife?' Geraldine asked softly.

John sneered at them. 'It's none of your business what happened between me and my wife. You think you're so clever, don't you? Well, you'll never catch me out with your tricks. As for those two girls, you've done the right thing arresting Paul. He was never good enough for Laura. It's taken a long time, but I knew I'd get him in the end. He's got what he deserves.'

'But his arrest had nothing to do with you, did it?' Geraldine said. 'Even you couldn't have made Cassie accuse Paul of behaving inappropriately.'

John shrugged.

'It would have been almost impossible to persuade her to accuse her teacher of molesting her,' Geraldine added. 'No one could have had that much influence on her.'

'It wasn't difficult,' John replied, laughing. 'That little slut would have done anything for me –' He broke off, realising what he had inadvertently let slip. 'In any case, why would I want to do that?' he blustered, but he knew he had given himself away.

'And then, to make sure Cassie didn't tell anyone, you killed her,' Ian said. 'Only she'd already told her friend, hadn't she? So then you killed Ella as well.'

'Yes, there's still the question of the two murders,' Geraldine said quietly.

'I don't know anything about that,' John said quickly. 'I don't even know who the victims are. I never saw them in my life. All I know is that Paul killed them.'

'That's what you want us to believe,' Geraldine replied. 'But we have a different theory.' She paused. 'We think you killed them.'

'My client denies ever meeting either of the victims.'

'That's not exactly true, is it?' Geraldine said. 'You just admitted that Cassie would have done anything for you. In fact, almost everything you say contradicts the evidence.'

She put images of Cassie and John on the table. John glanced at them with a baffled expression, and denied recognising either of the people in the photos.

'Let me jog your memory,' Geraldine said. 'Those pictures were taken in a pub car park, near Fishponds Wood.'

John shook his head

'That's you,' Geraldine said, pointing at the man in the pictures, 'and that's Cassie Jackson.'

'Who?' He turned to his lawyer. 'I've never seen that girl in my life, and that's not me.'

'That's not my client,' the lawyer echoed, after looking carefully at the image. 'It could be anyone.'

'We can't see his face clearly,' Ian conceded, 'but the man captured on CCTV in that image is wearing your client's coat.'

'His stepdaughter recognised it.'

John whispered furiously to his lawyer who nodded.

'There must be thousands of coats just like that one,' the lawyer said.

'It's just a coat,' John interrupted impatiently. 'That man could be anyone. It's just a man in a coat. You can't prove that's me.' He turned to his lawyer. 'They're clutching at straws. That bitch is so desperate to see me convicted. Some people just can't accept when they've got it wrong.'

'We found a coat just like this one, with exactly the same stain on the back, hidden in your shed in the allotment. DNA evidence has already proved that you wore it.'

John crossed his arms. 'It was stolen. She planted it there,' he said, staring in dismay at the image.

'And when we find DNA evidence proving Cassie Jackson was in your car?' Ian said. 'Are you going to try and fool everyone into believing my colleague planted her there?'

John's shoulders slumped and he dropped his head in his hands. He knew it was over.

'Why did you do it, John?' Geraldine asked him. 'We all know no one set you up. It was the other way round, wasn't it? You set Paul Moore up. Was it your idea for Cassie Jackson to accuse him of molesting her?'

'He had it coming,' John said. 'It was so easy to persuade the little tart to make the allegation against him. He deserved it.'

'What had he done to you?'

John raised his head and glared at her.

'All he did was marry your daughter,' she pressed on. 'He did nothing wrong.'

'Nothing wrong? Nothing wrong?' John echoed her. 'He took Laura away from me. He should never have been put in charge of teenage girls. He was a monster, luring my daughter into his life like that when anyone could see she was too young to leave home.'

'You were desperate to keep her for yourself, weren't you? Do you honestly think that was appropriate?'

'What are you implying? Whatever you're suggesting, it's not true! I never touched her! But he had no right to take her away from me. She was all I had.'

'You had a wife. But you arranged for Angela to be sent away so you could have Laura all to yourself. Only then she left you for Paul and you wanted to punish him.'

John shook his head. 'It was all his fault. After everything I did for Laura. I even dealt with her mother for her. They never got on, you know.'

'You tampered with her medication until she needed nursing care?' Geraldine asked, but it wasn't really a question that required an answer.

'It was the only way,' John replied. He paused, before adding, 'Those other girls had to be protected from him.'

'By being murdered?' Ian asked.

John glared but didn't answer.

'So his crime was to fall in love with your daughter and marry her?' Geraldine asked. 'You used Cassie Jackson to destroy his career and then, when she grew tired of the subterfuge, you killed her so she couldn't tell anyone what you had persuaded her to do. Only then you discovered Ella suspected you had killed Cassie, so you killed her too. What would you have done if any other friends of Cassie Jackson had discovered the truth? Would you have killed them too?'

John stared coldly at her. 'I only ever did what was necessary,' he said. 'If Paul hadn't taken her away from me, none of this would have happened.'

'You destroyed your wife before Laura married Paul,' Ian said.

John shrugged. 'She was never well,' he said. 'It would have happened anyway.'

Geraldine felt a renewal of the chill she had experienced when she was tied up and imprisoned. But this time it was different. John had been captured, not her. She rotated her shoulders slowly under her jacket, relieved that the pain was easing. Soon it would be gone altogether.

60

JOHN'S LAWYER HAD BEEN looking increasingly uneasy as the interview moved from the question of the three women his client had held captive, to the two girls who had been murdered. Fiddling with his glasses, the lawyer cleared his throat and requested a break in a voice that was shrill, and slightly tremulous. When Ian promptly terminated the interview, the lawyer exhaled loudly, as though he had been holding his breath for a while.

'We're happy to pause the tape at this point,' Ian said breezily. 'I think we're ready for a break too.' He nodded at Geraldine, who smiled thinly at the delay.

She was reluctant to complain about the dull ache in her shoulders or the raw stinging of her wrists, not only because she didn't want to be sent home, but also because she was determined her assailant wouldn't learn how severely he had hurt her. Where he was headed, such knowledge might serve to enhance his reputation, and she refused to be a part of that. Ian stirred beside her, and she was suddenly overwhelmed by a wave of exhaustion. She shrugged, and forced herself not to grimace at the pain the thoughtless movement caused her. The adrenaline rush she had been experiencing drained away until she could scarcely summon enough energy to speak.

'Suits me,' she said.

'Good. We'll pick this up again tomorrow,' Ian went on, addressing the lawyer. 'I think we're just about done for the day anyway.' He grinned at Geraldine as he rose to his feet. 'Do you fancy going for a drink and a curry on the way home?'

She glanced slyly at John as she replied. 'A drink and a curry sound lovely.'

'Or would you prefer a Chinese?' Ian asked. 'What do you fancy?'

'I don't mind,' she said. 'Either would be great.'

'Excellent. I'm hungry.'

They were both smiling as they left the interview room. Neither of them mentioned it, but Geraldine was convinced that Ian was conscious of John's miserable expression, and she felt a frisson of satisfaction. Looking through the window along the corridor on her way back to her desk, she caught a glimpse of Paul and Laura emerging from the custody block. Laura was limping slightly as they made their way to the car park hand in hand. Pausing to watch them, Geraldine heard footsteps and turned to see the detective chief inspector approaching her.

'How are you feeling?' Binita asked.

'My wrists are sore, but I'll be fine.' Geraldine turned back to the window. 'I wonder what they'll do now.'

'They're probably going home.'

'I mean, what's going to happen to them? Do you think he'll ever be able to return to teaching?'

Binita looked pensive. 'I don't see why not. It's not as if he's committed a crime, or even put a foot wrong. The whole thing was set up by his maniac of a father-in-law. Paul was completely blameless. Well, thanks to you we've got the real killer behind bars, and he'll never be released. There's no reason why Paul shouldn't return to his former life.'

'It might not be that simple,' Geraldine replied. 'Mud sticks.'

They both knew Paul wouldn't be able to walk back into his school and resume his teaching career as though nothing had happened. He would probably have to relocate to an area where his name wouldn't be recognised. But he was reunited with his wife, and in time would have the opportunity to settle somewhere new and start again. Geraldine sighed, recalling her own demotion, and the difficulties she had faced in salvaging her reputation and regaining her confidence after she had left London.

'Well, at least he won't be spending a long time in custody, while facing the possibility of years and years behind bars. And, like I said, that's down to your meticulous work. I want to congratulate you on doing a first-rate job on this case, Geraldine. But I also have to point out that you need to pay more attention to your personal safety in future. This isn't the first time you've put yourself in danger, is it? One day you're going to end up in serious trouble, if you're not careful. I'd be neglecting my responsibilities if I didn't have a word with you about the reckless way you behaved.'

Geraldine dutifully agreed to be more careful in future, even though she felt Binita's criticism was unjustified. John hadn't been a suspect when Geraldine had gone to see him, looking for Laura. But she was too tired to remonstrate with her senior officer. She was even too tired to go out to eat. Instead, she and Ian decided to go straight home, where he insisted she soak in the bath while he made dinner. After they had eaten, they discussed the outcome of the case, while finishing a celebratory bottle of wine.

'What happened to Paul Moore seems unfair,' Geraldine said. 'He was innocent all along, but now he'll be lucky to find another teaching job.'

'Fair?' Ian echoed. 'Was what happened to Cassie and Ella fair?' He frowned. 'Life isn't fair. No one gets through it unscathed. I made a complete hash of things, marrying the wrong woman when I was too young and stupid to know any better, and you've certainly had your share of problems in your career. We've both had a rough ride in our different ways, but we got through the difficult times, and I dare say Paul will too. He's young, and he's not on his own, and that makes a difference, doesn't it?'

He leaned forward and kissed her very gently on the top of her head.

'Yes,' she agreed softly. 'You're right. It makes a difference, knowing there's someone who's always got your back.'

'Here's to you,' Ian said, raising his glass and smiling.

'To us,' she replied, raising her own glass and returning his smile.

Acknowledgements

I would like to thank Dr Leonard Russell for his medical advice. My sincere thanks also go to the team at No Exit Press: Ellie Lavender for her invaluable help in production, Hollie McDevitt, Sarah Stewart-Smith and Paru Rai for their fantastic marketing and PR, Alan Forster for his brilliant cover design, Jayne Lewis for her meticulous copy editing, Steven Mair for his eagle-eyed proofreading, Andy Webb and Jim Crawley for their tireless work at Turnaround, and above all to Ion Mills and Claire Watts. I am extremely fortunate to be working with all of them, and really happy that Geraldine's career is not over yet!

It's hard to believe that Geraldine and I have been together for fourteen years now, along with my editor, Keshini Naidoo, who has been with us from the very beginning.

My thanks go to all the wonderful bloggers and interviewers who have supported Geraldine Steel: Anne Cater, A Little Mix Of Vix, Bookish Caterpillar, Bookish Jottings, Books Behind The Title, Books By Bindu, Books Cats Etc., Chaos Happiness Book Mama, Featz Reviews, Flicking Through Pagess, Flying Thry Pages, Joyful Antidotes, Lynda's Book Reviews, Miranda's Bookscape, One Creative Artist, Paterson Loarn, Penfold Layla, Scintilla, Stacey Hammond, The Bookworm Journal, The Reading Lot, The Word Is Out, Travelling Page Turner, Twilight Reader, What Janey Reads, 5 Star Books, and to everyone who has taken the time to review my books. Your support means more to me than I can say.

Above all, I am grateful to my many readers around the world. Thank you for your interest in Geraldine's career. I hope you continue enjoying my books.

Finally, my thanks go to Michael, who is always by my side.

A LETTER FROM LEIGH

Dear Reader,

I hope you enjoyed reading this book in my Geraldine Steel series. Readers are the key to the writing process, so I'm thrilled that you've joined me on my writing journey.

You might not want to meet some of my characters on a dark night – I know I wouldn't! – but hopefully you want to read about Geraldine's other investigations. Her work is always her priority because she cares deeply about justice, but she also has her own life. Many readers care about what happens to her. I hope you join them, and become a fan of Geraldine Steel, and her colleague Ian Peterson.

If you follow me on Facebook or Twitter, you'll know that I love to hear from readers. I always respond to comments from fans, and hope you will follow me on **@LeighRussell** and **fb.me/leigh.russell.50** or drop me an email via my website **leighrussell.co.uk**.

To get exclusive news, competitions, offers, early sneak-peaks for upcoming titles and more, sign-up to my free monthly newsletter: **leighrussell.co.uk/news**. You can also find out more about me and the Geraldine Steel series on the No Exit Press website: **noexit.co.uk/ leighrussellbooks**.

Finally, if you enjoyed this story, I'd be really grateful if you would post a brief review on Amazon or Goodreads. A few sentences to say you enjoyed the book would be wonderful. And of course it would be brilliant if you would consider recommending my books to anyone who is a fan of crime fiction.

I hope to meet you at a literary festival or a book signing soon!

Thank you again for choosing to read my book.

With very best wishes,

Leigh Russell

noexit.co.uk/leighrussell

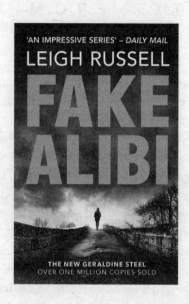

'AN IMPRESSIVE SERIES' – *DAILY MAIL*

LEIGH RUSSELL

FAKE ALIBI

THE NEW GERALDINE STEEL
OVER ONE MILLION COPIES SOLD

A wheelchair-using woman is strangled and her son, Eddy, is arrested. When his alibi falls apart, the police are satisfied that he is guilty. Only Geraldine doubts whether Eddy is cunning enough to kill his mother and cover his tracks so successfully.

The situation becomes more complicated when the girlfriend Eddy claims he was with at the time of the murder denies having met him. Shortly after the girl thinks she is being stalked, her dead body is discovered outside Eddy's house.

As the body count grows, the investigation team is getting desperate, pushing Geraldine to breaking point.

NOEXIT.CO.UK/FAKE-ALIBI

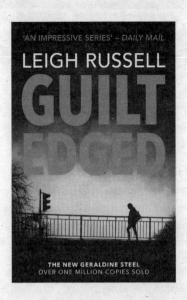

An inoffensive man is murdered in a seemingly motiveless attack. DI Geraldine Steel and her team are baffled, until DNA from an apparent stranger is discovered on the victim's body.

Geraldine is not convinced the suspect is guilty. When a witness comes forward to offer the suspect an alibi, Geraldine lets him go. That night, a second murder is committed. The evidence points to the suspect who has just been released.

As the story races towards a breathtaking twist, Geraldine is tormented by self-doubt, and struggles to focus all her attention on the case. Someone is lying and the police must uncover the truth before anyone else is killed...

NOEXIT.CO.UK/GUILT-EDGED